Revelation

Book One of the Eternal Series

Lena Kelly

Published in 2019 by FeedARead.com Publishing

Copyright © Lena Kelly

A CIP catalogue record for this title is available from the British Library.

This is a work of fiction.

The roots of this story began in a rather miraculous place. A story for another time.... by the fire with copious amounts of single malte. In variations and editing, to where this is now, still amazes me.

Enormous gratitude to Warren Layberry of DarkWater Editing in Canada for the early stages; for the gifts of your insights and talents, and a true education. It was a big bite, I hope I did it some justice.

Many thanks to my very patient friends (you know who you are!) as I consistently vanished down the rabbit hole into this parallel universe, and many others, over the course of years.

I'm not quite back yet.

Gabriel, with love and gratitude for all you give.
Kristian, my love, in the arms of whom I still find rest.

Lena x

I remember the sensation of sun-drenched marble
on the bare of my skin
the colour of the sky
the new moon
the eastern sunrise
from the steps of my temple
I can feel the heat of my tears
as they fall
like the dreams
of the absent rains
and I fall
into stardust
and time begins again

Prologue

Idra, 682 BCE

Anu watched as the moon rose. Hour by hour, she stood atop the ragged mountain, watching as she traced her way through the universal skies around the earth, pushing and pulling the tides as she journeyed.

I will see you again, Mamma. I will see you again.

She turned and tossed the twenty thimble-small crystals from her hand. They flashed briefly as they hovered in the moonlight, then vanished into the sea below.

In the blink of an eye
In the light of the day
In the light
as the moon shines high
Over us
Below us
Through us
Time crosses the skies
We are one time

we are one life
we are one dimension
Life
Seed us into the darkness
before the light of the day
Comes to greet us
We are but one time
we are but one life
we are but one dimension
Let it be done

Lilith staggered slightly, the weight of her body shifting awkwardly beneath her. Shimmering in a way that could only be through time, through dimension.

She froze.

This could only mean one thing.

The witch was alive.

one

Halifax, Nova Scotia, 2000 CE

Jon rolled over and felt the softness of naked flesh in his hands.

Selene.

Love was a funny thing. He couldn't reconcile in that moment where it began and where it ended. Time seemed to be passing at a rate of knots, and she was leaving in the afternoon. Forever. Not forever. But he couldn't lose the feeling of separations, endings and loss. The feeling that she was starting a new life without him.

Selene stirred slightly under his touch. He nestled in closer, pressing the back of her deeply into his body. He felt his arousal, and slowly slid his hand over her thigh and into the beautiful dark wetness between her legs. She moaned slightly, but didn't wake. His hand slid gently up over her side and fell softly onto her breast, rolling over her nipple, nudging it into wakefulness. He just loved the feel of her against his skin, in his hands, in his mouth. It was too much. He buried his face into her hair and nuzzled downwards to her neck. He knew she was waking now. Her breathing was becoming more and more shallow, and he could feel her heartbeat pick up speed with the telltale signs of desire rising. He reached back down into her depths and tolled the small bell, rolling her clit over and over, expelling the wetness within before he entered her. She arched her back and pressed into him, breathing shallowly but heavily, then rapidly as she came into her own with a soft cry.

"Marry me."

It was a whispered statement, rather than a question. Still dancing with ecstasy, breathy, hot, almost mindless-- Selene couldn't answer. Minutes later she rolled her head back to face the shadowy form in their bed, kissing his neck.

"God you are so hot."

"That's not a yes," Jon leaned away, his back on the pillow.

Selene rolled onto her belly and pulled her elbows up underneath her, staring deeply into his eyes.

"Are you asking me to marry you because you're scared you're going to lose me?"

"Maybe," Jon sighed and stretched both arms up over his head, running them through is short blond hair. "If I'm being honest."

Reaching up to kiss his prickly, unshaven face, Selene whispered, "I love you, but we aren't ready for this. You

10

know that. We just have to have a little faith that everything will be ok." Selene shifted closer, running her hand slowly down his muscled torso to his thigh.

Pulling her closer, Jon gazed deeply into the Aegean hue of her eyes in the dim light. "This isn't an end Lene. Tell me that much at least."

"I can't promise you that Jon. I just know I have to go. We've been through all of this.....the pull is so strong I can taste it. It's like salt. It whispers in my ears and shadows my sleep. It sings in my ear, it *calls* me. It feels like it's in my blood. I need to do this Jon. You need to be here, I need to be there. This is not an end as we know it, it's just a step forward in a direc--"

"Yeah, in a direction that pulls us apart." Jon interrupted, swinging himself away from her and out of the bed.

"I get it. *Really*."

Grabbing his shirt from the floor, he left the room and headed down the hall. Selene sighed, falling back into the soft pillow, listening as the refrigerator door opened then closed, and the kettle switched on.

How was she ever going to live without him?

Three years together. Two months since she accepted the place at Bournemouth's Parkwood College and started making plans.

And now he asks.

The clock was glaring a cringe-worthy four a.m.. Selene rolled herself deeper under the duvet and fell into a fitful sleep.

11

two

Bournemouth, UK

Barely two weeks had passed, but this new life was
beginning to wind deeply into her psyche already. Up at
dawn for a run, a quick bite at the cafe, then off to work
at the pub in Christchurch. She had even managed to
score a cheap car. It amazed Selene how easily one fell
into habits that had previously not been their own. The
nights were late at times, and with way too much drink
often involved. Still, she felt at home, and an ease in
herself that she hadn't felt for years.

The college was a five minute walk from her current
digs, and she had investigated the general layout and met
some tutors already. The one named Mark, had been very
welcoming, if not a bit flirtatious, and full of useful
information. The gothic library haunted her thoughts,
and definitely warranted more time and attention. It was
the oldest part of the college, and had a feel of the
ancients about it. There was even a pub inside the

college, very handy.

Now, more than ever, she really knew she had landed. She felt as if she was in the exact place she needed to be.

The sky was the colour of a deepening bruise. Selene couldn't remember ever seeing such a sky. The rain hadn't started yet, but she could feel the moisture in the wind as it rose and fell, and knew it wouldn't be long. She took one final look in the mirror and wished herself luck. *Day one.* She reached the open stone-gated walls of Parkwood Collge as the first drops let loose and the deluge began. Safely inside, she went straight to the office to complete her registration and collect her schedule. Then set about finding where she was meant to be.

The halls were rammed with students rushing in all different directions down halls and up and down stairs. As luck would have it (or not), her first class was mechanics of motion and rehabilitation. The infamous 'naked class' that one of the tutors had mentioned the other day. She took a deep breath, looked skyward with a small prayer, and pushed the heavy arched wood door open minutes before the hour. Already it was full of students greeting each other after a long summer break. She smiled shyly at a few of them as she made her way to a table that hadn't been claimed yet. A loud 'AHEM' from the front of the class drew everyone's attention, and Selene looked up and met eyes with the tutor she had met the other day, Mark.

13

"Good morning everyone and welcome back. We are starting off where we left off last term, entering the movement and mechanics of the pelvis. We have already covered the anatomy and physiology in depth, now comes the applied anatomy and biomechanics. Get yourselves sorted and we will begin with the large muscle attachments and their movements. Go!"

Everyone seemed to move at once, stripping down to boxers and bras and some very scanty lady-like lingerie. Selene hesitated, but slowly began to undress. The door suddenly opened near her and two late students rushed in. Seeing no other tables free, they approached her.

"Hi!" said a lovely blond, blue-eyed girl. "Sorry we're late, can we team up with you? I'm Ev. This is Morten."

"Selene, new girl." Selene grasped Ev's offered hand. "Delighted, I have no idea what to do here!"

"Good morning Selene." Mark was behind her and swirled around to face him. "Undress would be a good start. Don't worry, Ev and Morten will show you the ropes."

He winked at her, and she blushed crimson. She hadn't expected to stand before him half naked. He could see her discomfort, and laughed a little to let her know it was ok.

"Don't mind him Selene, he always likes to check everyone out." Morten laughed as he clocked Selene's obvious shyness around Mark. "I guess it is all new for you, we've been together as a class for two years already. Don't worry, by next week, you'll have met everyone and sussed out the whole plot."

14

"Right." Ev agreed. "Second nature, no worries. Come on let's catch up so we haven't missed anything."

Selene relaxed and found herself remarkably at ease motion-palpating half dressed students while she herself was in the same state of undress. By the end of the two hours, she felt she could have walked to the shops as she was, and it wouldn't have bothered her in the slightest. Amazing.

She looked down at her schedule and saw she had radiography lecture in the clinic then lunch, then radiology upstairs in the main college. *Good, half the day through already, and a relatively good start.* She found her way there and smiled as she realised that some of the same people were in this class with her, including Ev.

"Join us for lunch Selene?" Ev asked, as the class ended.

"Sounds great Ev thanks," Selene replied. "Did you bring food or are you eating at the canteen?"

"Canteen. Mondays are the safest days!" Ev said. "Freshest food and no leftover stews."

"Must remember that." Selene gave her a wry smile, as she followed her into the queue. Soon she found herself walking through the doors into the large lunch area. She followed Ev, who joined Morten and a few other third year students. They quickly introduced themselves and continued to chat.

"Hey Selene!" said Morten. "How did the morning go for you then?"

"A little nerve-wracking to be honest! First day at college entering in the third year and I have to spend the whole morning half naked!"

"Yeah, not for the faint hearted hehe." Morten grinned. "But, then neither is chiropractic. Being that we are on the leading edge and all, Selene."

"Oh give it a rest, Morten!" Ev said rolling her eyes. "I am so sure that Selene isn't interested in your politics. Give her a chance to settle in will you?"

Morten leaned over to Ev and kissed her on the shoulder. "Yes dear."

Ev groaned and pushed him away. Selene laughed. She wasn't aware of any politics at this stage, but she knew it would all come to light as the days wore on. She had come to this from her own experience with their local chiropractor in Halifax. It made sense to her that the body was capable of healing itself.

When the lunch room began thinning out, Selene glanced down at her schedule.

"Hey, where do we go for radiology?"

"Mmmm, follow me. We're in the same session." Ev swallowed her last mouthful and stood up. She kissed Morten on the head and motioned Selene to follow.

The day flew by, and by half past five, she was shattered and starving. The college pub was bursting at the seams with everyone out to meet and greet everyone else, despite the fact that it was only Monday night. She had learned that the college pub was named the Viking, after the rather high number of Scandinavian students. It was strange to see a pub located inside a college such as this one was, but it was nice and easy, overlooked the quad outside, and the funds went to the student council.

Freshers week had completed the preceding week, save the one last ritual, Guardian Night. It was the night that all new students were invited to a meal at one of the upper year homes. Even though she was in third year, she had been invited to one of the dinners on the Friday eve. She had rearranged her work schedule to be able to attend. She really wanted to get to know as many people here as she could. It was a relatively small college compared to the larger ones in the States. She was already recognising many of the faces, even if she didn't know their names. Most of the teachers seemed quite nice and approachable. So far so good. It was quite a different experience compared to her first week at Dalhousie, as the campus was so sprawling, she had had to run between classes to make them on time. It felt good to be in a smaller more intimate college.

Selene joined her last class in the pub for a quick drink before heading home. She really did need to eat. She could see Mark and another tutor, Pete, enter the bar from the far end. She smiled at them as they approached.

"Hey how did the day go?" Mark asked in greeting.

"Pretty good. Although it was a bit of a shocker to be in your class this morning. You could have warned me!" Selene genially punched him in the arm.

Pete chuckled. "Now that would have taken the fun out of it doll. Let the old man have his simple pleasures."

Selene blushed.

"Come, let me get you a drink. What will you have?" Mark asked.

"Guinness please. I'm starving so it ought to fill the

17

gap a bit."

"Crisps too then! On the way." Mark pushed his way through and began his order.

Pete smiled at her again and glanced around. "Met any new friends yet, Selene?"

"Yes thanks Pete. It's been a bit of a hectic day, but good I think. There are some really nice people here. It'll just take a bit of time to settle in. Everyone kind of has their cliques don't they."

"Here we go." Mark returned with the round and several bags of crisps and handed it across. "Cheers big ears! Here's to an exciting new term."

"Cheers all." Pete said dryly with a grin.

"So are you working over the weekend again Selene, or are you going to someone's house for Guardian Night?" Mark asked.

"Guardian Night. I have been told I simply cannot miss it," said Selene, a crisp halfway to her mouth. "I'm looking forward to it actually."

"Whose house are you going to then?"

"Ummmm, some people named Kjersti and Paddy?"

Mark glanced at Pete. "Good, good. You'll enjoy that."

"What? What aren't you telling me?" Selene asked having caught his glance to Pete. "Come on, give it up."

"Nothing. It's a big house, actually I think there are about six students living there, so it should be a proper party rather than a quiet evening."

Selene felt a bit relieved. "Ok, well I can live with that. You freaked me out there for a minute!"

Mark sipped the last of his pint. "Ah we're just playing with you Selene. Don't take everything so seriously. It gives you a chance to have an upper year student as a mentor for when you need help or to steal old notes. It will be fun and you will get to know a lot of the other students, its traditionally one of the best nights of the year."

"Ok then." Selene finished her pint. "Another round?" Both men nodded, but Pete held her back when she tried to make her way to the bar.

"Mine please Selene. Let us get these in."

"Thanks Pete, but only half for me please." Selene could see Ev and Morten at the far end of the room deep in conversation with a few other very hot blond guys. "Is everyone in this place like super stunning or what?"

Mark cracked up and nodded. "Well you are hand selected." He ducked to avoid her hand as she reached out to swot him. "I'm kidding, really! Seriously, I don't know. It seems that way doesn't it? I think the college has a large draw from Scandinavia, and in general chiropractors tend to be people who are quite into health and fitness. So I guess maybe that's why."

"Maybe." Selene said. "But it's still a little suspect if you ask me!"

"What's suspect?" A grinning man joined them in conversation. He was quite a bit shorter than Selene, with crazy cropped dirty blond hair and large tawny brown eyes. His face was full of conspiratorial mirth. It was obvious that he and Mark knew each other well.

"Why only the Inquisition, good sir!" Mark said with a

19

salute. He turned to Selene, "Selene, this is Adam, another teacher here. Although he is currently moving up in the ranks to director of academia, wanker." Mark said, letting *wanker* slide quietly out the side of his mouth with a sly grin.

"Hi Adam," Selene took the hand he offered and shook it.

"Welcome welcome. Always good to have a little fresh blood." Adam grinned at her and wiggled his eyebrows. She blushed a little but liked him instantly. His face was kind, and his eyes held a deep twinkle. There was something about his energy that sent tingles down her spine.

Pete rejoined them and offered Adam a pint as well. "Cheers mate."

The noise in the place was reaching deafening. Selene glanced around and caught Ev's eye. She beckoned her over to join them. Selene excused herself from the men and made her way through the packed space, even the halls were full to bursting, as was the quad outside.

"It's utter madness in here!" Selene exclaimed as she reached Ev.

Ev nodded. "It can be like this most nights post class, til about seven, then everyone goes home to eat and swot. Well, up until exam time, then it's a ghost town. How did your day go then?"

"Pretty good. I'm starting to feel like I'm really behind already, and it's only been like a day."

"Don't worry, you'll catch the groove, and everything will fall into place."

"I hope so. I'm going to make a move though, I need to eat and get organised for tomorrow. This week is going to break me otherwise! Thanks for everything today, Ev, I really appreciated your help."

"Hey, no worries. See you tomorrow, then."

"Goodnight all."

Selene waved herself off and saluted Mark and the guys, then left through the back entrance. The cool night air felt good and refreshing on her skin. She felt a little high from the Guinness and lack of food, but she wandered through the courtyard and around the college smiling to herself. The workload was going to be quite heavy, she could see that already, and she felt like there was a whole lot of catching up to do too. She had better get herself linked into a good study group, and fast.

three

Third year began as if the second year had never ended with a break for the summer. Within a few days Selene had enough homework and catching up to do to last her another year. And that didn't even include the first two years she had dodged by already having a degree. Finishing early on Friday, she headed home thoroughly exhausted, throwing her bag down onto her bed and collapsing. She quickly set her alarm for seven to make it to dinner for the Guardian Night. Staring up at the ceiling, she wondered what the hell she had been thinking, taking on another two full years study. Her brain hurt. She missed Jon, and her friends back in Halifax. Meeting new people was nice, but making real friends was really challenging. Her heart hurt. She suddenly burst into tears, and cried herself to sleep.

The rude bleep of her phone alarm woke her out a dead sleep. Dazed she rose and threw herself into the shower and dressed in jeans and a light turquoise top. She grabbed her bag and bottle of wine, the map, and headed out the door. She was really nervous and tired, but she knew she would feel better for getting out. She walked down to the end of her road, and headed across to find Ravine Road. Mark was right, the house was enormous, and she couldn't tell how many people were living in it. The music was already deafening, and she wasn't sure they would hear the bell if she rang it. She checked the handle. It was unlocked, so she let herself in.

"Hello? Anyone home?" she called out.

She could hear voices coming from around the back of the house through what could be the kitchen. She cautiously pushed the door open, and her face broke into a huge grin. She could see eight or nine people dancing around like complete maniacs in the garden. The kitchen smelled amazing, but she could see the BBQ roasting away outside as well. She walked through and stood by the kitchen door, waiting quietly as the song came to an end.

"Hey! You must be Selene!" A sweet ginger haired chap called out to her as he approached. "I'm Paddy, ye might'e guessed."

"Hi Paddy! Nice to meet you. Here take this." She handed him the bottle of wine and threw her bag down by the inside of the door. She stepped out into the garden to meet the others.

"It's the Scandi-Irish house this is. Three of each of us. A total madhouse. But I am sure you will enjoy tonight. Can I get you a drink? Red or beer?"

"Red, please Paddy. Thanks."

"This is Saoirse and Rune, Kjersti and Bronagh, and

Kristoff is upstairs still making himself pretty." Paddy quickly introduced her around. "These are my housemates, the other new students are freshers too. Margit, Signe and Fergus."

Everyone smiled and raised a glass to welcome her. They were a very lively group, already full of good cheer. Paddy returned with an excessively large glass of wine and turned to man the BBQ.

Everyone pitched in to set the table up outside, and gather the salads and rolls and everything else that was needed. By the time Selene sat down beside Signe and Kjersti, she felt she had known them for ages. Kristoff had finally descended to join them, with his arms full of bottles of wine and beer, and Selene caught her breath. He was almost god-like in his appearance, and she now understood that Paddy's comment was a joke. His skin was perfectly tanned against the shock of white blond hair, which fell to his shoulders. His eyes were so pale blue they almost looked white, like a husky. He was as tall as he was broad, but not over muscular, just fit, *really* fit. Selene was a bit tongue tied as he introduced himself with a kind shy smile. Kjersti and Bronagh clocked Selene's expression and burst into a fit of the giggles. They knew exactly how she felt, they had all been the same when they had first met him.

Kjersti leaned over to her and whispered in her ear. "Don't get your knickers in a twist over him, he's gay. Such a waste someone as hot as that! Terribly unfair to our sex!" There was a fair amount of humour in her voice. "He is actually one of the sweetest guys you could ever meet, though, truly."

Selene shook her head and took a very deep drink of her wine, grinning back at the girls.

"Yeah but at least we get to cop a feel in class!" Bronagh laughed and faked a swoon. Selene grinned at her, wishing that she could be in motion palpation classes with him too. College was definitely going to a very interesting experience.

The evening went really well, and it was long gone three in the morning, before Selene fell into her bed totally shattered from all the drink and dancing. After dinner more and more students had turned up, and it had turned into a full on party, just as Mark had predicted. Selene enjoyed every moment, feeling like she was part of things now, and relieved that she was actually getting to know people. Kristoff had turned out to be truly lovely, and had taken some time to chat to her about the course. Everyone she had met had made her feel very welcome. Ev and Morten had also turned up after midnight to join the party.

Guardian night indeed. So far, it was most definitely her favourite part of being here.

The weeks began to pass quickly from that point as the work piled on and free hours were sparse between working and college, and study times. Selene still hadn't been able to fall into a good study group. She knew she would cope well enough academically, but for the practical exams it would prove a problem. Her work schedule was starting to interfere a bit, and she knew that she would need to cut back. Finn, the pub landlord, was quite laid back about everything and took it all in stride, but his girlfriend Angela had had it out for her from day one. She wasn't sure what her problem was, but she went out of her way to make things difficult for Selene. She wasn't sure she would last much longer with the pressure Angela kept putting on her.

She had met the few Canadians and the two Greek students, and Petra, the other girl starting in the third year. Petra had fallen in with the rest of the German group and seemed to settle in so fast she almost disappeared from sight. Ev and Morten were lovely but were quite entwined with his Norwegian crew, so it was hard to catch them between classes or after college hours. Selene wasn't sure how long it would take to really find a true friendship here, but she knew she was good on her own most of the time. She kept occupied with work.

Her body ached at times from missing Jon, and the feeling of his arms around her. She caught her breath with the memory of being touched at times in class, when everyone was so open and touchy. She craved the closeness she and Jon had shared.

Late on a Thursday near the end of November, she found herself still snowed under an assignment at the library, when she felt the familiar cold sweep through her body. Just like the first time she had walked through this library. She shivered slightly and dropped her pen. She rose and

26

walked towards the spiral staircase and sacristy again with a smile this time, knowing that the spirits were about. She didn't fear them now, they had well and truly caught her off guard the first time though. Something or someone swished by her, and Selene spun around, coming face to face with Adam, and she jumped.

"Sorry to catch you off guard there Selene." Adam smiled, his eyes twinkling with knowingness. "What are you up to?"

"N-nothing. Just having a stretch." Selene said, catching her breath. "How's things?"

"All good. Bit late to be here though isn't it? Shouldn't you be out having a life or are you hoping to see a bit of the afterlife?"

Selene met his eyes. "Afterlife?"

"Just kidding. Though we do get the old sisters running around in here from time to time from the war days. This was a TB hospital at one time."

Selene didn't know whether to take him seriously or not. His energy was beginning to affect her again though, and she could feel the thrill of tingling running down her spine. How did he do that? He seemed to sense she could feel something as well, and his smile widened.

"Come. Pack up, and let's go have a drink," he said, placing his hand in the centre of her back. It had been aching solidly for weeks, but with the softness of his touch, the ache literally vanished, and Selene looked up in surprise.

"The bar is still open," Adam's eyes rested on hers. "And on a Thursday night there will be lots of others out and about, even if you feel you have no life at the moment."

Selene nodded and went to gather her stuff. How would he know how she was feeling? She wasn't sure what to make of any of this, but she liked Adam, and it felt good to know they could just hang out. Whenever she did run into him, he was always kind and genuinely interested in how she was faring. And the ache, it was gone. She followed him out of the library and into the pub, and sure enough there were loads of familiar faces. Selene smiled at many, and realised, she was probably isolating herself by doing so much work at home instead of at the library, then coming out for a break afterwards. *Note to self.*

"What can I get you, luv?" Adam asked as they found a small table in the corner.

"Something dry and red, and perhaps a glass of water too if you don't mind?"

"I don't mind Selene." Adam met her eyes again, and then headed for the bar.

Selene grabbed her kit and reorganised the bag so that the books fit a bit better. So much to carry. She also dug out a banana to fill the hunger gap as it burned through from so much brain work. Her back was still ache free after Adam's touch. She wondered if he was some kind of healer, but was too shy to ask or say anything.

"Here you go, drink up!" Adam settled himself and his pint at the table.

"How long have you been teaching here, Adam?"

"Too long. Probably over five years or so, like Mark

28

and Pete. I just wanted to stay in the area. Seemed like a good idea at the time." He leaned back in the worn out old chair and drank deeply. "Why here?"

"Why Bournemouth, you mean?" Selene asked and he nodded. "I don't know really. I guess Jon, he's my boyfriend back in Canada. He lived in Brighton for a while and really loved it. And I know it might sound strange, but I started having all these weird dreams. I knew I wanted to study and work with my hands in healing terms, but everything kept calling me here. I can't explain it, but when I got the acceptance, it just felt right."

"Makes sense." Adam said. "How are you settling in?"

"So far so good. The workload is heavier than I thought, starting half way through. There is a lot I am having to catch up on, and everything is different test wise and assignment wise, so it's learning a whole new way of doing things. I'm missing Jon a lot, it's hard not being able to speak to each other or write or anything."

"Why can't you write or call?" Adam asked.

"Jon took a job up north, in a very remote community. He's pretty much incommunicado."

Adam looked at her for a minute. "Must be difficult." Selene nodded.

"And home? How is your accommodation working out?" Adam sipped his pint and looked deeply into her eyes. He could feel the sadness and the loneliness around her.

"Ha! It isn't really. I am still looking for somewhere else. Eyes open all the time."

"Have you thought to ask Drew at the café? He has a

lot of local contacts, he might be able to hook you up with somewhere."

"That's a great idea. Thanks Adam, I'll ask him when I see him next." Selene stifled a yawn, trying not to appear rude. She was so shattered.

Adam leaned forward and touched her hand. "Come on, I'll see you home. It would be better for you to rest tonight. You've put in enough hours."

Selene nodded and they gathered their things and left.

Osian and Kristian found themselves following a safe distance behind Adam and Selene. So far, their time here had been easy and peaceful. Selene had settled in well, and they had had nothing to raise their guard over. But they weren't sure what to make of this man. He wasn't human like the rest of the teachers at the college, but he didn't carry a lower demon signature either. They looked at each other in confusion and shrugged. Time would tell who he really was, and what he was up to with Selene. They watched as they reached her house, he leaned over and kissed her cheek, wishing her a good night. She turned and entered and the lights followed her upstairs to her room. Adam watched for a moment, then turned back in the direction from which they came. He stopped before them and paused for a moment.

"Don't worry boys," he said. "She's in safe hands with me, you have nothing to worry about. I may not be able to see you, but I can feel you are here. I'm glad too. She needs all the support she can get. She's really been suffering over the last few weeks, and there will be more intense changes in the years to come. Be seeing ye."

With that said, he walked by, eventually disappearing into the night.

The angels looked at each other in mild alarm. "What do you make of that?"

"I don't know," Kristian replied. "He must be a seer or some kind of warlock, but he doesn't seem to carry a demon signature. Maybe a creature of some sort.... how strange. Well at least he means her no harm, I feel that to be true, but he obviously knows something we do not, it might be worth speaking to Raphael."

"Agreed."

They raised their left hands skyward and vanished within the glow.

The weekend passed quickly between work and studying, and Selene found herself back in her motion class Monday morning preparing for the exams. Ev and Morten had agreed that she needed a bit of extra time to practice and said they would help. Mark had taken a back seat through the term, knowing that it would be inappropriate to be seen to be giving extra attention to one over another. Adam had been his usual genial self, and it hadn't gone unnoticed by Selene that her back hadn't ached since he had touched her in the library. Things were warming up for another great college tradition. The Christmas Review show would take place in the coming week. Each year group was responsible for

31

putting on a series of skits, the show was basically an excuse to take the mickey out of everything and everyone, drink excessive amounts and party. She hadn't seen much of the group she had met at the Guardian night, but Paddy had made an effort to see her and make sure she was handling life in general, as had Kristoff.

Needless to say, the exams came and went, with great relief to Selene, she seemed to fare well in most of them. The show was an absolute riot of fun and laughs, although she couldn't quite remember the ending. Far too much merrymaking. Christmas was just around the corner, and she decided she wanted to take some time out and travel a bit. She was desperate for a real break. She booked a cheap fare to Dublin from Bournemouth for a few days, and then would return to London to spend her first UK Christmas with her brother, Mathios. They hadn't spent a Christmas together since he had relocated to the UK a few years ago.

The break couldn't come fast enough. Work agreed to give her a few days, but Angela was really nasty about it in general. Selene already knew that after the new year she would need to find other employment, it was just getting too stressful.

four

Ireland

Selene made it to the great dirty bus seconds before it pulled away from the airport stop. It was lashing down with rain. She knew it would be a good few hours before they would reach the Galway city centre, so she settled in and relaxed. Minutes later she slept.

The sudden stillness of the bus woke her, and she stretched her arms up and over her head. The bus was full now, and a young girl sat beside her listening to music at full blast on her iPod. They were at the station in Galway, and there was a line of people slowly gathering their belongings and exiting the bus. Selene reached up and grabbed her backpack, and slung it over her shoulder as she followed the queue in its slow march forward. She already had the directions to the hostel, and quickly made her way across the road and down the street.

Selene finished the simple paperwork, grabbed the key from the receptionist and headed up the stairs to the dorm room. There were six bunks, but only two people booked in, counting herself. The other two rooms were fully booked out, but the entire place was empty. *Curious.* She dropped her bag onto the top of one of the bunks opposite to where the other person was staying. She returned to the desk to ask where was good to grab a bite before wandering around a bit, still having a little time before sundown. The main city area of Galway was smaller than she had expected, and most of it was fairly walkable. Glancing at her map, she turned left outside of the hostel and walked down towards the Neachtains pub. It wasn't far, and it was just filling up with the after work crowd as she arrived. She managed to grab a spot at a small snug by the bar and ordered a meal. Within the hour, it was heaving, and she felt quite fortunate that the bartender was friendly and flirty, and so found she was rarely short of a drink as a result. The music was just kicking off as she finished eating, and saw a few lads approaching.

"Can we share up with ye or are ye waiting on someone?" the tallest of the three said with a grin.

"No, please." Selene smiled back and waved her arm over snug and stools. "Have a seat."

"I'm Donal, and these are me brothers, Ciaran and Patrick." Donal held his hand out as Selene extended her own.

"Selene." she said and nodded at the other two. "Are you from Galway?"

Ciaran smiled and pulled the stool up closer to where she sat. "We live in Birr, in Offaly, not far from here. I'm studying pre-law at the college there, but we are up to see Donal, here at the Uni. So rather than drive back and forth we thought it better to stay the weekend."

Selene smiled. He was lovely, tall, with short dark hair and unwavering deep blue eyes that held her gaze. She felt the colour rise a bit in her cheeks, and lowered her head to sip her drink. Donal reappeared with a round of drinks for all, including Selene.

"Thank you kindly," she said.

"Slainte!"

The boys raised their glasses, and Selene raised hers to join them.

"So where're ye from?" Ciaran set his pint down on the small table.

"Originally Greece, but I lived in Canada for almost seven years. I'm now studying in the UK."

"Well travelled girl then! Must be getting me passport in order!" Ciaran smiled, and settled back into the snug, as the music took over. There was silence between them as they listened with ease, and Patrick and Donal were into a deep and meaningful discussion about something, but neither Selene nor Ciaran could make sense of it over the music.

"So why are ye travelling through here at this time of year then Selene?" Ciaran had to shout over the music.

"I finished the term, and had a few days before work started for the proper holidays. I thought it would be fun. I've always wanted to see Ireland. I've had a lot of very close friends with Irish blood, and now at college, there are a lot of Irish students."

"Yes, well, we are the sort you'd want to be around now."

"Yes," Selene met his eyes, "I'm beginning to think so."

Ciaran held her gaze for longer than a moment, long enough for something deep inside to connect between them. They tried to talk more, but gave up in the end as the music was overwhelming.

The lilt of the Irish fife seemed to carry Selene back in time, it's mystical quality opening something somewhere in her heart. She felt herself drifting and swaying to the music. Time shifted and she found herself with a different crowd, dressed in clothing of a different time. The walls were darker and candles were lit, there were no lights. She shook her head slightly closing her eyes. When they opened again she was back. She felt Ciaran watching her with interest, and the colour rose in her cheeks. He smiled and continued to enjoy the sound washing over them. It was getting hard to sit still, as the music rose and fell, continuing to ascend in its percussive urgency. By the end of the set, everyone was up dancing, in spite of there being little room to move. Everything built to its final crescendo, then slowed, and slowed again to its rightful end. The entire pub erupted in a cheer.

The boys stood and began to make their way through the crowded room, Selene with them. Finally outside, Ciaran reached for Selene's hand.

"Let me walk ye back to your hostel Selene, 'tis late

and I don't want anyone getting the wrong idea and getting ye into trouble now!"

Selene laughed deeply and took the hand he offered, following him out of the pub.

"If you insist, well then..."

"Where ye stayin?"

"Kinlay House by Eyre Square."

"Never!"

"Yes, why?"

Ciaran laughed and pulled Selene close. "I guess this is meant to be! We are staying at the same place!"

"You're joking!" Selene stayed wrapped under his warm arm. "Well then, lead on!"

The two laughed and joked through the streets as they made their way back to Eyre Square. It was so easy to be with him. Everything just felt so natural and right. Nearing the entrance, Ciaran suddenly stopped and looked into Selene's eyes. Face to face, he lowered his gaze, and bent to kiss her. Selene froze for a moment, the image of Jon floating in the forefront of her mind, but the drink had loosened her enough to respond. And suddenly it was like a dam exploding inside of her, all the loneliness and emptiness, lack of Jon's presence, lack of communication, the need to be held and touched and loved, it all hit her all at once. Small tears rolled down her cheek, but she wiped them away and pulled Ciaran closer and deepened their kiss.

Ciaran eased back to catch his breath a few minutes later. "You are gorgeous. I can't believe ye were sat there all by yer own."

Selene smiled but said nothing, and he kissed her again. Minutes or hours later, they still stood outside, now feeling the freezing cold penetrating through their coats.

"Come, you're cold I can see it. Let's inside now." Ciaran placed his arm over Selene's shoulder and opened the main door. They collected their keys separately, then compared notes.

"Which room?"

Selene looked the key number. "Six."

"Never!" Ciaran exclaimed again. "Same hostel, same room even!"

"No way!" Selene couldn't believe it. How could that be? She felt a bit flustered now, after their long and deep kissing, that they would now suddenly be sharing a room.

"Come, let's away then." Ciaran took her hand and led her upstairs to the dorm room. They entered and went to their prospective bunks. No one else was there. The other beds still lay empty.

"I'm going to wash up and change, see you in a min then." Selene took charge of herself, gathered her things and left the room. When she returned, Ciaran had done the same, and they both looked a bit sheepishly at each other in their night clothes. They each climbed into their own bunks and closed the main light. It was dark, but the small nightlight meant that they could just about make out their faces from across the way.

"Ye alright there, Selene?"

"I am Ciaran, thanks. I've really enjoyed tonight." Selene rolled over and pushed herself up on her elbows to see him. "Tell me more about your family."

"Ach no, that's nay talk for a night like tonight. Tell me where you went when you were listening to the music earlier in the pub."

Selene looked up at the ceiling and smiled.

"I didn't go anywhere," she said. "I just felt like the music was drawing me back into time. Back when there were no lights, just candles, and we were all dressed differently. It was all very dreamy."

"I swear on me whole heart, Selene, that for an instant in time, ye did disappear. I swear it!"

"Ciaran, really. I think that's the drink talking."

"If ye say so, but, I know what I saw! Come on then, tell me what ye plan for tomorrow now."

"Well, given that I only just arrived, I wanted to see some sights. Thought I would see what the weather was doing in the morning. I have two days here and then off to Dublin, then back to London for Christmas Eve with my brother, Mathios."

"Ah, that's good. Hmm, for today, I guess it depends on what you like. The Uni is nice, and there are a few churches and all, and the Spanish Arch. Kirwans's Lane and the city wall are cool. 'Tis a nice town, and to be sure you'll be well occupied. If you fancy it we're going up to buy a bodhran from up in Donegal."

"Thanks, but I won't be caught between three brothers! I would really like to stay here and see a bit, as the next day I am off already."

"Ye're too far away, come be with me." Ciaran said suddenly. "I want to kiss you again Selene. We don't have to do anything more."

Selene let her head fall forwards into her hands and considered it. *Trouble, trouble, trouble* sang its way through her mind, but so did please yes, and she rose and climbed down one side and up the other to reach him. Snuggling in beside, they found each other in arms and kissed deeply again.

"Beautiful. Best. Night. Ever." Ciaran whispered holding her close. Selene smiled and closed her eyes. They fell asleep together between talking and kissing, still wrapped in each others arms.

"G'morn beauty." Ciaran whispered into Selene's ear. It was quite light outside, and they could hear the buzz of the hoover outside and people rushing about to start the day. Ciaran glanced at his watch, "Half past nine. Better get a move on before they kick us out!"

Selene stretched out beside him, her long torso exposed. Ciaran looked down at her and ran his hand over her skin. His touch set fire to her system and she inhaled sharply. He leaned down and kissed her, and she pulled him deeper into her embrace. His hands continued their exploration, and she allowed her own to run freely over his body. Time lost between them, they didn't even hear the door open, and it wasn't until they were blasted with pillows that they realised Ciaran's brothers had arrived.

"Wake up, enough of that!" Donal shouted laughing. Selene flushed a thousand crimson shades and buried her head under the pillow groaning, then suddenly sat up and launched it back at him. Patrick was grinning ear to ear, and Ciaran was as flushed as Selene.

"Well well little brother, leave ye alone for a moment and look where ye end up!" Donal winked at Selene, which only served to make her blush again.

"No room for the Holy Ghost in dere boy!" Patrick chimed in.

"Ah leave us alone boys, we're busy!" Ciaran said, pretending to be angry. But it couldn't hold, in seconds they were all dissolved in laughter. "Come now, out both of ye, let her catch her breath. We'll meet ye in the breakfast room."

Still laughing with knowing faces and little winks between them, Patrick and Donal nodded and walked out. Ciaran looked at Selene with a small smile. "Sorry about that. They can't help themselves."

"It's ok, it was pretty funny. I have an older brother too. Come on, let's get on then. You need to get on the road, and I have sights to see."

"Are you staying again tonight?"

"I had planned to yes. Then head off tomorrow to Dublin."

"Why don't you stop half way and stay at ours in Birr? Come tonight, and tomorrow we can play a round of golf, hit the pub....there aren't any sights as such to see really. Maybe a bit of hurling?"

"Hurling? I don't fancy that!"

"Whatever do you mean you don't like hurling? It's the

41

greatest sport ever invented!" Ciaran looked shocked.

Selene burst out laughing. "Where I come from, hurling means vomiting after too much to drink!"

Ciaran fell back on the bunk in gales of laughter. "Never!"

Selene giggled. It was funny how different countries used similar words but had completely different meanings for them. They got themselves sorted and went down to breakfast with the boys. The teasing was endless, but for the first time in a long time, Selene felt a sense of home and belonging. It felt like warm sunshine working its way through her soul, just being part of this lovely band of brothers.

"What are ye thinking?" Ciaran whispered to her from across the table as he leaned forward and took her hand in his.

"Just enjoying spending time with you. It's nice to be here and not so on my own. It gets hard sometimes."

"So that would be a yes, then?"

"Yes?"

"You'll come back to ours and see Offaly," Ciaran stated. The boys nodded in collusion. "We're going to teach her how to hurl like the best of us boys!"

Selene erupted with laughter, Ciaran joining in, especially as Patrick and Donal appeared totally confused.

"It means something else where she comes from!" Ciaran explained. "Vomiting from too much drink!"

Donal and Patrick shook their heads in dismay and mock disapproval that anyone could taint their hallowed sport.

"Listen Selene, spend the day seeing what you want to see. We'll collect you from here about four o'clock, and we'll be back in time for dinner at ours."

"Ok, sounds good," Selene said. "Are you sure your parents won't mind?"

"Sure enough!" Donal exclaimed with a wicked grin. "They'll be delighted now he's come home with a girl! We were all beginning to wonder...."

Ciaran swatted him hard with his backpack and turned back to Selene. "Seriously, it'll be fine now." He bent to kiss her softly and smiled as he pulled away. "See ye here at four then."

"Ok. See you then. I'll be here."

Selene waved them on and headed out towards the St. Nicholas Church, Spanish Gate and the medieval city wall. Most of the day was fairly drizzly, so she replotted her route to maximise the time and distances and keep them short. She bought a few postcards at a shop by the Church and found a quiet café to sit and write home. It had been ages since she had spoken to her parents, and she felt a little guilty about choosing to not return home for Christmas, but it truly had been extortionate airfare no matter who paid it. Selene imagined that her dad, would like the Church of his namesake, for it really was beautiful. She tried hard to keep busy and immersed in the day, but her thoughts kept wandering back to Ciaran, his kisses and the feel of his body against hers. It had all happened so naturally, like they had known each other forever. He was so kind and genuine. She really was a little worried about turning up at his parents' house with him, unknown and uninvited by them. Her thoughts turned to Jon, and she wondered what he would be doing over Christmas, and if they would finally have a chance to talk. Time was rolling on, and the days and nights apart were getting harder not easier. The novelty of space and time alone to grow had worn a bit thin in the deep dark of winter, and she found herself wishing the next few months away. Roll on spring she thought, as she licked the stamps and replaced the cards into her backpack. She rose to leave and headed back towards Eyre Square continuing her walk down Kirwan's Lane.

At half three she found a little pub and sat with an Irish coffee in hand while she waited for the boys to return. *Courage. It is just a bit of courage,* she reassured herself with a chuckle. Her mother had always liked single malt whiskeys, and Selene was proving to be a little like mother like daughter in this regard. She was on her second when they finally arrived at quarter past the hour.

"Well, well me lover, that is a good start. Careful I don't end up having to carry ye over the threshold now, I don't know what me mam would think to that!" Ciaran laughed as he greeted Selene with a kiss.

Selene blushed. "I will try to behave, I promise!" She drank up quickly and followed Ciaran out to the car. Donal was back at the Uni, and it was just the three of them now, heading back to Birr.

"Settle in now, it shouldn't take us long, about an hour or so." Ciaran said as he clicked the seat belt in beside her, leaving Patrick alone in the front like a chauffeur. It was already dark as they left Galway behind and crossed through the countryside. Selene leaned on Ciaran's shoulder. It wasn't until she felt a little nudge that she realised she had fallen asleep.

"Oh God sorry! How long was I out?" Selene asked.

"Not that long, sure 'tis alright now, 'twas quite lovely." Ciaran said. "Look here now. We're coming through the main part of the town called St. John's, and there beyond is Birr Castle. It's dark, but you can see the walls anyway. Ah, there's the golf club where we'll go tomorrow to play, and not far ahead is home."

Selene sat up and readied herself, gently wiping her eyes and hoping the little makeup she had put on earlier was still on and presentable. It had been a very long time since she had met parents of anyone, especially as a stranger coming to stay.

five

Distinctly unwelcome would be the politically correct
expression Selene would have used to describe their
arrival, or rather *her* arrival with the guys that night. They
had rung ahead, but as terribly polite as Ciaran's mother
was, she was all snow and suspicion the minute she laid
eyes on Selene. Dinner was uneventful and pleasant, Mr.
Hanny was full of hilarious tales, which only served to
wind up his wife more. Selene helped with the dishes as
Ciaran set a bed up for her in the lounge. Everyone said
goodnight, and Selene was left to her own devices. She
could hear Mrs. Hanny in the kitchen going on about
"that wan"; and how someone had turned up "with one
arm longer than the other". But she didn't really
understand most of it, until she heard the last bit, "sure
are there no local girls now." She covered her mouth
with her hand and laughed quietly to herself, then turned
back to her bag and looked for her night clothes.

An hour and a half later, she heard the door slide open.

"Budge up then Selene," Ciaran said as he crawled into the bed beside her. "'Tis freezing in this bloody house sure 'tis now."

Selene obliged, but began to panic. "What if your mother catches you in here! She doesn't exactly approve of me you know!"

"Oh no, you didn't hear her going off on one in the kitchen earlier now did you? Never mind her Selene," Ciaran laughed quietly. "She hates every girl we bring home, you'd have thought she'd have given it up by now being that there's three of us boys!"

That made Selene feel better. She did remember how her mother was around new girls that her brother Mathios had brought home at times. And how hard things had been with Jon's mother. A stab of guilt ran through her at the thought of him, and she shivered. Ciaran snuggled closer to her and kissed her neck as a result. Selene began to relax, and they faced each other in the darkened room. His hands found her face and held it closer to his, and he kissed her softly.

"Make love with me Selene," he said. "I know we've only just met, and you're leaving already tomorrow. It's too short a time to be sure, but it just feels so right to me. I want to be with you."

Selene already knew she was fighting a losing battle between her brain and her heart. Her body had already responded to Ciaran as it should, with love and affection, however misplaced it was. Her entire being ached to be

47

held and loved.

"Do you have anything?" she whispered, and she felt him nod and reach for it.

She leaned into him and kissed him, letting her hands slide up under his shirt and onto his muscular chest. She felt him exhale and relax into her body, and still holding her close and tight, he too allowed his hands to freely discover her. Gently and silently they manoeuvred around items of clothing, not daring to undress for fear of anyone walking in, keeping their expressions of pleasure to changes in breathing, holding and squeezing.

The mattress was so small they had to hold onto each other for fear of falling out. Selene rolled Ciaran underneath her and he caught his breath. He could barely see her, the room was so dark, but he could feel her power as she slowed his thrusts with her core, taking his control. Her hands held his over his head, and their lips deeply engaged. Of all things, he could kiss her forever. He lowered his head and caught her nipple in his mouth and she gasped. At the sound of her pleasure, he felt his body heave with such sudden release that he almost shouted out loud. Selene squeezed his hands and fell heavily onto him as a reminder to be quiet, and began to giggle.

"Shhhh, you'll have the whole house in here in a moment!"

"God I can't help it. I want to shout from the rooftops. Ye feel so good. I can't believe it now. Here we are. Kissing you last night was heaven, and this is more than that if that's even possible."

"You're mad." Selene chuckled quietly. "Beautiful, but mad."

They held each other for a while, gently resting in each others arms as they stole a kiss here and there. Ciaran's hand rested lazily on her breast, still gently massaging her.

"Tomorrow we'll hit the golf club and play the nine. That should take us well past lunch. I'll need to be driving ye to Athlone to catch your bus to Dublin then, I have a practice tomorrow night."

"Sounds like fun. You and Patrick must teach me to hurl though, whatever that is!"

"Ah yes, can't let ye go without that now!" Ciaran rolled off the bed and gathered up his things. "I had better go, if I fall asleep here, no matter how much I want that, we'll both be hanging come morning. Can I tuck this into your bag for ye to dispose if that isn't too awful? If me mam finds it there will be hell up." She nodded and he tucked the wrapped bits tightly in tissue and stuffed it into the front pocket of her bag. "Don't forget it there now. Will ye be ok Selene?"

"Yes Ciaran, go now. I'll see you in the morning. What time is everyone up?"

"Early. Da leaves at half five, but no need for ye to wake for that. He won't disturb ye. The rest of us will be up around half seven or so."

He bent forward and kissed her deeply one last time. "In the morning then."

"Goodnight."

Selene listened as he made his way back with stealth to his room. Once he had left the lounge, she wrapped

49

herself up deeply in the duvet and smiled. It was a beautiful moment in time, and she was glad they had met. Her heart felt guilty when she thought of Jon, but she breathed deeply and let it go for now. It was a momentary respite in months of loneliness, and she was grateful for it. She closed her eyes and breathed in the joy.

When she next opened her eyes it was only just daylight. She could see the pale glow of the sunrise beyond the dining room curtains, and could hear the sounds of the house waking. There appeared to be no central heating here, and she was next to frozen. She reached over to her bag and grabbed another jumper. She had just thrown it on when she heard a knock at the door.

"Hello lovely," Ciaran said warmly as he entered with a steaming cup of tea. "Drink, and run up and grab a shower. If ye wait til Patrick is through it will be too cold. Best beat him to it!"

"Right then," Selene said and threw the covers back, taking the tea in hand, she grabbed her kit and headed straight up, stealing a kiss from him on the way. She rounded the corner just in time to run into his mother. "Good morning."

"Good morning, did you sleep well now dear?" Mrs. Hanny asked coolly.

"I did thanks, and thank you again for allowing me to stay." Selene said. Mrs. Hanny smiled tightly and continued on towards her room. Selene jumped in and out of the shower and was dressed in minutes. It was freezing in the house, and she didn't think she would warm up, but the heat of the shower had helped. The remaining tea was already cold so she threw it down the sink as she left the room. When she returned to the lounge, the bed had already been cleared and the table laid out for breakfast. Her bag off to one side, she reclaimed it and packed up.

"Ah, that was quick," Ciaran said as he entered carrying hot potatoes, sausages and eggs.

"Coffee is on the counter if ye can grab it for me." He set everything down and followed her back to the kitchen. When they returned Patrick and his mother were already seated and waiting. Without a word Selene poured out and everyone began to help themselves. It was a sedate affair, barely a word spoken.

"So, hurling." Selene began, breaking the silence.

Patrick smirked and looked from Selene to Ciaran knowingly. "Ah yes, let's have a little go outside then before ye head off. It's a great sport, Selene, I cannot believe ye haven't heard of it even."

"I haven't! I guess it didn't make it to Canada, and my Greek side claims no knowledge either." Selene replied laughing.

"My boys are county players, Selene. Did they tell you that?" Mrs Hanny said proudly with a cold smile.

"Well, then, I guess if I am going to learn, at least it's from the best." Selene replied as she finished her last bite.

Plates cleared, Mrs. Hanny ushered them out to begin the lesson, saying she would sort the clearing up. Selene was pretty sure that it was the easiest way to get rid of her sooner rather than later, not that she minded.

She joined Patrick and Ciaran in the garden behind the house, where they had laid out a few sticks and balls. It looked like a cross between lacrosse and field hockey, and with a few short words, Selene was engaged in full play, able to throw a decent distance and receive well enough to pass. Patrick and Ciaran were impressed, and it was a great start to the day.

"Well, if ye play golf like you hurl, then we are in for a good morning on the course Selene." Ciaran said as they jumped into the car.

It was absolutely freezing on the course, and despite the sun making its best efforts, the two chose to retire when they reached the fifth hole. The pub was warm and welcoming, and Ciaran ordered Irish coffees and a huge platter of food to share. They ate in comfortable silence, sitting close together and hands touching. Neither seemed to want to break the day and make the move towards Athlone.

"It was a nice night last night," Selene said with a shy smile.

Ciaran leaned back into the seat and looked at her. "That would be the understatement of the year for me Selene. Meeting ye, spending time with ye, and making love to ye, all in the last forty-eight hours. I can't remember feeling so happy."

Selene sipped her coffee. "Me too. Moving to a new country, starting a new course, making new friends, travelling alone, it's all been a real challenge, much more so that I had thought it would be. The last forty-eight hours have felt like coming home. It's been bliss."

Ciaran reached for her hand and kissed it. "Come now, we must get on the road or ye'll miss your bus. Not that I would mind-"

"Ah but your mam would!"

Ciaran roared with laughter. "Perhaps. She's not all bad trust me. She just wants her boys set up in life before we settle down that's all. She doesn't dislike ye, she dislikes the timing of ye."

"If you say so." Selene grinned at him, and he smacked her lightly in jest on the arm.

"Go on," he grabbed his coat and then her hand, and they walked out to the car.

The drive to Athlone was less than half an hour, and time was running out. Practice would begin soon enough, and he had to be back on time.

"It feels awful to leave ye here," he said pulling up to the stop she needed along the Dublin Road.

"I'll be fine, I was travelling on my own before you, and will continue to do so from now."

Ciaran smiled and pulled her closer and kissed her passionately. "Ye were my first Selene. Could ye tell?"

"First?" Selene repeated, then clued in to what he meant. "No Ciaran." Selene said with genuine surprise. "You're beautiful and so loving. You're a natural." She giggled a little on the last word and he rolled his eyes. "No, seriously. Being with you last night was very special to me. Knowing this makes it even more so. I felt very well-loved. I would never have known had you not said, really truly."

"I guess I was just waiting for it to feel right, and with ye it just did." Ciaran reddened slightly. "I know we live in different countries and lead very different lives Selene, but is it ok with ye to stay in touch, be friends like?"

"I would love that Ciaran. Yes." Selene smiled and reached into her bag for her phone, and they exchanged details.

"I really have to go now." Ciaran kissed her again and held her in a tight embrace, neither really wanting to let go. He finally released her and stepped back. "Good bye Selene, stay in touch now my girl. I'll be dreaming of ye tonight."

"See ya Ciaran." Selene waved him off and turned towards the bus schedule. The bus they had hoped to make had long past, and there was another three hours wait for the next bus. She decided to wander through the town and look for somewhere warm to hang out. It was getting colder again as the sun was low in the sky now.

six

Glancing across the road, Selene saw a sign for the Athlone Chiropractic Centre. *Brilliant.* It was already the twenty-third of December, she wondered if they would be open. *Well, three hours to kill, if they are open, I will beg for an adjustment!* She walked across the road and down a little further, and entered through the glass door. It was jam packed with people of all ages, laughing and jostling each other, kids running around, total chaos. Selene made her way through the large room to the lady at the reception desk.

"Hi. I'm Selene. I'm a third year chiropractic student at Parkwood in Dorset, I wondered if your chiropractor could fit me in, but I--"

"Course she can. Don't look so worried, it really isn't

chaos, it's just organised to look that way. Grab a seat. I'm Eileen. Dr. Anna Jane will be out shortly and I will introduce you. It might be a while before she sees you though is that alright?"

"I have three hours before the bus, so I hope that will be ok?"

Eileen nodded and pointed to the last seat in the row. Selene made her way to it and dropped her bag. She suddenly remembered the stuff in the front pocket and blushed. She had better dispose of *that* before hitting airport security. *Now that would be mortifying!* She relaxed into the chair, and took in the office. Along the walls were many pictures, all hand drawn, about health and wellness. Some about choosing drugs and surgery last, about living life to the full, the power of innate intelligence and how the power that made the body healed the body, and keeping the body free of interference. Selene felt very at home here. She had definitely landed in the right office.

Forty-five minutes later the office was almost empty, with most people having come and gone. The momentum was natural and flowing, and Anna Jane seemed to have time for everyone. They all chatted and laughed the whole time. There was a really great energy in the place. Finally, Eileen looked up and waggled her finger at Selene, entreating her to come forward. Selene left her bags as they were and rose, as Anna Jane came back out with another young man.

"See you in the week now, luv. Make sure you take it easy on those lifts Santa," she was saying, and he nodded and waved as he departed. He smiled at Selene and tipped his cap. She wasn't as tall as Selene, and had medium length blonde hair, which looked a bit mussed up, like she had just woken up, but in a sexy way that Selene could never manage with her own hair.

"Anna Jane," said Eileen. "This is Selene, she is a chiropractic student in dire need. Do you mind squishing her in?"

Anna Jane chuckled and stepped forward to shake Selene's hand, her deep green eyes holding her own. "Where are you studying then?"

"Hi. Bournemouth, Parkwood College." Selene replied, returning the iron grip handshake with a grin.

"Cool. Come on in and let's check you out."

Anna Jane turned and motioned Selene to follow. They entered a smaller room with a large chiropractic bench in it, and more hand drawn posters framed on the walls.

"Your office rocks. I love the energy here." Selene said.

Anna Jane smiled. "Me too. It's a great community, I really like living here."

"Where are you from originally then?"

"The deep south, the Carolinas."

"When did you move here?"

"Almost five years ago now. I always wanted to live in Ireland, it always felt like I was called to be here for some reason. I used to have all these dreams about it. I always thought it would be Dublin or Galway, and here I am mid-country, but I like it."

Anna Jane motioned her to lie prone. She went about checking everything then made two manual adjustments. Selene was aware that Anna Jane was standing close to her and just observing her, but she wasn't sure what she was looking at. She chose to just relax and go with it.

"I'm going to do a bit of network stuff is that ok?"

"Yeah sure. What's that then?"

"Really low force energy type work. Just relax and follow your breath ok? What's the story with your thoracic spine, dude? It's like, out there."

"Chronic ache around T6/7, that is why I started seeing a chiropractor. It hasn't cured it per se, but it has settled it, I can breathe properly after an adjustment. The doctor kept saying it was asthma, but my mother never believed it. She wouldn't let them load me up with drugs and the like, as they could never prove it was necessary, or that it would change anything. It only aches when I am in a stressful situation now, or something needs my attention as far as I can gather. It is literally a thousand times better than pre-chiro. That's for sure." Selene rearranged herself a little and let herself completely relax.

Anna Jane looked over at her grandmother, who had appeared in the corner, and was shaking her head. *She doesn't know Anna Jane. Don't push it. She is one of them--*

Anna Jane looked at her grandmother with raised eyebrows and grinned. *Selene was one of them alright.* She could see the deep emerald and turquoise coloured roots entwined around the parallels of her spine easily. She just couldn't figure out how Selene couldn't know they were there. Time to dig into that later. Anna Jane lightly touched a few areas on her spine, and gently instructed her to breathe, and allow the breath to come through fully, especially through the middle of her back between her shoulder blades. She smiled as Selene involuntarily raised her arms by her sides, then extended them outwards and back, loosening the folds between her shoulders. Grandmother nodded and disappeared, and Anna Jane lightly tapped Selene to let her know she could sit up when she was ready.

Selene sat up and stretched. "Awesome. Thanks! I so needed that! That was pretty cool, I feel like I can really breathe deeply now."

"So what are you doing in Athlone, then?"

"I'm just passing through. I was in Galway, then met some friends, stayed a night in Birr, then from here I have a night in Dublin before heading back to work for the rest of the holiday."

"Fancy a party in Dublin tonight? I'm going to a masquerade ball at the 'Den of Iniquity' of all places."

"Is that a place or someone's house?" Selene laughed. "That sounds amazing, are you sure? I don't have a costume."

"My friend, Ydris' house," she said. "I can sort that. It will be fun, loads of weird and crazy characters. You'll love it."

Anna Jane led the way back to the front office where Eileen sat, having closed up the office. "Eileen, Selene is going to come with me tonight, so you can relax. You don't have to worry about me being all by my lonesome in the Den!" Anna Jane looked at Selene with a smirk.

59

"Eileen doesn't approve. She doesn't like the shady characters in Dublin!"

"Girls you have no idea what you are getting yourself into there." Eileen all but waggled a finger at them both. "Anna Jane likes to walk the line a bit, Selene dear. There is darkness and danger with that lot, they are not to be trusted! All of me bones are telling me now!"

Anna Jane grabbed Eileen into a huge bear hug. "Don't worry ma'am. I'll be back in two days, if not, send out the cavalry!"

Eileen harrumphed and loosened herself from her grip. "Mark my words girls, be on your guard. Especially you, Selene." Eileen added pointedly and glanced hard at Anna Jane. "Lovely to meet you. See you anon! Merry Christmas all. Do try your best to not meet an untimely end!" Selene heard her mutter under her breath as she waved, and was out the door quick as a flash.

"Come on." Anna Jane grabbed her bag and flicked the lights off. They locked up and headed back to her place on the outskirts of town. Anna Jane drove a large 4x4, distrusting of the tiny euro cars everyone else seemed to prefer.

"Deathtraps," she stated firmly, "already died in one of those once!"

She grinned at a confused Selene.

Died?

"Right then, off to mine to gather costumes, then a quick bite to eat and we are off! The party doesn't start until eleven tonight, so we have loads of time. We'll crash there tonight. I always have a room there, but don't panic

60

if there are lots of extra bodies! It's the party of the year! It's quite cool that you can come. All the wilds will be out!"

Selene smiled at that. She wasn't sure what Anna Jane meant by *the wilds*, but she was pretty sure that this would be a night to remember.

seven

A few hours later, they were standing by the enormous stone gates awaiting the valet who would take their keys and car from them. A horse and carriage waited to bring them down to the manor house. Selene was in awe of just about everything at this point. She felt a bit like Cinderella, taking a carriage to the ball. The dress, the horse and carriage, the coachman, the size of the house-- it was absolutely enormous and very old indeed. The gardens wrapped around the entire house, with the manor situated deep in the valley, then descended further into the hill overlooking Dublin. It was perfectly stunning. Through the floor to ceiling vaulted windows, she could already see that the ballroom to the right of the house was heaving with people. If it were not for the cars, she would have felt she had crossed back in time. In fact, as they crossed the threshold into the foyer, it felt they had. Everything was lit by candlelight, with no electric lights to be seen. They were greeted by a butler at the entrance and shown towards the stairs.

Anna Jane ascended with Selene following, to find the room she usually stayed in when she was here. Apparently she and the host were quite close friends.

"Glad you came?" Anna Jane grinned, looking at the expression on Selene's face.

"I am. This place is unbelievable, Anna Jane. Thank you for inviting me."

Selene took one last look at herself in the mirror and fidgeted with the low neckline of the dress. It was a stunning blue sapphire silk, floor length dress, but it was very revealing up the top end. She was utterly in love with it. Anna Jane had a similar style, a little more ornate, but in a vibrant silk red with an overlay of gold lace around the breast. It was breathtaking.

"Anytime doll. It will be a unique experience, I can guarantee that much! Come on, let's join the party!"

They descended the main staircase and walked through the crowded foyer and into the side room where there was a large bar set up. It was crowded as well, but Anna Jane managed to weave her way through and within minutes, both had drinks in hand. Anna Jane led them back to the main ballroom, and Selene caught her breath. She had never seen the like. It was like stepping into the mid-nineteenth century, the costumes were incredibly elaborate. There were seven musicians in the live band playing from a raised platform, and the music played on and on, with the dance floor full of people moving in ordered sequence. Selene felt a little dizzy with it all. She began to wonder if they had stepped back in time, it all felt a bit too real. There had to be over a hundred people in full costume in this room alone. It was truly remarkable.

"Dr. Malone!"

A deep male voice commanded from behind, and they turned to see a large man, dressed not unlike a king, enter the ballroom. Selene imagined Henry VIII, would have looked much like this. It might not have been the right century, but the likeness was compelling. Anna Jane ran forward and embraced him. He swung her around and held her close.

"I've been searching for you. Delighted you are here at last."

He nuzzled and nipped at her neck and inhaled deeply, and she swatted him playfully away.

"I'd never miss it, my dear. Come, meet my friend Selene." Anna Jane motioned to Selene to join them. "Selene this is my very dear friend and Lord of the House, Ydris."

Ydris looked at Selene with his exceptionally pale skin and dark beady eyes, and grinned, his nostrils flared with her fresh and rare scent.

"Welcome new friend. You are *most* welcome here. You are amongst friends. None of your *kind*, mind, but no matter, you shall enjoy all we have to offer."

Anna Jane's head whipped round as his comment met her ears, but she remained silent.

Selene smiled, feeling a bit confused and uncertain, and nodded. "Thank you most kindly, my Lord."

"Ydris, please! I am quite simply Lord of the manor, nothing else, and tonight is the night for that title to be in full effect! Go forth and be merry!"

He gave a very pointed look at Anna Jane, and with a quick glance at Selene, walked on to address the next adoring crowd.

"Did I miss something?" Selene asked. "What did he mean by *your kind?*"

"You really don't know do you?" Anna Jane mused under her breath. "Oh, never mind him. There will be all kinds of creatures out tonight though, make sure no one tries to kiss your neck whatever happens, there are those with a fetish for blood here, and it's a bit creepy. But most of them are really cool. I don't imagine that anyone will give you a difficult time. Don't worry!"

Selene stared at Anna Jane wide-eyed. *Blood fetish? My oh my oh my, where the hell am I?*

"You are in Dublin, my pretty, Howth, to be precise." A deeply accented and very sexy voice from behind her answered her thoughts. "Welcome to the evening ladies."

Selene jumped with the sensation of the warmth of his breath on her neck and the sound of his voice in her ear, yet he was a good few paces yet away. Their eyes met momentarily, and she blushed furiously and looked away.

Anna Jane stopped in her tracks, speechless. Although he wore a simple decorative mask across his eyes, both came to the very quick conclusion that he was one of the most attractive men they had ever seen. He was tall with long dark hair, and very muscular, which they could see even through his elegant black and white costume.

"And you are, kind sir?" Anna Jane asked in her best southern drawl.

"I am the Lord of Misrule, my lovely," he bowed deeply before them. "Please do not keep me at such a disadvantage, do reveal your names dear friends."

"My name is Selene," she said softly, still not meeting his eyes again.

"Anna Jane."

"Beautiful and enchanting. So lovely to have you here for the gathering."

His voice was soft, and he reached to kiss each of them by the hand, a small white rose appearing and then quickly disappearing where his lips had met their skin, as he did so. The girls gasped with surprise, and stared up at him.

"I will leave you to your mixing, but I will be seeing you later on. Enjoy yourselves tonight." He grinned at Selene, holding her gaze for more than a moment, and disappeared into the crowded dance floor.

Selene looked at Anna Jane, who still looked starstruck. "The Lord of Misrule huh? Well, he can misrule me anytime!" Anna Jane laughed, grabbing Selene's hand. "Come on, let's dance!"

Selene let herself be willingly pulled onto the dance floor to join the sequenced dancing. Her hand was still fluttering with electricity from where he had touched her. From time to time, she could see him at various corners of the large ballroom. And each time their eyes met, she returned his smile with a blush. *What's gotten into me? I shouldn't be flirting with anyone. Else.*

His expression was soft and inviting, and she felt quite drawn to him. It was like she couldn't help herself.

The dancing was easier to follow than it looked, and it was well over an hour later when she finally set herself free and headed towards the bar again to refresh herself. Anna Jane was lost in the moment and enjoying it all. She remained dancing and smiled as she watched Selene leave the set.

Finally holding a large glass of red wine, Selene made her way towards the open garden doors and stepped outside. Their Lord of Misrule was nowhere to be seen. The fresh air was frosty, and the garden twinkled like a fairyland with the combination of the frost and candlelight. There were several enormous candles planted into the grounds along the large paving stones, a stunning effect. She relaxed against the doorframe and sipped her drink.

The Lord of Misrule, stood not far away, silent and unseen, in the shadows. He knew she was not human, but she seemed totally unaware of this fact. She behaved like a human. She was the spitting image of his dear friend of old-- a taller and younger version. His mind was burning and working overtime. How could this be? Had Merope had another child after the fall? It was possible, the timeline worked. It had been over twenty years since she had fallen, and this girl was in her early twenties. He debated with himself as to whether or not he would engage her in conversation, in order to find out more about her, but he held himself back. He had other more pressing things that he was here to deal with tonight.

She was beautiful, but a lamb to the slaughter here. Too naïve to play with just yet. There would be time for her, but he needed to find out more first, and play his cards close. Something told him there was a lot more to this story. If she was indeed the daughter of Merope, her parentage was in question, as no human bond could have produced an immortal child. No, he would keep watch. For some reason he couldn't name, he felt very protective of her. He must ensure that the lamiae stayed well clear. All he needed was an upsurge of demonic interest in her. That would be very unfortunate indeed. *I need more time.*

"Dear girl!"

The voice boomed from behind her, making Selene jump and spin around, almost losing her footing. She wasn't used to these crazy shoes that were a part of her rather revealing costume. The whole plunging neckline thing didn't work for those on the smaller chest side she decided. She simply wasn't used to revealing so much. Ydris stood in front of her and grinned.

"Come! I will show you the house whilst the rest of the beasts are well entertained."

The Lord of Misrule rolled his eyes and looked back towards the upper master chambers. He knew that there would be a private party already in full swing up there, and the motley collection of lower demons would be in full play. He quietly followed them through the house, his protective senses alerted. She would have no idea what she was walking into.

Selene smiled weakly and took the arm he offered. She followed him through the main foyer again, and then down several stairs into a large kitchen area. He grabbed a couple bottles of champagne on the way through and opened the French doors leading to another wing.

"After you," he said with a slightly leery smile.

Selene was a little unnerved by Ydris. Following him to a seemingly abandoned area of the house with the party in full swing at the other end seemed a bit crazy. But she didn't know how to turn back without sounding rude, so she stepped through and began to ascend another large staircase. He reached ahead of her again and opened the large double doors, to reveal yet another large room, and another party in full swing. Selene's eyes widened with surprise mixed with relief. The room was packed with people in various stages of undress, however, and that quickly set her on edge yet again. They walked through to the far side and Ydris set the bottles down on the large oak sideboard. He smiled at her again, lifted a bottle and popped the cork. A cheer went up in the room and music began to play from the speakers that were set high into the five corners of the room. Selene could see that there was another room leaving off from the right side of the doors from which they had entered, and she watched as people filtered in and out. She looked

around at the décor, which was heavy and dark in deep
scarlet reds and navy blues, with aged squares of oak
panels, and a huge old oak sleigh bed buried under people
clambering over each other. It struck her as very odd that
the room was in the shape of a pentagon. It reminded
her of some of the older castles she had seen.

"Come, I will show you around,"

Ydris handed her a glass, and walked back across the
room, cheerily greeting the people they passed. Selene
was becoming more aware of the strange shapes of the
people, the colours of their eyes, and the faces around
her, and noting that some were totally naked at this stage.
In fact, they were *all* naked once they entered the next
room. She wasn't sure whether they were all drunk or
drugged, but something didn't sit quite right. The
atmosphere was highly charged, but it wasn't clear
whether it was just sensual or something else entirely.
The spa-like room was completely white, tiled with many
shapes and sizes of tiles, and many mirrors, and a large
chandelier was the centre point. There was still no
electricity, and the room was bathed in the warmth of the
many candles set into recesses of the walls. It was
beautiful. On the far wall was a hot tub in the shape of a
half moon, the largest she had ever seen, and it was
overflowing with naked bodies, laughing and talking,
kissing and generally playing around with each other.
Selene wasn't sure whether the whiteness of the room
paled everyone so much, or that they weren't just
naturally the 'Irish white' that was a common joke at the
college, but some almost appeared blue even in the

candlelight. The women in particular were quite beautiful, with their high cheekbones, wide eyes and long flowing hair. Further along was a glass wall, and beyond it a steam room. They all looked up and greeted Ydris with affection, some holding glasses up to be refilled, to which he merrily obliged.

"Shall we join them then my little angel?" Ydris grinned at her, pulling her closer to him with one hand, and loosening the buttons on his long ornate coat with the other. "I feel the need to relax a little now, it's been a very busy few days, and now that everyone is finally here, it feels only right to be getting on with this."

Selene blushed and stepped back, releasing herself from his grip. She had no intention of disrobing and jumping into the tub, with him nor anyone else.

"I, uh, I think I should go and see where Anna Jane is, Ydris."

"Pah, never mind her. She will end up up here soon enough. Come child, shed your mask and let us see *all of you*."

His voice husky and edged. His eyes remained beaded and frank, greedily taking in the shape of her underneath the sapphire costume.

"Your warm flesh is calling to me Selene," he taunted, and Selene shivered a bit and stumbled back into someone.

"Come now, I want-- "

"Ah we meet again my beauty," a soft male voice said from behind her, embracing her as she fell into his arms. "Selene,

71

Anna Jane has been looking for you. Come with me, and I will take you to her."

He gazed deeply into her eyes. Slightly breathless, Selene could only nod. She didn't even turn back to look at Ydris.

"It's a good thing you are the Lord of Misrule my friend, or we might be finding ourselves outside," Ydris growled.

He did not respond at first. He only glanced up at Ydris with a raised eyebrow. They locked gazes, Ydris took a step back and bowed his head.

"Stand down Ydris. *This* one is not for you. Should harm come to her in any way, I will find you, and you will answer to me. This warning stands for everyone. Let that be known."

Ydris nodded silently and turned away, his face red with anger. The lass was quite a beauty, and she would have added quite nicely to his rather growing collection of sirens. He looked down as he felt a hand slide up underneath his half undone shirt, onto his bare chest.

"Come Ydris, come play with us," she sang sweetly and led him away deeper into the room to continue undressing him. He glared back at the door where the Lord of Misrule had taken Selene, then sighed. It would be much more pleasurable to just give in, so why fight it? There would be time enough yet to find out why he had such a strong interest in the girl.

Selene breathed a huge sigh of relief once they had descended the stairs and crossed the threshold into the

72

kitchen area.

"Thank you. I wasn't really sure what to do, short of run."

He still held her gently by the arm, and she didn't want him to let go.

He looked down at her and smiled kindly. "Selene, this is not a place for you. What are you doing here? You obviously haven't much experience with these worlds. You need to be on your guard a little more. There are creatures here who would cause you harm, some intentionally, but all the same. You will be safer staying with the dances, and closer to Anna Jane. I will need to leave soon, my business here is almost complete, but I will keep an eye on things until then."

They reached the ballroom again, and Anna Jane ran forward to meet them. Her protector turned silently, kissed Selene on the cheek and bowed his exit. Selene held her hand up over her cheek where he had kissed her as she watched him go, deeply wishing he wouldn't.

"Where ya been?" Anna Jane giggled merrily, watching the tall, dark and very mysterious man as he left the ballroom.

"Ydris found me and took me up to his chambers." Selene said frowning.

"Oh my! Bet it's full of all kinds this time of night. He's a bit of a character, our Ydris," Anna Jane nudged Selene back towards the bar.

"That would be and understatement! Everyone is like, naked up there. Is that normal?"

Anna Jane laughed. " 'Fraid so. Ydris has some pretty

wild friends. They party pretty hard on all levels, if you know what I mean."

"What did the Lord of Misrule.... God, I don't even know his name...what did he mean by creatures? *It's all so surreal!*"

Anna Jane tossed her head back slightly, but she didn't reply right away, she shrugged her shoulders. "I'm sure I don't know. Likely just a bit of drama, don't you think?"

Before Selene could respond, Anna Jane stepped forward to accept another glass of wine for Selene and champagne for herself. "Have you seen anyone you know?"

"Anyone I know?" Selene asked. "Here?"

"Sometimes Ydris' brother is about, he studied at Parkwood, but I don't think he practices anymore. But I don't think he......" Anna Jane trailed off as someone beckoned her from across the room.

Kristian and Osian stood by the open window, listening with relief that Selene hadn't stayed up in the chambers with Ydris. How she had managed to get herself into this situation was beyond them. She was far too trusting. They could slide in and out unseen, but it was tricky, as some could see through their glamour, and they didn't want to alarm a room full of vampires, demons and lamiae with their presence. Anna Jane hadn't been able to see them, but she did sense their presence, she knew *someone* was watching. They would have to be extremely careful.

"Six more hours of this and she will be on a plane back to London. We just have to keep her safe until then." Osian said, and Kristian nodded.

The Lord of Misrule - or Lord of Chaos, as he was known to them, had also taken a special interest in her safety, which was very interesting and disturbing at the same time. They had watched him as he had watched Selene, and then covertly followed her as she was led upstairs by Ydris. They weren't sure what he was doing here, there were many sorts of creatures here, but mostly all lower demons and vampires, not the types they had thought he would be associating with. Perhaps he was up to something himself. The angels looked at each other and decidedly settled in for a long night. If any one of them got a taste of Selene, things could become very serious indeed.

Selene was yawning.

"Why don't you go up and crash," Anna Jane said. "You know where the room is right? I'll be dancing a while longer yet!"

Selene nodded and headed back to the bar to grab some water to bring up with her. She waved good night and then turned to go up the stairs. Her Lord of Misrule was standing there waiting for her.

"Calling it a night then my lovely?" he said.

"I am. I'm shattered, it has to be after four in the morning!"

"Indeed it is. May I?"

He reached for her hand, holding it as they ascended the staircase together.

"Do you have a name? Other than the Lord of Misrule, that is?" Selene asked as they reached her room. They both still wore the masks of the evening, and neither had made a move to remove them.

"I have many names, but you may call me Ios," he said, and held her gaze. "It has been my pleasure to meet you, Selene."

Selene caught her breath for a moment, his eyes were so intense and so dark, so deep blue they looked like night. With stars, little flecks of glowing white dotted through the darkness. All she wanted to do was to fall into them, and feel the touch of his lips on hers. She shook her head a little to clear the thoughts that were beginning to form.

"Thank you again for rescuing me from Ydris," she reached up and removed the small mask on her face, and stared into his eyes.

"Try not to find yourself alone with him Selene," Ios said. "Let's just say that he can be very persuasive."

He stepped back to look at her without her mask. She was indeed the image of Merope, he could really see it clearly now, even in spite of the fact that their eyes were a different colour. It unnerved him somewhat, for her eyes were a rather rare Aegean shade, and he knew he had seen those eyes somewhere before.

Selene nodded and turned to open the bedroom door. She wasn't sure she wanted to be left alone, but she knew that she needed nothing more than to crash out completely. Her body was aching with exhaustion.

"Good night, my Selene. I hope we will meet again sometime. You should be safe enough here now for the night, dawn isn't far around the corner. Just keep the door shut and no one should disturb you."

Ios reached down and kissed her softly and slowly again, on both cheeks this time, and gently squeezed her hand.

"Thank you. Goodnight Ios."

As she closed the door behind her, her knees felt weak. Every cell in her body burned, everything felt like it had been set alight. She couldn't *ever* remember feeling that before. Barely out of the dress, she grabbed her nightclothes and fell into a deep sleep across the bed by the window, her body still tingling with his touch.

eight

Anna Jane was asleep, wrapped around a very tall dark haired man in the bed by the window. There were three figures piled into each other on another bed, and two more sprawled out on the floor of the room.

Selene smiled to herself as she picked her way through them, grabbed her wash bag, and went in search of a shower. The house was deathly quiet, not a soul moved. If she had known better, she would have thought not a thing breathed, but her mind wouldn't let herself go there just yet. The word *creatures* still crept around, unwelcome, inside her head.

She found the shower room and scavenged a large towel. The heat of the water felt completely renewing. She thought back to the previous night and wondered why had Ios taken it upon himself to protect her, and wondered what he was actually protecting her from?

She vaguely recalled the fierce warning he had given Ydris. None of it made much sense to her, but thoughts were beginning to niggle in the far corners of her mind that all was most definitely not what it had seemed. She didn't know Anna Jane that well, but sensed she had been deliberately vague, when she had questioned her about what was actually going on.

Selene dressed and packed up her bag - it would be time soon to be getting to the airport. She wondered if she should wake Anna Jane or whether she should just ring a taxi. She had no idea where she was, nor how far the airport would be. She decided to check out the rest of the house to see if anyone else was up to help her first, before waking anyone.

Selene descended the staircase and deeply inhaled the beautiful aroma of fresh coffee as it assailed her senses. Thank goodness, she thought, someone was up, she just hoped it wasn't Ydris. She walked through the French doors into the kitchen, and saw a lone figure at the table leafing through a newspaper.

"Hi." Selene said softly.

The man at the table leapt up in surprise. "Ye scared the life out of me!"

Catching his breath he stepped towards her and smiled. "Wasn't expecting anyone up at this hour. I'm

Eoin."

"Hi, I'm Selene," she was relieved to see him smile. He was cute. Tall, with shaggy blond hair, a scraggly beard and big blue eyes. She couldn't really tell how old he was, but he seemed close enough to her in age. "I'm a friend of Anna Jane's, but she is out cold, and I need to find a way to get to the airport."

"Time for a cuppa?" Eoin grabbed a mug from the shelf as she nodded. "Enjoy the party last night?"

"Mostly," she said coyly. "Interesting crowd."

"Yes, my brother has a rather tortured history, and as a result some very interesting friends."

"Your brother?"

"Ydris, Lord of the Manor. I am the younger brother."

Selene raised her eyebrows, they were nothing alike in character, and they hardly resembled each other. She decided not to ask about Ydris' tortured history. Eoin poured her coffee and handed her the mug.

"I don't suppose I will see anyone before I leave to say goodbye?"

"Unlikely. Most won't venture out again until at least sundown. Some of the others may be up a little before, but judging by the state of the place, it won't be anytime soon!"

Selene sat down across the breakfast table from him. "You don't really look like brothers."

"Yes well, same mother, different fathers," Eoin said with a grin.

Selene smiled back and sipped her coffee. She

80

thought for a moment, weighing what she dearly wanted to ask, then thought, *oh hell*.

"What kind of *creatures* were up with him in his rooms?"

Eoin stared at her for a moment. It seemed odd that she didn't already know, but she had seemingly been up there, and come out relatively unscathed as far as he could tell. He couldn't see any marks on her neck or wrists.

"Who was up there with you?"

"Ydris took me up with him well after midnight, and there was another rather private party going on. Naked people, everywhere." She blushed a little admitting to it. It had been rather exciting, but she had been pretty freaked out at the same time. "I didn't actually stay with him very long, Ios came to find me and bring me back to the ball."

"Ios was *here*?" Eoin seemed surprised.

"Well, I guess you can't have a proper masquerade ball without the Lord of Misrule." Selene gazed into her coffee.

"Interesting." Eoin said quietly. "Well, to answer your question, Ydris has a collection of sirens, women he keeps close to him. He didn't try to taste you?"

Selene stared wide-eyed at Eoin as she registered the words. Her expression said it all.

"Anna Jane didn't tell you did she?" he asked, already knowing the answer. That was careless, and stupid, and he felt the anger rise in his blood.

"Ydris is a vampire, Selene."

81

"A w-*what*?"

But even as his words hit her, she knew in her heart that it was true, and that blunted the edge of it somehow. Had she sensed it last night? Maybe she had on some level. It had all seemed so crazy. She felt stunned, but relieved at the same time that she was not losing her mind. Selene fell silent and stared at Eoin. *Vampires? Sirens? What-the-actual-fuck?*

"You heard me. Many of the creatures here last night were a mix of lower demons; lamiae which are like vampires, but controlled by another higher demon, and the sirens that Ydris keeps with him. There's a weird kind of hierarchy. It started ten years ago, it was all like a fetish thing, but somehow it all turned real, *very* real at some point. I rarely see him now unless it's after midnight. It's all very sexy and all, but I don't want to lose my shit and become one of them. I prefer to keep my wits about me when I'm here.'

Selene was nodding now. "Anna Jane mentioned something about blood fetish thing. I didn't think she was serious. Does she know it's a real thing, or does she still believe it's just a fetish thing?"

"A real thing for sure, she knows better. She and Ydris have had their fling. She knows the truth. They've become quite close actually over the years. I cannot believe she brought you here and didn't lay it out for you though."

There had better be a bloody good reason.

"Yeah, a heads up would have been a friendly thing to do really, but to be fair, I only met her just yesterday as I

82

was travelling through from Galway."

Selene was still in mild shock, but she could feel even that fading. She actually didn't know what to believe. She closed her eyes for a moment and thought of Ciaran, just to touch base with reality. But Ios smiled back at her in her mind's eye. Her eyes suddenly flew open.

"Is Ios a vampire?"

"No." Eoin answered in short, giving no other detail.

Selene felt quite relieved, at least the one seriously hot and very friendly and protective man wasn't one of them. That was a good thing.

"Do you go up there often - to the whatever they are, chamber parties?"

"Not often, but sometimes."

"Is it always so..... *sexual*?"

"Yes."

Selene let this information sink in. She hadn't ever really had much experience save being with Jon. This was way out of her league.

"And you have sex with them?"

Eoin looked at her silently for a while. He wasn't quite sure what she was getting at, or why she was asking so blatantly, but he supposed she was just curious.

"Well, they are demons Selene. They like sex, it's easy and detached. Purely physical release, it's like a drug that keeps them stable for being very unstable elements. Spending time up there is kind of like being in a living version of most men's wet dreams really."

"Oh."

Selene gazed back into her coffee, her cheeks

83

reddening, and Eoin smiled. She was very attractive, but seemed wholly unaware of it. He couldn't believe Ydris had let her get away so easily, but he figured that Ios probably had something to do with that.

"What time is your flight?" he asked.

"Two hours from now. I should get going. Is there a cab I can call? I don't want to wake anyone." *Especially now.* She looked up at him finally, his intense blue eyes taking her in. She was grateful for the change of subject.

"No bother, love, I'll take you."

"Really? Thanks." Selene said. "You really aren't a vampire then?"

Eoin threw his head back and laughed. "No. Not a vampire. Human."

"Well that's a relief," she said. "Me too." *As far as I know.*

"Come on, let's get a move on. It's a good half hour from here across the city."

"I've never been here before. Shame that I have missed out, but I guess I will make it back at some point."

"Your only night in Dublin, and you end up here? Unreal." Eoin shook his head. "Some girls were just born lucky I guess!"

Selene grinned and reached for her coat. She followed Eoin out through the main door and they climbed the hill back up to where the cars were parked. He pointed to the black Land Cruiser, and they hopped in. He proved to be quite a tour guide as they wove through the city route towards the airport, and Selene felt quite satisfied that at least she had seen something of the city.

84

"Thanks a million, Eoin. I really appreciate your helping me out," Selene said as she stepped out.

He reached into the back, grabbed her backpack, and handed it across to her. He walked around the car and pointed to the entrance she would need. "Straight through there and you should be homeward bound."

"Brilliant. Please say goodbye to Anna Jane for me. No doubt I will see her again at some stage. I will text her later when I get back to London."

Eoin stepped closer to her and smiled. "If you ever change your mind about the goings on in the chamber and want to give it a go--" he couldn't keep a straight face as she blushed. "No, seriously though, here is my number. No playing now, if you come back to Dublin you can always crash safely at mine. It's totally in another part of town."

"Thanks Eoin. I'd better be going now." Selene reached up, kissed his cheek and backed away.

She turned and crossed over the road and entered the departure lounge with her head spinning. She looked back and he waved from the window of the Landy, and sped off back to Howth. She made it through the security and onto the plane without incident and promptly crashed out, not waking again until she felt the stewardess nudge her shoulder.

nine

Selene knew from long experience that Mathios was late for just about everything. She looked around for a tall, dark-haired man with mad curls that could resemble him, but no joy.

"Brothers!" she muttered.

She exited the arrivals area, and headed for the café. More coffee was definitely in order. Too much had happened over the last few days, and she felt the need for headspace, an internal debrief, and serious caffeine. She settled herself where she could see him when he eventually did arrive, and slowly sipped her short black and nibbled on a freshly baked chocolate croissant.

Bliss.

Mathios snuck up behind her and grabbed her up into a tight embrace.

"Welcome back sis!"

"Thanks Maty, it's good to see you."

She held on just an extra minute, letting the events of the last few months fall away. She really had missed him, they had always been so close. It felt strange that he was only two hours away and yet they still had barely a moment to see each other at times.

"Nice timing as usual!"

"Everything ok?" Maty asked, not minding the extra squeeze, but noting that it wasn't her usual thing.

"Yeah. I'm pretty shattered though. I ended up at this wild masquerade ball in Dublin last night. Mental wild. Totally like being in a nineteenth century vampire story! I crashed at four, but I don't think anyone else did until gone dawn."

"Wow, that's brilliant! I would have loved that!"

Selene thought of Eoin's comment about men's wet dreams and flushed crimson. She didn't think that would be Maty's scene, but how would she know anyway? It didn't bear thinking about.

"Maty?"

"Yep?"

"Do you think vampires and creatures and the like are real or stories?"

Mathios stopped in his tracks and stared hard at her. "Why do you ask?"

"I dunno, was just thinking that's all."

"Wild party huh." Mathios grabbed her in a light

87

headlock, rubbing her head.

"Hey!" she laughed and pushed him off.

"Come on Buffy, let's get home and you can crash out for a while. Some friends might get together at the local a bit later, it's usually a busy night out Christmas Eve and all that. But we don't have to go if you are pretty wiped."

"Thanks. Let me grab some sleep and see how I feel, is that ok? Sorry to be so crap."

"No worries, we can chill out, it doesn't matter to me either way."

They changed trains a few times before making it back to Notting Hill. It was a huge old building on Princes Square. Selene had no idea when it had been built, but Mathios had bought one of the maisonettes almost ten years ago with their parents' help. He had done a brilliant job with the décor, very masculine and earthy, definitely bachelor, but welcoming at the same time. It was light and airy, not unlike their home in Greece had been. It was only a one bedroom, so she would be camping out on the large pullout in the main room. She loved the photos and paintings he had collected over the years, it made her feel so at home every time she managed to visit.

Mathios suggested she sleep in his room for a bit, so he could watch a film and relax while she slept. He checked in on her a few minutes later and she was sound asleep. He was still quite disturbed by her questions about vampires and other creatures, and thought it might be a good idea to get a few answers. He called out quietly to Kristian and Osian, who quickly appeared by his side.

"Hey," Mathios said, trying to not be completely

unnerved at how quickly they could just appear. They had been watching over them ever since Merope had appeared in their lives all those years ago. "I am going to assume that you have actually been with Selene all this time?"

"We have, Mathios. It's been a bit sticky. There were loads of lower demons, but also some others who could have seen through our glamour, so it was very difficult to stay near her." Osian said.

"Where the *hell* was she?"

"At a ball given by one of the younger vampires, it happens every year around this time. She met a new friend who invited her along. Your sister is entirely too trusting, and so unaware of how attractive she is to them. Her energy signature is so strong, and her naïveté doesn't help that."

"She can't help what she doesn't know. Vampires?" Mathios swore under his breath. "You are kidding me."

"We are not. She had a pretty heavy introduction to the netherworld last night Mathios, but she handled it. Mostly as she didn't seem to get it, her human reality is so strong, she couldn't make the pieces of the puzzle add up until she met Eoin this morning, who spelled it out for her."

"Eoin?"

"The human brother of Ydris, the vampire in question."

"Right, of course," Mathios said with no small measure of sarcasm. "I should have known that."

"Look, she is alright, isn't she?" Kristian said. "We

would have interfered if she had been in any danger, but remember that there would have been consequences to that too, Mathios. In any case, the Lord of Chaos, a very powerful demon, has taken a liking to her. He protected her from Ydris' advances last night, and also set a firm warning that she was not to harmed in any way. So I do not think we need to worry at this point about anyone coming to seek her out."

"Really? A powerful demon likes Selene, and that's a good thing?"

"Neither good nor bad at this point, Mathios. Demons have many ranks and associations, not all are bad. Not all are Edomites," said Kristian. "He has offered her his protection in their world, and no one beneath his association will act against him. He is that powerful, yes."

"Ok. Ok. This has just thrown me a bit. She was supposed to be having a short holiday, not meeting up with the entire bloody realm!"

"We know. Calm down. She is fine. She will have questions, but we must do what we can to answer them honestly without delving too deeply into it."

"Ok. So when she asks me if I believe in demons I can say yes, but I have never seen one myself?"

"It's mostly the truth, isn't it?"

"It is I think, I mean, I've seen you all of my life, but I'm not so sure if I have ever seen a demon, not a real one anyway." Mathios mused. "But I guess if *you* exist, then anything is possible."

"Good, then let's just see how this plays out. We will

keep an eye on her in this world, and our demon ally can keep his world away from her." Kristian nodded at Osian, and they raised their palms, disappearing in an instant.

"Mathios?" Selene said sleepily from the bedroom door. "Did I hear voices?"

"No, just the telly," Mathios said as he turned and quickly flicked the kettle on in the kitchen. "You hungry?"

"Starving. What's the plan?"

"Hit the shower and we can hit the pub and grab a bite with some friends."

"Okey doke. Sounds good to me." Selene grabbed her kit and hit the shower for the second time.

Mathios paced around the kitchen, still unsure of the whole idea of a demon lending his protection over Selene. It unnerved him. Somehow the thought of demons wasn't nearly as unsettling as the thought of vampires actually being real. That had set him on edge completely.

ten

Eoin stormed upstairs to find Anna Jane upon his return. He was still steamed and a little disbelieving that she had allowed someone like Selene to just walk into a den full of vampires and demons with no warning.

Anna Jane was still half underneath McPhee, out cold. He shook her shoulder and she groaned. He shook it a bit harder, not above thinking that a splash of ice cold water would serve her right, but he didn't want to wake McPhee. This was between them, and he didn't want to involve anyone else. She had a thing for danger, Anna Jane did. She held no fear and stood solid ground with any and all of the creatures she had come to know over her time in Ireland. He knew she was a seer of sorts, even if she was human herself. He had a lot of respect for her, but she had seriously crossed a line, and he wanted answers.

"Anna Jane!"

She groaned again and opened a bloodshot eye, which couldn't really focus on him.

"What is it?"

"I need to talk to you, *now*."

"Ugh. What time is it?"

"Irrelevant."

"*What fucking time is it!*"

"Half past one," he said without sympathy.

Anna Jane groaned and gently shoved McPhee off her arm. She sat and steadied herself on the edge of the bed. "What do you want, Eoin?"

"We need to talk about Selene."

That got her attention.

She looked around the room. Selene was gone. She could have sworn she was in the bed by the window when she had come up with McPhee at dawn.

"Where is she?"

Eoin turned towards the door. "See you in the kitchen in ten. And go wash up, you're looking like you've seen better days."

Anna Jane glared and gave him the two-finger salute behind his back.

She rose in her own time, gathered her things and threw herself into the shower. Leaning against the shower wall, she let the heat steam the alcohol out of her system. *What the hell had happened, and what did Eoin want to talk about?* Her brain went into overdrive. She had met Ydris on a very crazy late night out during the first week she had arrived in Ireland for a holiday, back in his fetish days, before he was a vampire - in the days when she really had been looking for trouble. That was eons ago, a few years before her move, and it had been five years now since they had slept together. Ydris had the persuasive glamour of a vampire, and had almost had his way with her before she had recovered her senses. Miraculous really. They had been rather cagey lovers on and off for a few months, five years after the change, which had gradually given way to a real friendship again, despite their obvious differences. There was no way a warmblood was going to survive long term in his company.

She and Eoin had only met after his graduation two years ago, when he had returned from the southern UK. The attraction had been instant-- and all-consuming. They had spent every waking hour together until Eoin had found out that Ydris had been with her first. Eoin had never forgiven her, though she had known Ydris for years. But the past history with Ydris had stood firmly in the way. She couldn't have changed anything if she had wanted to. It didn't stop her from loving Eoin, but it had built a stone wall around his heart where she was concerned.

94

Eoin was sitting at the table inhaling more coffee when she entered. She poured herself a large one and sat across the table.

"Where is Selene then?"

"I took her to the airport earlier. She says goodbye." Eoin said coldly. "Why didn't you tell her about Ydris?"

"I didn't think it was necessary. No one would have tried anything with her." Anna Jane avoided his gaze. She had thought Selene not being human would have been protection enough from the vamps. But she had been wrong. She would never have admitted it to Eoin, but she was eternally grateful that Ios had shown up when he had.

Eoin looked up at Anna Jane with eyebrows raised. "What do you mean? Obviously Ydris tried."

"She isn't human Eoin. Although she doesn't seem to realise that fact." Anna Jane said, amazed that after all this time, Eoin still couldn't feel it.

Eoin was silent for a moment as he considered this new information. He sat back and exhaled. *How did I miss that? Well, she had distinctly told me she was human, and I believed her, that's why. Idiot.* She was also beautiful, and had a rare aura of innocence about her, a naivete.....and that had disarmed him. He was still annoyed with AJ for having been so careless with her though. He hadn't seen her in over a year. He had kept his distance from her, simply because it was just too hard to be around her. Ydris never missed an opportunity to let him know how she had felt and how she had looked in his hands - what she had *tasted* like. It was just too much. Ydris may have been all about the taste and the sport fuck, but Eoin had loved her. And deep down somewhere he couldn't acknowledge, that he probably still did.

"What is she then?"

"I don't know." Anna Jane said, playing her cards close to her chest. She wasn't entirely sure in truth, but nor was she ready to give up what she did know. "Ydris knew. He took her upstairs and he was going for the whole seduction scene apparently, when Ios interrupted."

"Why didn't you tell her about Ydris, Anna Jane? That was careless and a bit cruel really, don't you think? What do you think would have happened if Ios hadn't intervened?"

Anna Jane rolled her eyes at Eoin. In truth, she wasn't sure herself why she hadn't been clear with Selene about the party. It felt like she hadn't been supposed to, like there was something bigger unfolding here. It had been a while since she had had any visions, but the appearance of her Grandmother usually meant something was coming. She just didn't know what.

"Who knows?" she said, masking her uncertainty. "I think whatever she is, she needs to know. She really believes that she is human, and she isn't. I don't get it. I don't get how someone like her goes through life not knowing."

Eoin met her eyes and held her gaze. They were at an impasse and they knew it. The skies were darkening again with the day long of shadows. They could hear stirrings of movement upstairs, and knew it wouldn't be long before someone appeared.

"So what was with Ios being here, the Lord of Chaos?"

"I don't know. Damn he is something else though." There was a dreamy quality to her voice that irritated him. "He had this energy--"

"He is a pretty powerful demon, this wouldn't be his usual stop on the party train."

Anna Jane glared at him peevishly.

"And *you* would know - "

"I make it my *business* to know Anna Jane. My life depends on it." Their eyes met. "You play it like a game. But this is life and death. These are creatures that can turn on you at anytime. They have no humanity, they have no conscience, AJ. Don't kid yourself."

Ydris appeared at the entrance to the kitchen. "Ahh my two favourite humans. I was just feeling a bit parched." He laughed heartily at his own joke, stretching his arms long and wide, ignoring the unamused reaction of Eoin and AJ.

"So, Anna Jane, wherever did you dig up that little delicacy last night?"

"I didn't bring her here for *you* Ydris." Anna Jane stated without emotion.

"Then why was she here?"

"Chance. Fate? You have heard of it? She came in to the office yesterday, we chatted, shared some time, I liked her, I invited her. I didn't realise what a shit storm it would cause."

"Well, it did. And not just for me. Ios, our Lord of Chaos or Misrule or whatever, very gallantly protected

97

her. In fact, he never took his eyes off her the entire night."

"Did he not?" Anna Jane said drily.

"Did he not, indeed. I know I am considered young for a vampire, but I have never received such a powerful warning before to stay away from a particular creature. I would say he was very interested. She has been noticed now, and it won't be the last we hear of it, mark my words."

Eoin pushed his chair back and stood to make more coffee. He was lost in thought. Nothing made sense. He needed to figure out why Ios had been here in the first place. Had he known Selene would be there? Or had he other reasons to be here, and her appearance had been a surprise to him? And Selene. A trip to Bournemouth was definitely in the offing. He needed to gain more insight, to know who or what she was. Her innocence made him feel quite protective over her as well, and he knew that she would be in need of a good friend in the days to come.

Ydris sidled up to Anna Jane and kissed her hand. "So, what else is on the agenda, then, lover?"

Anna Jane felt Eoin stiffen then cringe as he heard the words. It was almost as if he stopped breathing.

"Have you been sharing our secrets, Anna Jane, telling our Eoin all about our little adventures together?" Ydris grinned at her and ran his hand down her leg. "Shall we head back up and relive the good old days?"

Anna Jane leapt up, her chair crashing back on itself. Now it all made sense. She slammed her hands on the table. "So *that's* it?"

She glared at Eoin and then back at Ydris.

"This stupid penis waving cat fight between you two? Jesus, Ydris, it's been over five years. Surely you've had better, your sex life has become bigger than even you could have imagined. It's been five years for fuck's sakes. Give it up!"

She turned to go and stopped at the threshold, turning back to meet Eoin's shocked eyes, her expression hard and angry, and her eyes liquid with emotion. She quickly turned to go before the tears began to fall. *Enough now. Enough. There's an end to it.*

Ydris shrugged his shoulders and glanced up at Eoin. "Do ye really want her, Eoin?"

"I don't need your permission nor your approval to be with anyone, Ydris." Eoin said coldly, grabbing his keys and storming from the room.

Ydris sighed and leaned back in his chair. "'T'was only a bit o' fun really."

Elba slunk back up the stairs before Ydris could discover her. Her mistress would most likely share their growing curiosity about who this new creature actually was, and where she belonged in their world. Especially after the warning that the Lord of Chaos had given Ydris. The power in the room had been palpable, many of them had never experienced anything like it. All of them had cowered under his threat. Yes, her mistress would be very interested indeed.

eleven

Time had passed far too quickly as far as Selene was concerned. Christmas with Mathios and some of his friends, and then the entire week and New Year's Eve at work at the pub. Ireland and vampires seemed a million miles away, lost somewhere between radiology and pulling pints. Being back to serious study at college, even with the short break in Ireland. Even with the rather bizarre time spent with the undead and the sirens, it already felt like she had never been gone.

Selene threw her keys on the side as she entered the house, quickly surveying the lounge to see if Daron was home. He wasn't. It had been a really long day. She was loving radiology, but it wasn't loving her. She kept seeing things that weren't there, and missing things that were, and it was driving her crazy. She needed to hit the books and get some serious time in and fast. The February exam set was only just around the corner. She poured herself a glass of red and headed back up the stairs to chill out for a bit before dinner and hitting the books again.

The phone was ringing downstairs, and as she lifted her head from the pillow where she had inadvertently fallen asleep. The house was in darkness, so she knew Daron was still not home. She leapt up and raced down, catching it just on the final ring.

"Hello?"

The line was bad and thick with static interference.

"......lo? May I speak...." there was a bright buzz of static......Selene Kostan......."

The voice sounded a million miles away, but she recognised it all the same.

"Jon!" Selene shouted in reply. "Is that you?"

"Hi Selene! Yes, it's me! Sorry for the ....static, the line is bad..... it's a CB phone, at the Ranger's office. It's the first chance I've had to ring...........you ok?"

"I miss you! I'm so happy to hear your voice!" Tears caught in the back of her throat as she realised just how much she was missing him.

".... too. How is studying going?"

"It's ok, it's hard, a lot harder than I thought."

"I'm sure you will kick ass sweet..... always do. You're too hard on yourself."

"Ha. Well, I hope so. How is life out in the boonies then?"

"All good..... hard. We really are in the middle of nowhere........ lies are getting a bit low, the snow is really heavy this year, and there have been some pretty long weeks where it hasn't stopped ....it makes it hard to get out. I haven't even been able to post a letter to you yet."

"I can't believe it. I still don't have your address either you know. Can you give it to me now?"

"Don't bother love, it wont get here by ...... ice thaws anyway. Write and keep me a little journal .... can catch up over the summer together with it. I really miss you too. Especially at night, when I ....think. I can't wait.............you........... Selene."

"Jon? I missed most of that. I love you so much. I can't wait to - "

There were three loud clicks and the line went dead.

Selene sat back on the sofa and burst into tears. The sound of his voice had made the last few months of missing him so achingly real. How was she going to last the next six? She had already ended up sleeping with Ciaran. She had thought she was the strong one, the one who wouldn't break, and it had certainly not turned out that way. Dreams of Jon had given way to dreams of Ios at times, and she really didn't know how to feel about that either, other than to just chalk it up to fantasy. Hearing Jon's voice had re-opened her heart, which she hadn't realised was so deeply shut down. It had been a very long first term, the workload had been heavy. This term had kicked off just as heavy. She had had to do a lot more

102

catching up from the skipped two years than she had been told. She had friends, but she wasn't really close to anyone. She missed her life in Halifax, and the friendships they had both had there, and the life they had had there together. Whatever it was that had called her here, had better come right. She knew she couldn't change course, even if she wanted to, there was something driving her to be here. Lonely as she was and as hard things seemed at times, she knew she was where she needed to be. She let the tears slowly come to a halt. The she rose, grabbed a sandwich and cuppa from the kitchen, and slowly climbed back up the stairs.

It was close to midnight when she finally reached over and closed the light, brain fried and exhausted.

twelve

The new moon made the darkness ever more present, and the skyward flow of fiery lava from the Halema'uma'u crater effervescent against the strident remains of sunset below the blackening sky. Lilith leaned across the solid wood frame of the hot tub to reach for her wine and drank deeply. The volcano shuddered underneath her, and she smiled and sighed with satisfaction. Eden House had been her favourite place to hang out for more years than she could remember. Over the last century, she had slowly accumulated percentages of what had been a hut-come-luxury five star hotel, until she had owned it all outright. And then she closed it down and made it her residence.

In all of the many lifetimes she had slid across and endured, this present time was good. Very good. For longer than she could remember, she felt a freedom here on this island and in this house, that she had felt nowhere else since her creation.

"Madame," said a soft deep voice from behind her, and Lilith turned her head to see her manservant Claude standing by the open French doors. She nodded at him and he stepped forward into the night.

"Elba is here to see you. She apologises for the late hour; however, she has travelled quite a distance."

"Hand me my robe Claude," Lilith rose from the heated waters and held her hand out for his as he helped her step up and over the edge. He gently held the robe across her naked body, and allowed her to thread her limbs through it.

"I will see her in the main library when I am ready."

"As you wish." Claude replied, and followed her back into the house.

Elba sat on a low settee by the entrance, waiting patiently. Exhausted by the long flight and the many delays, she almost dozed off. Many weeks had passed since the masquerade ball in Dublin, and she had been able to find very little information of use to add to what she had overheard. She hoped that the information would be of interest to Lilith, as it was a rare thing indeed to find an immortal and an eternal being on the ground, let alone in a den of demons. She had assumed this new creature was possibly angelic the way Ydris had spoken to her. He had quite pointedly called her *angel*, and spoke about no one else being of her kind. She wondered what Ios knew about her, why he had been so protective. She had been very surprised to see him there. Elba knew from past history that Lilith was always interested to hear news of Ios. She knew too, that they had not been in contact for almost a century.

Claude appeared before her and nodded, indicating that she should follow. She left her bag and stood up, stretching out as she trailed behind him through the great stone lodge. It was a spectacular dwelling, right in the middle of a national park, on the edge of the volcano itself. Claude showed Elba to the large library and took his leave.

Elba looked around. It was stunning and felt new agey-old, not like the libraries in England or Ireland, but old enough to have the scent of the centuries-old books that filled the shelves. She wondered if Lilith had actually read any of them, or if they were just for show, or for others to research things. The large windows overlooked the lower floor, which led out to the long sweeping deck that surrounded the lodge. She walked towards the table and poured herself some water, then stood by the window, watching the majestic flume of the volcano as it continuously sputtered into the darkness.

"Elba-iae." Lilith said coolly from the doorway. "What brings you here this night child?"

106

Elba caught her breath as she watched Lilith enter the library and seat herself by the large fireplace. No matter how long she had known her, centuries uncounted by now, her very presence still blew her away. She was as breathtaking as ever, her long flaming red waist length hair still wet from the bath, was twisted into a soft plait, which fell over her bare shoulder. Her olive coloured skin contrasted with her large bright green eyes, and fine delicate features. She was wearing a strapless figure hugging emerald silk dress, and she was simply stunning. Elba found herself at a loss for words. Lilith arched an eyebrow; then seemed to understand and smiled softly, appreciating the reaction. She waved her hand indicating that Elba too should be seated.

Claude returned with a tray of mixed drinks, handing Elba a small goblet of something warm, sweet and pungent. Elba looked up at him in surprise and at Lilith with gratitude. She was hungry, and it had been a good few days since she had had the freedom to feed properly. She drank deeply then placed the goblet on the small tray in front of her.

"Thank you Mistress Lilith, I am very grateful for your kindness. I was ever so hungry. I apologise for the lateness of my arrival, and lack of notice."

Lilith nodded and waited for her to continue.

"I was attending a masquerade ball given by a rather wealthy young vampire in Dublin before the Christmas, and I came across someone that may be of interest to you. The vampire had brought her up into the more private rooms, intending to seduce her I guess, and he

107

referred to her as *angel*, and I had overheard him greet her earlier in the same tone, indicating to her that although there were none of her kind present, that she was most welcome in his home. I had never come across her before. I might not have taken much notice, but Lord Ios was there too, and he was very protective of her. In fact, as Ydris was trying to seduce her enough to feed on her, Ios intervened. He gave a grave warning that she was not to be harmed, and let it be known that his warning stood for all demons, lamiae and vampires. It wasn't the type of party or place that I would have ever come across Lord Ios either. I just thought you might be interested to know that's all."

Lilith sipped her wine and relaxed back into the soft red leather chaise. *Interesting indeed. A new creature, and perhaps an angelic. This was news.*

There had been literally none of their kind born for millennia. But why ever would one of them be earthbound?

"What did she look like child?"

"She was quite tall for a female, and had long dark brown hair. Her eyes were.... unusual."

Lilith sat up a little straighter and placed her glass down on the table beside her. "Unusual how?"

"Like the colour of the warm Aegean seas of Greece. Almost crystal-like. She was very pretty actually. And the other odd thing was that she behaved like she was just a simple human. As if she didn't know who or what she was. She showed no power or resource."

"Interesting," Lilith said, still sitting upright. "Thank

you, Elba. I appreciate your coming and informing me. I will have Claude show you to one of our rooms, and you are welcome to take your leisure here for a few days to regain your strength after your journey."

"You are most kind, Mistress Lilith. Thank you for seeing me."

Elba rose understanding that she had now been dismissed, and followed the ever present Claude out of the library.

Lilith stood and walked to the large window, raising a glass to her reflection. *Could this be what I have been waiting for?* All the years that had passed since she had blown that sea nymph forward into time, baiting Gabriel. How she hated that creature, beautiful as he was, perfect as he was. Her heart ran cold. *Perhaps. Perhaps.* More information was needed. She grinned with delight at the thought of a new diversion.

It was definitely time for a little Chaos.

thirteen

"Guinness Selene?" Henrik asked from behind the bar, when he saw her enter.

"Yes thanks, mate."

She spotted Ev down by the sofas on the other end of the room. Morten was with her and they seemed to be having a bit of a tete-a-tete. Selene tossed her bag by the window and hung out, not wanting to interrupt.

Phew. Copying done, papers almost done. Easter break a few days away. Whew!

The sun was shining for a change, so she wandered

out into the hallway and took the long way round to the courtyard. A bit of fresh air was just what she needed. She opened the heavy wood exit door and stepped down to the ground and came face to face with Eoin.

"Selene!"

"Hey Eoin! What are you doing here?"

He grinned and gathered her up in a hug before setting her lightly down on the grass outside. "Down for a bit of Easter sunshine. The Emerald Isle is still in the doldrums I'm afraid."

"How long are you here for?"

"A week, maybe a bit longer, a month? Depends. I might take on a few locums to keep the dough rolling in, y'know."

"Please let me get you a drink, Eoin, to say thanks for driving me to the airport."

"Ack no, let me go, Selene. Thanks for the offer. I'll meet ye back in the sun in a sec." He stepped back through the college door.

The sight of Eoin both cheered and unnerved her. All that she had left behind and stuffed into a mental box labelled *'to be dealt with later'* suddenly flew open. He had cut his hair and trimmed his beard back significantly, and he looked quite handsome. She could see now why Anna Jane had fancied him. He really was the polar opposite of Ydris, in both looks and in personality. He was very thoughtful and kind as well. He would be a welcome friend to have for sure.

Eoin rejoined her, taking a deep swig of the Guinness in hand. "Ahhhhh, that's more like it now," he said with a satisfied sigh. "Do ye live close, Selene?"

"Darracott Road. But I've been looking for new digs as my landlord is a bit creepy."

"Ah, well, I did live here for five years, I can ask around for you see what comes up?"

"Thanks Eoin, that would be brilliant." Selene relaxed and closed her eyes in the glaring sunshine. The heat of it felt good on her face. *Bring on summer.*

"Penny for your thoughts." Eoin said, watching her.

"Bring on summer."

"Yes, couldn't agree more," Eoin smiled as he inhaled the fresh air around him. "Seriously now, how've ye been?"

Selene met his eyes and registered his meaning and his sincerity. "Ok. I've been ok. It's not like there is anyone I can talk to about all the stuff up there, Eoin. In all honesty, I haven't had time to blink since I got back, and until I saw you just now, I hadn't really given it any more thought."

"Filed under unexplained mysteries then?" Eoin grinned.

"Something like that, yes." Selene sipped her drink. "How's Ydris?"

Eoin remained silent for a moment. "We haven't spoken since ye left."

Selene nodded silently as if she understood, but she didn't really. What had really happened, then? There had been an argument between them, the three of them, Anna Jane had said as much over the phone, but hadn't gone into any detail.

112

"I gather AJ isn't speaking to Ydris at all. Does that mean you and she aren't speaking either?"

Eoin nodded. "AJ and I go way back. We have a bit of a history too."

Selene regarded him for a moment, taking in the look of loss in his eyes. "Do you love her?"

Eoin looked up at her question. Unexpected, but he couldn't lie. "I did. I still do, but I just cannot see a way forward with her. Her history with Ydris is just something I cannot get out of my mind. Anyone else Selene, anyone. But him?"

Selene reached out for his hand and squeezed it. "I get it. That's a hard one to swallow. But it was in the very distant past, before she ever knew you."

Eoin groaned and rolled his eyes. He knew all that, but his heart and mind just could not find any resolution. "He's me brother Selene, and a living-dead one at that."

She looked up as the college door opened and Mark stepped out with Pete, pints in hand.

"Hey all. Nice bit of sunshine then?" Mark said jovially, before he clocked Eoin. "Hello Eoin. What brings you to these parts then?" he said, suddenly cool.

"Hey Mark. How's t'ings?" Eoin smirked. He knew that Mark couldn't stand him, and it made him laugh inside.

"Oh, you know each other, then?" Selene said, trying to break the ice a little bit.

"It's a small world, Selene. Mark and I go way back, hey Mark?" Eoin said.

Mark looked away as he took a long draw of his pint.

"So, why you here, Eoin?"

"Came to check in on my friend, Selene, and locum work. Was hoping to run into Adam actually, is he about?"

Mark and Eoin held each other's gaze for a few more minutes before they turned to Selene rising, leaving Eoin's question unanswered.

"Well, if we are finished measuring whatever you boys feel you need to measure, I'm after another pint. Anyone need anything?"

Pete chuckled quietly as he sat by the next table and lit a fag. *Good girl.*

Mark shook his head and moved off to sit with Pete, and Eoin nodded a yes. He followed her back into the college and turned up the stairs to use the facilities.

As Selene entered the bar, Morten stormed out without a word. She turned back to see Ev in tears.

"Ev! What's happened?"

"Oh nothing, just the usual selfish prick ass guy bullshit." Ev reached for some tissue in her bag. "He wants me to go on this big camping weekend with everyone, and I don't want to go. It's our only long weekend before exams, and my Mum hasn't been well. I want to go home and spend some time with her. I don't get how he doesn't get that."

"Me neither. Shit. That's not the Morten I thought I knew, that's for sure."

"Yeah, I guess he doesn't want to be the only single there, it's all couples. I get that, I do. Sorry, or I would have asked you to come Selene. But you wouldn't have

114

been comfortable in that situation, never mind the whole language barrier thing."

Selene smiled. It was kind of Ev to say she would have invited her along. "Let him sweat it a bit, he will come to his senses. Come on, there's someone I want you to meet. Just let me grab some drinks."

Selene grabbed a round for the three of them and followed Ev outside. The sun was just about to vanish over the edge of the building and the temperature was dropping along with it.

"Brrr! Better drink up or head inside soon, it's getting cold out here!" Selene handed Eoin his drink and turned to introduce Ev. "Eoin this is my lovely friend, Ev. Eoin is down visiting from Dublin. He has already graduated, but he's down looking for some locum work."

"Hi Eoin, good to meet you." Ev smiled and looked back to Selene. *Nice one.* Ev wondered what was going to happen when Jon actually did make an appearance here, whether he would stay or go back, whether they would keep doing the extreme long distance thing. It all seemed so hard, and so lonely. "It is actually quite cool out here. Shall we reconvene inside?"

"Yeah let's go." Eoin said. Giving a little salute to Mark and Pete, he followed the girls inside. It turned into a large grin as he overheard Mark comment, "*smarmy bastard*", as the heavy door closed behind him.

The girls sat on the small sofa, and Eoin reclined on the larger one facing them. "Eoin is going to help me find a new place, Ev."

"About time. You *do* need to get out of there. That

115

guy is harmless, but way creepy!" Ev grimaced.

"Seriously? Has he tried anything?"

"No Eoin, I don't think he would either. He just drinks an awful lot and leers at me. It's gross." Selene said. "I think I should find my own space really. Jon will be here in the summer, and I hope that he will decide to stay on. It would suck to do this for the next two years, I hate being so far apart."

Eoin smiled and drank deeply. "Yeah, distance doesn't *always* make the heart grow fonder now does it."

"Well, it makes it grow harder that's for sure, and that's not a good thing." Selene said.

Ev reached over and squeezed her hand. She knew it had been really hard, especially with the lack of contact. She couldn't imagine having to do that. It felt so wartime. She finished her drink and rose. "Well, time to hit the last of the papers and finish it all off."

"See ya in the morning, mate." Selene said.

"Nice to meet ye. See ye again soon Ev." Eoin said warmly.

Ev nodded and left the two. Selene gathered her belongings up and looked at Eoin. "Fancy a quick bite at mine? I have to print the last paper, but then we can hang out a bit if you don't have any other plans?"

"Sounds great Selene thanks. Jonas is working tonight so he won't be back to let me in until at least nine. I was just going to hang out somewhere pub-like. Yer offer is a hundred times better!"

"Great let's go then."

They rose and waved their goodbyes to Henrik at the bar and left through the library entrance.

fourteen

"So. Anna Jane. Tell me all about it." Selene poured them each a second glass of wine as dinner cooked.

"Ah, trying to gain truth through drink I see." Eoin winked at her. "'T'won't work!"

"Come on. What happened there, really truly. I mean, I know her about as well as I know you. What do you have to lose by throwing your cards on the table?"

"Ye don't mince words do ye Selene?" Eoin leaned back in the chair. "Right then. I loved her. From the minute I saw her I thought all me Christmases had come at once. We fell crazy in love, spent all of our time together, then Ydris put his oar in and announced to the world that his little brother was having his seconds. It was *humiliating*. And he didn't stop. Every chance he got, he would reminisce about shagging AJ, and how good she tasted. It made me sick. I just couldn't cope anymore so I ended it. He did it again the morning ye left, but in front of AJ, and she went nuts on him," he paused. "I hadn't seen her for a year before that morning."

"That's insane. What an asshat." Selene said. "But weren't they just on again off again, like over five years ago? I don't get it, what's his hang up? Why would he do that to you? It's ancient history."

Eoin just drank his wine. He didn't have an answer. He hadn't really ever considered the why behind Ydris' behaviour. He was a vampire for fucks sake. And to be honest, he'd always been a selfish prick, even well before the change. Who knew why they did anything? He had just reacted. He met Selene's eyes and half smiled at her. She remained silent for a while as she too considered the why.

"I think, he is jealous of you." Selene said.

"Bollocks!" Eoin shouted with a hard laugh in response. "What has he to be jealous of? He has everything any man could want."

"Really?" Selene asked and leaned forward, gazing deeply into Eoin's eyes. "Really? Think about what a *man* wants."

Eoin raised his eyebrows in surprise. What a *man* wants. It took on a whole different meaning when she said it. He opened the second bottle of red and refilled

119

their glasses.

"He has immense wealth, bequeathed by his paternal grandmother, which is why I am working and he is not, aside from the vampire issue. He has immortality, he will never age, or get sick. Endless sex on tap with some pretty hot creatures, an awesome house, freedom." Eoin began.

"Does he now? Keep going."

"Loads of friends, power...."

"And?"

Eoin stilled. He really didn't know what else to say, so Selene began to fill in the blanks.

"Is that really what a *man* wants? Really? Are those things all you want? Is that that is important? How many of those people are true friends Eoin? Or are they just hanging around for the party? When does endless sex get boring without the intimacy that comes with truly being with some*one*? Loving and having love truly and deeply returned?"

Eoin looked up and met her gaze.

"Where is the love? Where is the sense of purpose? Of belonging? Of contributing?" Selene leaned forward again and reached for Eoin's hand. "He has nothing of the things that make us human, not anymore, limited as we may be." She stared deeply into his lovely blue eyes. "He has sex, but no love and no intimacy. He will never father a child. He will never create a living family. He will never take his kids to the park or to school. Can you see where I'm going with this? Life as he has always known it to be, all that he took for granted all those many years, has irrevocably changed. He is *undead*. He must kill to survive, or bleed those he entrances. He might fall in love if he ever cops onto himself. But he is too deep into his ego and all of its fine promises at the moment. Immortality may grant him that, it may give him centuries to mature. But it will also give him loneliness, as he will continually need to create new lives when he has outlived the human span. Can you see why he would be jealous of you? You are *living. Living!* He will never feel his heart race ever again. He will never be able to do all the things you can do. He will never feel all the things that you can feel, that you can touch. *You* are the one who is free Eoin. Not him."

Selene squeezed his hand. "Your love for Anna Jane showed him all that he has lost forever, and all the things he doesn't have. You held up a mirror, and there was literally nothing to see. And whether he understood it or not, this is how he reacted, by taunting you and teasing you and breaking you apart."

Selene sat back and sipped her wine, still holding his gaze. "You cannot let him control your life like this."

Tears fell from his eyes as her words broke through the barriers around his heart. The wall had shattered well and truly. He could hear the truth profoundly and deeply. He stood and grabbed her up in a warm embrace. She responded in kind and felt the tears in her own eyes.

"Thank you," he said and held her close. It was ages before they broke apart with the soft laugh of joy that comes with such release.

"Slainte Selene, for making me see what is real." Eoin

raised his glass in a toast to her. "God, so much time has been wasted. I just never saw it that way. I hadn't even considered it."

"Delighted, Eoin. Delighted." Selene sat back in her seat with a Chesire wide grin. "So, ya gonna call her, then?"

Eoin threw his head back and laughed. "Ye don't think t'is a bit late? She wouldn't still want me after the way I've treated her."

Selene shrugged. "Why don't you tell her to come down, or better yet, I will ask her to come, and you can meet her at the airport and take it from there?"

"Star. Would you really? Now *that* is a plan. But what if she doesn't want to see me?"

"She will Eoin, but she will give you a hard time, you know that, right? But she loves you and you know it. Take the time to talk it out, and for goodness sake be totally straight with her or you won't stand a chance. Being away from home and Ydris is a good time to clear the air."

"Right then. You ring her, and let me know the details, I'll take it from there. Well, I'd better push off and let you get some kip. Thanks Selene, it's been a lovely evening with ye. Ta for listening and all. Here I was thinking ye could use a friend after all the Dublin malarchy, and wow. Thanks a million."

They embraced again, and Eoin stepped into the dark night.

Ios reclined in the large cream leather chair in his study, and sipped the single malt in his hand. Selene. He sighed, letting his head fall back into the cushion. He hadn't been able to stop thinking about her since their chance meeting. Touching her had sent a sharp jolt of electricity through his system, catching him off guard. He could still see her looking back at him with her translucent Aegean blue eyes. Those eyes. He suddenly sat bolt upright. *Eternal.* She couldn't be. Who was she? He knew he had better find out soon, there was no way the warning he had given would go unnoticed in their world. He had felt the fear, the resistance, and the resonance. Where to start? He stared absentmindedly at the large ancient painting of Chios and smiled.

Anna Jane hadn't needed any convincing to fly south for the Easter break, as the weather in Ireland had been foul, compared to the long sunny days they were getting in the southern UK. Selene just hoped she would forgive her for setting her up with Eoin.

Selene borrowed an air mattress just in case, and an extra duvet from Ev, let Eoin know the flight details and tried not to hold her breath. She knew AJ would be livid, but she didn't see any other way of breaking down her defences. In the very short time they had known each other, they had already discovered that their friendship was as deep as it was wide. Somehow, they just seemed to know each other instinctively. Selene knew that through the hurt she would be as stubborn as Eoin had been. All she could do was hope and let the chips fall where they may. Her bag began to pulse, and she reached deeply into it and found her phone.

"Hello?"

"Hey sis, what's happening?'

"Hey Maty! What's up? This is a surprise!"

"Thought I might head south for a couple days over the Easter weekend, whadd'ya think?"

"Brilliant! It might get a bit crowded in here, but I am sure we can manage! Anna Jane is coming from Dublin too. Eoin is already here. It would be fab if you can come!"

"Are you sure?" Mathios was mildly alarmed, but equally curious, as these had been the people that had involved Selene with the demons and vampires.

"Absolutely! It's about time you came down really. It's really nice, and if the weather stays as it is, we will all be beach bound."

"Perfect. Anything for a break from the city!" Mathios said. "I'll head down for dinnertime Thursday and probably head back up Sunday after lunch if that's ok."

"Perfect. Bring beach kit. I have towels here though. Call me if there are any problems. Let me know what time to pick you up ok?"

"Ok Lene, see you Thursday!" Mathios said and ended the call.

Selene was delighted. A weekend full of friends and

124

her brother too, instead of just work and study. Suddenly, it was all looking up. A great time to blow off some steam from the heavy few weeks that had just passed, and before the final weeks leading into the exams. Brilliant. She jumped up and started a list of things to do in her head and got busy.

fifteen

Adam looked up as Eoin entered the café, saluting Drew as he made his way to the back.

"Doc," Eoin held out his hand. Adam grasped it firmly and gave it a good friendly shake.

"What brings you to these parts again Eoin? Thought we were well rid of you." Adam's eyes twinkled with merriment.

"Well, ye know yer never really rid of my sort now are ye!" Eoin said. "Another cuppa Adam?"

Adam nodded and grinned at Eoin. Two years had passed since they had seen each other, and he hadn't changed one bit. Maybe a bit more professional and less student looking, but his humour remained the same. Adam remembered how deeply grief stricken Eoin had been when he discovered the truth about Ydris and his crossover to the undead. It had nearly destroyed him. Looking at him now, however, he could see that he had come to terms with everything.

"So, what's happening then?" Adam asked as Eoin sat across from him.

"Selene," Eoin said, watching Adam's face intently for any reaction.

"Lovely girl, what about her?" Adam asked, meeting Eoin's eyes directly, but giving nothing away.

"I met her at Ydris' Christmas party. I think she might need some help and some guidance, and someone to talk to, someone that knows about us."

Adam nodded, understanding. "She's a special girl."

"In the not so human type of way, is that what you are saying, Adam?" Eoin leaned forward as he spoke softly. "Has she said anything to you?"

"No. I don't think she knows, Eoin. I've kept a close eye on her, and while she seems to be very aware of the energies around her, and her own energies, she hasn't made the connection yet. She hasn't opened her mind enough yet." Adam paused and sighed as he sat back in the chair. "I'm not sure whose child she is, but she is well guarded."

"Guarded?"

"Everyone has guardian angels Eoin. But she has *warrior* angels watching over her, two of them in particular. Big guns. No messing. And," he paused thoughtfully, "I believe, that the truth is being purposefully kept from her."

Eoin sat back in shock. "Really?"

Adam nodded. "I've thought a lot about it, and that is the only thing that makes sense. It won't last as a secret, she is evolving, and has done so quite a lot over the year already. People become aware of her when she enters a room, and I have overheard students talk about the quality of her touch. I will be here for her; you can tell her she can trust me, and that I was there for you. But let me reveal my full self to her in my own time."

"I will, Adam. Thanks. She's a lovely girl. It's good to know she is protected, even if we don't know from what or who or why."

"Well, we all know how you love a good puzzle. How's things up in Howth?"

"Good in general. I've been getting to know the ins and outs of the underworld fairly well now. I know who's who and what's what. Not any like you around though. One of the higher demons was at the Christmas party Ydris gave - the Lord of Misrule, or Ios as he is known. He was quite protective over Selene too. I'm not sure what he was doing there, not his usual thing to be sure. No shortage of lower demons though!" Eoin paused and sipped his coffee.

Adam was watching him closely, but showed no response to Ios' name.

"Fell out with Ydris, so we haven't spoken in months now. Not a bad ting 't'all, mind. Just been getting on with getting on. Selene really helped me to see a few things more clearly, so I'm going to try to get back with AJ if she'll have me."

Adam smiled and sipped his coffee. He knew AJ was a seer, from one of the old American families, but he had yet to meet her. "Will she be joining you here, then?"

"Yes. I'm to collect her shortly from the airport. She doesn't know I'm coming though, unless she's had one of her visions, so if ye feel a little groundshaking of the not good kind, ye'll know why!" Eoin sank the last bit of coffee. "I do want ye meet her though, will ye be around the weekend, now?"

"I will be, yes. You have the number, maybe just let me know where to meet you all for a drink or something, keep it casual and low key." Adam grinned and did a nudge and wink with his finger to his nose.

Eoin laughed and returned the gesture. "Done. Right then, better be getting on. Don't want to keep the lady waiting now, not when I'll be on me knees from the start!"

"Later, matey," Adam said and waved him off. "Good luck!"

He looked up at Drew and raised his cup. A three-cup morning already. *Not a good start to the day.* He hadn't reacted in front of Eoin, but the mention of the Lord of Chaos had set him on edge a bit and upped the ante as far as Selene was concerned. His own family had had dealings with him indirectly over the centuries. They had better find out who she was - and the sooner the better.

Selene wrestled with the air pump fitting as she tried to blow up the mattress she had borrowed from Ev. Every time it filled up, the fitting popped out, and the air rushed back out again. And the expletives were becoming more than just four letter words. She finally gave up and decided to let Maty sort it out. He would be arriving shortly at Pokesdown Station, and she couldn't wait to take him out and show him around. She had arranged to meet Ev and Morten for a meal in Bournemouth town, and if all went according to plan, Eoin and AJ would meet them too. Although there might be a lot of make up sex happening, so Eoin had indicated a possible no show. Selene had laughed and promised to not hold it against him.

Selene could see the tall curly head as it crossed over the train bridge towards her. "Maty!"

He looked up and waved back at her with a grin. "Hey sis!"

"Welcome to Bournemouth, well kinda sorta, this is the outer bit." Selene smiled and embraced him warmly.

"So what's the plan, then?"

"Drop your kit, and off to dinner in town. My friends will meet us there. We thought we would just do simple Italian if that's ok?"

"Perfect, I'm starved. The train food was diabolical. Hideous." Mathios smiled and followed Selene up and over the road and down a smaller road towards her house. It was a lovely red brick townhouse, not big, but nice enough. Inside had the familiar smell of damp that

130

many of the older homes had, but at least it wasn't overpowering. They dropped his stuff and headed straight back out to meet the others.

La Strada was tucked away on the other side of the triangle side of town, and the others, including AJ and Eoin, were already there when they arrived. Selene made introductions and they relaxed into an easy friendly atmosphere. AJ tried to give Selene a hard time over Eoin collecting her, but it was so transparently untrue she gave up with a fit of giggles. She was really happy that everyone was so at ease. She watched as the banter made its way across and around, and enjoyed the laughter. She also noticed that Ev hadn't taken her eyes off Mathios for most of the meal. It was very subtle, as was the blushing colour of Ev's cheeks, but Selene smiled as she took it in. Mathios appeared indifferent to her attention, but in his own way, she could see he was drawn to Ev himself. After the meal they decided to stop at the offy and grab a few bottles and head down towards the beach. The sun was just setting, and they wanted to sit outside and relax. The night was warm and already full of stars, and no one wanted to be stuck inside a loud club.

Eoin held AJ back a moment and sent a quick text to Adam. He could meet them by the pier, casually out for a walk by the sea. That would work. AJ read it over his shoulder and smiled, then tugged his hand to catch up with the others.

The night was unusually still as they made their way slowly down the boardwalk and onto the soft sandy beach, walking a little ways away from the large pier. The sun was just completing its descent, and the remaining rays wavered like a kiss of fire on the darkening horizon.

Selene had finished pouring out the wine, and turned to sit beside Mathios when she spotted a lone figure walking serenely along the boardwalk. She recognised him right away. "Adam!" She waved. He glanced up and smiled, shifting his direction to join them on the beach.

"Good evening, Selene, everyone," Adam said. "Ah, sure, yes thank you," he added as Mathios offered him a drink.

"Out for a late evening walk then Adam?" Selene asked as she made herself comfortable on the sand again.

"Oh you know, lovely warm night, good for clearing the head."

The others remained casually spread out along the beachfront, while Mathios walked a little ways away with trousers rolled up and his bare feet in the sea. Ev quietly followed and the two remained chatting as the water lapped their feet.

"Nice to see you again, Adam," Eoin said as he leapt up, reached out and shook his hand. "I'd like you to meet Anna Jane."

"Ah yes, the infamous AJ. Lovely to finally meet you, my dear."

"Pleasure is all mine Adam. Thank you." AJ laughed and shook the hand he offered. "So where does your family originally hail from?"

Adam met her eyes and held her gaze for a moment before answering. He knew what she was asking, but he didn't want to give too much away just yet. "Originally from Mesopotamia region, in times gone by, but obviously we have moved onwards and westwards over the centuries."

"Cool. Opposite side of the planet from where I come from, but my family goes way back through Celt times and then into Vikings before we lose the thread." AJ replied with a shy smile. "All the good stuff runs down my maternal side."

"As do most good things my dear, as do most!" Adam chuckled, and AJ relaxed. It was impossible *not* to like him. His energy was serene and very peaceful, unlike hers, which could be fierce and a bit unstable at times, even with her heart on her sleeve.

"Are you around over the weekend, Adam? I would love to hear more about your family if you are." AJ said as nonchalantly as possible. She felt incredibly drawn to him, and wanted to know more about him. Eoin hadn't said much, other than that Adam was a little like her. He was more than a *little* like her, he was a full blown warlock, and she knew it the minute he had touched her. She might be a seer, but unlike him, she held no power, other than being able to channel. This was one man she was going to be friends with for a very, very long time. She suddenly turned and kissed Eoin happily on the lips. He looked quizzically at her, but didn't say a word.

"What? Ye mean ye don't plan to be spending every waking moment with me, then?" Eoin interrupted, pretending to be offended.

Before AJ could answer, Ev and Morten stepped forward to say their goodnights to the group. Mathios

133

stepped away a little, and once Ev had said goodbye to everyone else, she took a moment to speak with him again while Morten was chatting to Adam.

"It's been lovely to meet you, Mathios, I hope you can make it down again soon, sometime." Ev said blushing a little.

"It's been lovely to meet you too Ev," he said, and reached out and held her hand, longer than he should have, then slowly leaned in and softly kissed her cheeks in the Greek fashion. "I hope I can make it down soon too. Looks like any time down here would be a welcome break from city life."

Out of the corner of her eye, Selene caught AJ's eye and grinned back at her. If electricity were visible, then there would sparks flying all over that action. But none said a word. Selene grabbed Ev into a huge bear hug and swung her around to break the moment, before Morten noticed. "Goodnight hun, I'll ring you tomorrow night. If it's sunny we'll just be hanging on the beach here anyway."

"Cool sounds great." Ev smiled. Glancing back at Mathios, she blushed and waved, then waved over at Adam, AJ and Eoin.

"Hmmm, looks a little fireworky there Maty!" Selene poked Mathios in the ribs.

"Whatever do you mean, angel?' Mathios asked innocently. He was smitten. No point in trying to hide it from her. But he was the kind of man that wouldn't make a move unless there was a clear way through, and Ev was clearly involved with Morten. As he called her *angel,* six pairs of eyes flew over to look at Mathios, something that he did not miss. *Curious* he thought.

"What? What did I say?"

"Nothing, nothing Mathios. I think we all thought we heard something different. Did you mean Ev angel or Selene?" Adam laughed softly, taking the intensity out of the question. But Adam already knew by his expression that Mathios, whilst human, knew a lot more about Selene than he would ever let on.

"Ah come on guys give me a break. She's a nice girl but she's with someone, so forget it ok?" Mathios said looking down and out to sea, a little embarrassed to be caught out by all. *Had it really been that obvious?*

"Yes, Maty," Selene said. "It was pretty obvious to everyone but Morten I'm sure."

Mathios paled a little in the starlight. That was definitely not good.

"Don't worry, mate. It will all come to rights. What is meant to be will be. Right?" Eoin chimed in.

Everyone started to make their way back up through the town and towards the taxi rank, as no one had driven in.

Adam dawdled a little with Selene, trailing up behind everyone else.

"Listen, Selene." Adam said. "Eoin told me that you had a pretty interesting introduction to the *otherworlds* up in Howth over Christmas."

Selene stopped short and whirled around to face Adam. *Otherworlds.* "What did he say?"

"He said you met AJ and then Ydris, his vampire

135

brother. And the Lord of Chaos as well."

"So you know all about them?" Selene was awestruck.

"Yes. I was here and really helped Eoin through the transition of losing a brother and gaining an undead brother a few years ago. I just wanted to say, that if you need anything or need to talk about anything, anything at all, please come to me. There is nothing you can say or tell me that will surprise me."

Selene reached out and held his hand as they continued up Old Christchurch Road.

"Thanks Adam, that means a lot. Sometimes I don't know which way to turn or what to think about anything. Especially the whole reality of demons and vampires and the like. It was pretty overwhelming." She loved just being near Adam, she felt completely protected and safe, and she liked the way his skin tingled next to hers.

"Are you a demon too then?"

Adam laughed. "No Selene, something else, but let's save that for another day shall we? Suffice to say, I am here, whenever you need me."

They had reached the taxi rank, and Adam reached over and kissed her on the cheek as he said goodnight. He waved his goodnights to the rest and set off down the old sea road on the opposite side of the roundabout.

Selene was quiet all the way back, lost in thought. The whole party at Christmas had been so much fun, but also so eye opening. The fact that an entire other world existed frightened her as much as it excited her. The middle of her back began to tingle again, and she wondered briefly if there was a connection, before laughing the thought off.

The rest of the weekend was easy, and everyone enjoyed just hanging out together in the sunshine on the beach. AJ and Eoin were totally back on, and a new sparkle existed between Mathios and Ev. Selene felt totally refreshed and renewed inside, and finally ready to face the last term.

Almost.

sixteen

It was Friday afternoon mid May, but already most of the students were starting to disappear. The annual Viking party was happening at one of the larger student houses that night, and the buzz was electric.

Ev waited for her with Morten on the street corner in the early evening, looking rather frightening and stunning at the same time. Her hair had been teased up and out with her Viking horns on top, and heavy eye makeup and very sexy costume.

"Wow!" Selene said. "You look amazing!"

"Aw thanks mate. It's only a bit of fun really, but prepare to get very very messy." Ev laughed.

Morten grinned and kissed Ev's hand, then gently grabbed her by the hair in mock taking fashion and began to lead the way to Ravine Road.

The party was in full swing already, and by ten o'clock it was heaving with hot sweaty and very drunk students dancing like maniacs both inside and outside the house. By midnight Selene was feeling a bit heady and went in search of water to cool down and sober up a bit. She fell into Kristoff when she finally made it to the kitchen, feigning exhaustion.

Kristoff smiled and handed her a large bottle of water, and led Selene upstairs to his room. "It's quieter in here. We can just chill out for a bit. It's all a bit hectic down there," he said as he closed the door.

Selene wandered around the room, taking in the décor, the posters and paintings. He was a very unusual guy, Kristoff was. She tossed her Viking hat aside and opened the bottle and drank deeply. She threw herself down across the bed and breathed in the stillness of the air. Kristoff joined her and they sprawled comfortably together. He reached over and grabbed the joint on the nightstand, and lit it. He inhaled deeply and breathed out slowly, leaning back into the pillows. Selene smiled up at him and took a drag. She had never got much out of pot, but had a go anyway. She inhaled, coughed, and inhaled again, giggling as she did so. Kristoff laughed and rolled her swiftly into his arms and kissed her. It was a gentle loving kiss, which held no more promise than the lovely friendship between them. Selene relaxed completely in his arms and felt her body lighten, a feeling not unlike flying slowly overtaking her senses.

She stretched out on the ornate chaise and lifted the glass of wine to her lips. The child beside her lay in a deep sleep, dreaming. He was as beautiful as Kristoff, just a younger version, and she somehow knew he was the close friend of her youngest son, who also slept beside them. She reached over and gently massaged his head, playing with his blond curls as she did so. She looked around the palatial room of pale stone and enormous pillars. Behind her she could see the Aegean Sea, it's colour spectacular and unmistakeable, through the arched windows of the castle. She rose and left the sleeping children, wandering towards the hallway ahead of her.

She could hear voices directly across the hall, behind the closed door. She paused for a moment, then softly pushed the door open a sliver. She froze, seeing two people deeply, roughly and very passionately grasping at each other. It was her husband the King, and the apprentice sorceress, his distant cousin who had arrived the year before. She knew she should be shocked, but she felt nothing. Nothing at all. As she turned and pulled the door to, the apprentice Elysia, glanced up and met her eyes with a dark, cruel and self-serving smile. She walked away and returned to where she had left the boys. Reaching for her wine, she kissed the top of each head and left them, making her way back to her own rooms.

The sun was shining in her eyes when she woke, fully clothed and sprawled across her own bed, having no recollection at all of how she had ended up there.

The term wound up into a frenzy as it approached the final exams. Everyone was maxed out on caffeine and stress. Selene was *particularly* stressed as she had never had to write exams like these. Many of the University exams in Canada had been the multiple-choice sort, so at least if you had some inkling you could make an educated guess. These exams, however, were all full written and essay type, so either you knew the answer or you didn't.

Ev looked quite bleary eyed and exhausted herself as she took her place across from Selene at the lunch break.

"Fighting again?" Selene asked concerned.

"Yep. Same old argument. I didn't go on the trip, which was bad enough, now he is upset that I want to spend the summer in Edinburgh with my folks. Mum isn't well. And quite frankly, I don't actually give a shit what he thinks. I am trying to pass these exams, and this isn't the time to be stressing about anything else."

"True." Selene swallowed the last bite of her sandwich. "Come on, a few more minutes and our last few hours to freedom will be counting down."

Selene stood and tossed the wrapping in the bin and turned to wait for Ev, who rose slowly and gathered her things.

"I think I will go home and collapse after this one, never mind be social."

Selene reached over and hugged her gently around her shoulders. "Don't worry. Just keep your focus for a few more hours, then we are home free."

Ev nodded and followed her into the hall and took her seat. *It might be a bit of a struggle to stay awake at this point, let*

141

alone focus.

The clock started and instructions were given, the final three hours of their last exam began. Selene prayed they would all make it through with no re-sits.

Three and a half hours later the pub was jam packed with exhausted but happy students, celebrating the end of another year. Selene felt that she had passed, if only just, and that was good enough as far as she was concerned. Ev begged off and headed home, but Selene felt like a little socialising was in order after the last few weeks of intense brain strain, and stayed on.

The next day Selene rose quite late to the phone ringing. She felt into her bag and found it, catching it on the very last ring.

"Hello? Is Selene there?" It was an elderly voice she did not recognise.

"Speaking."

"Hi Selene, I am a friend of Eoin's, he said you might be looking for a place to live for a while."

"'Yes, I am. Who is this please?"

"Oh I am sorry, my name is Tom O'Hallorhan. My very elderly mother lives on Darracott Road, and the tenant we had upstairs has now vacated. I had said to Eoin that I would let you know if it came free, and it has."

"Really? That's fantastic! Is it a studio, shared or one bedroom?"

"It's a one bedroom. I need to do some repairs and all, but it should be ready in about two weeks. The rent is sixty pounds per week plus bills."

"'When can I come around to see it please?" Selene asked, it was a little more than she could manage, but she would find a way, especially if Jon stayed on with her.

"This afternoon? I will be there for a few hours, cleaning and painting."

"Fantastic! I will pop by, I'm just down the road, which number is it?"

"Sixty-two. Fine then, just pop round when you can."

"Thank you ever so much, I will see you in an hour or so." Selene rang off and jumped out of bed and into the shower. She then sent a message to Eoin to thank him.

Selene already knew she would take the place, no matter what. It was the right location, and a chance to live fully on her own for a while until Jon arrived. She met Tom and they agreed on the rent and a moving date. She returned and left notice for her landlord and began to pack up. Two more weeks. Fortunately she was already double booked with shifts at the pub pretty much until he did.

There was a huge end of year celebration on the beach the next day before the students headed off home for the summer, and Selene was excited to meet up with everyone. She had finally settled into some good friendships, and she felt accepted as part of the year group as well. Maty had thought he would make it down for the weekend, but had been called in to work instead. Ev was quite disappointed but didn't really say much. She and Morten were still at odds at the beach party, and

Selene took it in stride, trying to entertain Ev with tales of crazy things. Adam, Mark and Pete made a brief appearance for a few drinks before quietly disappearing into the background.

"Have a good summer Selene, try to get some time out, don't just work twenty-four-seven." Adam advised.

Selene grinned at him. "I won't, but I do need to get some serious cash in before Jon arrives, he is here for three weeks, and I have cut down a lot to be able to spend some time with him. We've only spoken once in almost a year. It's going to feel really weird."

"It will." Adam said. "But just be open to possibility, and see what comes of it. I think if you try to force anything, it will make things difficult for both of you."

"Thanks Adam, true words." Selene swallowed Adam up in a huge bear hug. "Thank you for being here for me."

"Bah, nothing. All in a day's work, my girl." Adam was blushing. "You have my number if you need anything, and I may see you at Drew's anyway through the summer. By the way, he is thinking of opening up some evenings for dinner in the fall, maybe ask if he can keep you in mind?"

"That would be amazing!" Selene said. "I will, I promise. Anything to get out of Angela's mean line of fire, I tell ya, that woman has it out for me."

The party continued through to the early hours of the morning, with bonfires raging and music blaring by the Hengistbury Head. Selene was amazed that no police bothered them at any time. A great night was had by all, and most were more than ready to head home in the early morning, scattered to the four corners of the earth for the next three months.

seventeen

A visit to London was just what the doctor ordered as far as Jon was concerned. After eight months in isolation with bears, moose, seals, snow - endless snow - and a few other teachers - enough was enough. And a dry community at that. Time for some city life, Guinness and a good shag. Smiling to himself as he stepped off the plane, he was already envisioning a good start to the month ahead.

Selene was barely breathing. The heady mix of total anxiety and the thrill of seeing Jon again was making her crazy. Memories of the year gone by were seeping out of her pores. They hadn't talked much about seeing other people let alone sleeping with someone else. It had been a hard, long and lonely year, and finally giving in to the physical contact with Ciaran had saved her from isolation and despair. But guilt was its own demon threatening her from within. Looking up, she suddenly saw him. *Dammit all to hell!* Lovely and fit as she had remembered-and forgotten, and those gorgeous baby blue eyes - *just breathe girl!* For a moment she began to wonder what had possessed her to ever leave him in the first place.

"Jon!" she shouted, waving to catch his attention. He smiled his beautiful smile and walked over, dropping his bag and engulfing her in a huge bear hug.

"Hello darlin'!" he grinned and planted a kiss on her forehead. Then slowly and gently touched his lips to hers.

"I missed you," he said, his eyes holding hers captive.

"Me too. I'm so glad you're here. It's been a long year, too long." Selene pulled him closer as her voice broke emotionally, and she tucked her head into the nape of his neck. "Much too long. I didn't expect it to be so hard."

Jon smiled. *Good. A very good start indeed.* "So where we to then?" he asked, squeezing her tightly then releasing her to lift his bag.

"Car park, then south on the M3 to the sea."

"Sounds perfect. Does that include some food? I'm

147

starving! The plane food was shite. Thirsty too, actually."

Selene chuckled. "For what, Guinness or water?"

"Aye, you know me so well wench," he replied in his best Scottish brogue. "Fed, watered, bedded. Aye, that would be home then!"

An unexpected blush coloured Selene's cheeks. Jon almost did a double take in surprise. *Yes, time. Definitely too much time apart. Well, no time like the present to sort that right out.* He tossed the bag over his other shoulder and grabbed her in a sudden embrace, deeply kissing her, and taking her breath away. *That's better.* He continued the walk with his arm over her shoulder. They reached the car and drove for a while in easy silence, and Jon found himself dozing as she drove. Selene didn't mind, relieved to be lost in the silence. She needed time to think, her body still fizzing with the electricity of that kiss. Should she tell him about Ciaran? It was an affair, not a relationship, and they had remained friends. But she had broken, and she had thought she would be the strong one. She had no idea how he would react. *Breathe,* she instructed herself. *Just let it be, wait it out. See how things go. Its been a long time....just see how things feel when we get back to the flat.*

It was a gorgeous day, and the drive was fast and clear. Making her way down the M3, signs of late spring were everywhere, and the colours were beginning to blossom, making everything look radiant. Finally with some warmth in the sun, it looked like the entire natural world was out to play. The endless undulation of the hills along the motorway always amazed Selene. How was it that there were so many more million people here, but so much open space? It seemed like everyone lived on top of each other clustered in cities, towns, and villages, leaving miles of fresh open fields to be admired. It seemed to breathe eternity on a day like today.

The rest of the journey was uneventful, the car had been absolutely brilliant. One of Vinnie's friends at the pub had been selling it cheap, and it seemed like a perfect solution. She had been working a lot of late nights at the pub and taxi fares were adding up. So two hundred and fifty pounds later, she had a small purple Yugo car that worked perfectly well. Selene smiled and patted the steering wheel. Soon enough they were rounding the corner to the flat. Darracott Road. It was funny to have ended up back here on this street of all streets, and almost directly across from where she had spent her first few months with her old landlord.

"Jon?" Selene jiggled his ribs a bit to rouse him. "We're here. Do you want to hit the pub to eat, or crash first and eat later?"

"Mmmhmmm."Jon mumbled as he came to. "More sleep yes......." He flicked the door handle and pushed the door open with his head, and reaching for his bag, stepped out of the car. Looking back with a half smile, he said, "Where the hell did you buy this insane thing? I cannot believe we made it all that way!"

"Are you insulting my car? Barney is not amused!" Selene laughed. She was used to people staring at the purple Yugo. It was an unusual car, never mind the colour! "It's my two-hundred quid special. I treated myself after the first two weeks of needing a cab to get back from a late shift from the pub. It's been worth it, for sure."

"Ugh," Jon stretched out fully. "I'm awake now. Let me just wash up and let's grab some grub, I'm growling!"

Selene led the way through the small gate and up the steps to the front door. They stepped through and continued up the spiral stairs to the first floor. Selene opened the door and felt the sense of anxiety return as she showed Jon quickly around the small one-bedroom flat. It didn't help her nerves when he grinned wickedly at the sight of the rather enormous bathtub. Turning so he couldn't see her blushing again, she grabbed a clean towel and threw it at him.

"Here you go. Why don't you grab a quick shower and then we can head into town? Wash the airplane dust off ye."

"Sounds about right. Won't be a sec." Jon dropped his bag in the bedroom, and grabbing his wash bag flicked the shower on and disappeared.

It was all Selene could do to sit still. Pacing around the flat wasn't going to help matters at all. *Maybe I should just jump him now. We haven't seen each other in almost a year, is it supposed to feel this strange?* She didn't know how to feel, let alone behave! *ARGH!* She paced again around in circles in the small lounge. She heard the shower stop and the door open, so she sat down. Then, thinking better of it, went to find her keys and money. *Better to be waiting to go.* She wasn't quite ready for the naked bedding part yet.

"Ready freddy!" Jon appeared at the door with a little

dance – smart, casual and gorgeous as ever in a t-shirt with shorts and slaps. Selene smiled in appreciation, a look that didn't go unnoticed by Jon. Relief flooded through him. She had been so distant it was weird. The year had been hard, and with so much isolation on all counts via phone, online and post wise on his part, contact had been so minimal. It had obviously taken its toll. All he could hope was that there was no one else waiting in the wings for her, that he still had a chance to win her back. And he was willing to do whatever it took. The visions he had had were too literal and lucid, but non-sensical as well. They had started after the first sweat lodge, and they had just kept coming. He had so much to tell her it felt overwhelming. And most of it made absolutely no sense to him. Aside from the night of passion with the other teacher, which was the only thing that had been and felt real, there was nothing else. And he had no intention of bringing that up anytime soon.

It was a sunny breezy day, and they held hands as they walked down the road towards the beach café. Selene pointed out things of interest and general street names that needed remembering. Easy, chatty, happy. Selene smiled, and relaxed into the space of just being together. Jon asked many questions about the area, trying to get the feel of being here, the culture, the pubs, the beach, the surf, the students, the lifestyle. He had already lived a short time in Brighton, and things seemed to be pretty similar on all counts, although the town here was quite a bit smaller and a lot less London like.

151

They ended up taking the bus back from the main town, not realising how far they had walked, and Jon was shattered. He fell into the bed not even pulling the covers back and was out cold in a matter of seconds. Selene smiled and made her way into the kitchen, making herself a cuppa and settling into the cosy corner chair with a good book. Hours later she wasn't sure whether to wake him up for some food or to let him sleep it all off. She remembered how exhausted she had been on her arrival. The lead up, packing and lack of sleep had all taken its toll, never mind the extremely emotional goodbyes between them. She decided to let him sleep. She readied herself for bed and gently shoved him over so she could get the blankets free enough to cover them both. He reached over and grabbed her into a spoon and promptly disappeared back into the land of nod.

eighteen

"Selene is the daughter of that sea-nymph, the one
Gabriel was always watching over before he vanished.
Do you remember? The falling star you blew forward in
time for Gabriel to chase, trying to keep him busy while
we were up to no good." Gamaliel grinned and reclined
back against the wall of the house, drawing deeply on his
rolly. "Although, I cannot remember what it was we were
up to back then--"

Lilith cackled. "Those were the good old days, weren't
they? Things seemed so much easier in so many ways

back then, we were so much more imperceptible. We had a freedom of movement through time and space that has become far more difficult these days, all these modern technologies."

"True. True," he sipped his drink. "He *did* chase her though, through time. I don't know what happened next, however; we had both lost interest by then. But the nymph did have another child, what we don't know is whether it's Gabriel's or the human she then took up with."

"All in good time, all in good time," Lilith said. "I think the first thing we need to do is isolate the girl. We need to get her living alone, so we can infiltrate without resistance."

"Well, that might be tricky. She does have the usual guardian angels about, but she also has two warrior angels that were assigned to her by someone higher up."

Lilith met Gamaliel's eyes in surprise. "If that is true, then I believe we have our answer, my dear. Let's play a little game shall we?"

"Anything your heart desires, my lady," Gamaliel replied and bent to kiss her hand. Lilith stood and walked towards the edge of the balcony overlooking the still sputtering volcano.

"Let us set play to the Labyrinth shall we? Let's find out who the girl is currently with and break them up." Lilith fell silent in deep thought for a moment. "I will send that Elysia. That black witch that lived in the castle when the sea-nymph was Queen. She was nothing but a menace, and it did come back to me that she was ever so

154

demanding and self-serving. She would be a good choice for this. I am sure Manto will be delighted to be rid of her. Offer her a sweet enough deal that buys her silence in this time, and whet her appetite. Of course certain death is the answer to any questions she may have, including failure to succeed. Go back and find her in Chios. We cannot afford anyone to trace this back to us. And we need her cunning to pull it off." Lilith clapped her hands gleefully. She knew Ios would have been capable of planning just this kind of thing. Where *was* that handsome demon? She was yet to discover what role he played in this story. She couldn't figure out why in Edom he would chose to protect this girl. It didn't make sense. And the more she thought on it, the more she wanted an answer.

Gamaliel nodded in agreement. "That sounds like some strategy and game playing. It's been a long while since we have set a Labyrinth. It shouldn't be too hard to break them up. We can send the boy to a place where there are no modern communications, and he can sit there for a year, with memories of Elysia and of Selene. We will need Elysia to weave her spell before we send him off, to give him a reason to think about her. She must be in play immediately. Then we can play them off against each other on his return!" He paused as Lilith grinned. "I will make it so my lady, fear not. The first set of the Labyrinth is laid. *Isolation*."

He opened his chest with a deep breath, and released his wings, taking her into his arms and wrapping her closely, kissing her passionately as he did so, then just as suddenly releasing her and vanishing.

Lilith remained gazing out at the fire with a smile. Games were afoot, and oh how she loved a good, good intrigue. It had been a long time since she had used the power of the Labyrinth on anyone, and it sent shivers of real excitement through the darkness of her veins. It was after all, Ios who had taught her the art of strategy and the gifts of patience and cunning. Perhaps it was time for a little party of her own. She called for Claude and had him send out a summons to the Queens. She would need their cunning and sorcery. Yes, time to play and set a few things in motion. And then there was Sariel. Her Sariel. She never quite knew which side of the deck he played, being cast an enlightener, but she knew that she had to play her cards and see what he could offer. If this girl was an immortal and a possible eternal, there had to be some use for her that could benefit their kind.

nineteen

Selene could hear Jon snoring from the bedroom. She smiled to herself. It had been nice not waking alone. She had forgotten what that felt like too, having a warm body beside her. Through the kitchen window she could see it was another gorgeous day, and she didn't have to work at the pub until five. She set the kettle on boil, and grabbed the cafetiere and the day old croissants. She hummed softly as she prepared a simple breakfast for them both in bed.

Jon was already awake when she returned. "Mmmmm

I could smell that coffee brewing," he smiled, still a bit dozey. "Awesome, thanks."

Selene bent down to kiss him on the lips. She retreated before it could become more and turned to pour the coffee. "Best eat a little something, you crashed so hard last night you missed dinner."

"I could think of a few things I would rather eat," he said with a grin, but reached for his croissant instead.

Selene rejoined him under the covers and they snuggled together while they ate, drank, and leafed through the morning paper. She felt herself relaxing into his arms and enjoying being there again. So many good memories. It felt good to be together again.

Jon reached over, lifted the tray off the bed and shoved the papers onto the floor. Leaning on an elbow, he looked down at her, unsure of what to do next. Selene ran her hand down the side of his body, and he lowered his head and found her lips. Kissing her, he allowed his own hands to rediscover what he had fantasised about for months. The softness, the smoothness, the feel of her strength, the smell of her.....all of it.

He realised he was nervous. It had been so long between them. And with so little communication over the year, he felt unsure. He slid his hand under her neck and inhaled deeply, feeling himself come alive against her thigh. Her hands reached up to his face and held it. She looked into his eyes before kissing him again. Jon lifted her shirt over her head and pushed his own clothing down and off.

Everything felt new and strange, like the first time,

knowing each other so well, but seemingly not at all at the same time. Jon followed the line of her neck over her chest onto her breast, resting there a moment to feel her breathing and watch her nipples harden and pink up under the pressure of his fingers. He lifted his head and rolled his tongue over the other nipple, listening to the changes in her breathing. He used to be able to make her cum just by working her nipples into ecstasy. He was pretty sure he wouldn't be able to last long enough to do that just yet, he could feel his own body losing control in its need for release. Jon let his hand run further down into her wetness and gently massaged the swelling button with ever increasing firmness.

Selene arched her back into his hand and her breathing became rapid and shallow. She had missed this. Missed being naked with him, the sex, the closeness, the knowing how to bring her to this edge.

He pulled away before she could climb any higher and pulled her up and over top of him. He placed her back to his front, and reached down between her legs, entering her as she lay on top fully exposed. Once inside, he rocked her back and forth, holding tightly onto her breasts with one hand and her clit with the other. Selene could barely contain herself, and then she couldn't. She shouted out suddenly and came hard pressing down into him. She then lifted herself to sit up and she rolled forward onto her knees with him still inside her and rode him, she sank lower and pressed hard then released and rose repeatedly until he lost control and grabbed her tightly and shoved himself hard and fast into her a few times as he came.

Selene smiled as she turned around to face him. Jon lounged back with his arms under his head, then he reached out and pulled her back down on top of him and kissed her. In a matter of seconds he was asleep again, and Selene chuckled to herself as she rose and went to the bathroom. Just like old times.

The days began to blend into each other, as they spent as much time together as they could, between Selene's working hours. She had tried to cut them down a bit while Jon was here, but she was painfully aware that she really did need the money to cover the rent and food, never mind try to save for tuition fees. There were a few rocky moments, but mostly it was unfolding as well as it could have considering how much time they had had apart. Selene was starting to feel the pressure build up, the need to come clean and tell Jon about Ciaran was burning her thoughts. It was also really hard being his only friend here, work was her only respite for time alone, and she wasn't alone with Angela constantly on her back.

It was well past the yardarm when she finally woke again, Jon was still beside her snoring away. She smiled and looked at his face, her eyes following the lines of his eyes and the soft edges of his nose, his whiskery chin and lower down towards his neck and chest. All of it felt strange but home at the same time. She had missed him until her heart had bled at times. Yet at other times, she'd been able to forget completely that he had existed. How was that possible? Loving someone as much as she loved him, yet able to be so separate, so alone and so self consumed. Love confused her so totally at times. Making love to him now still felt almost like making love to a complete stranger, even though their bodies remembered each other. Her heart felt strange. *What is wrong with me?*

She rose and stepped into the shower, letting the heat absorb her restlessness. After a year of next to no communication, a year of waiting – holding the space in her heart – the ache, the loneliness. All of it overwhelmed her and she began to cry.

Jon opened his eyes in the bedroom a bit dazed, taking a moment to realise where he was. He could hear the shower running, and he could hear Selene, crying. His heart contracted and he sighed deeply, pressing against the pillow and raising his arms over his head in helpless frustration. He imagined she felt as he did, a little lost and unsure. He rose and made his way into the bathroom, where he stepped into the shower with her. Selene turned around and looked up at him in surprise, her eyes red.

"I'm sorry," she leaned into his shoulder as he embraced her.

"What's going on?" Jon asked.

"I-I didn't think it would be like this."

"Yeah, I kinda thought we would just pick up where we left off y'know?" Jon sighed. "Doesn't seem to be the case, does it?"

Selene shook her head in agreement. "We've both

changed so much over the year, and grown so much in different ways. Can't you feel it? And we haven't been able to share any of that space together."

"Yeah I do. Not being able to share this year and all the experiences, I think that's why we feel a bit weird about things."

"We feel like strangers, but not strangers." Selene said, the tears building up again. "I don't know what to do, but nothing feels right, and I just feel like there is so much pressure to be where we are not."

Jon held her in silence as he considered what to do. He didn't really know what to do either. Break up? His heart instantly recoiled at the idea. Instead he said, "Let's just start again. Let's be friends. Let's go back to the very beginning and see where things take us."

"Back to the beginning? As friends?"

"Yes, let's start over."

They held each other a little while longer then got out to dress. The atmosphere was lighter but weirder, neither sure what to say or do. Selene made her way into the kitchen and made some more coffee and a few sandwiches. The calm after the storm, like the relief they all used to feel when the humidity broke after a thunderstorm at home.

"I have to go to work. Will you be ok here? You have a key, so you can make your way around and familiarise yourself with the area or whatever."

"Yeah sounds good. Scout around, maybe head down to the beach for a swim or something."

"Mmm good idea. The water's lovely actually. I can

162

draw you a map again so you don't get lost, it's a bit of a windy trip to the coast road from here, its easy to get turned around."

"Cool thanks. What time will you be back?"

"Not late, the pub closes at eleven tonight, so I should be back shortly after if its not too busy."
Selene grabbed her keys and bag, and leaned down to kiss him as he sat on the sofa. "It feels weird to just leave like this after that conversation."

"It's ok. Probably be good to get a bit of headspace right now. I'm still pretty jet-lagged too, so I'll go for a swim and clear the cobwebs. See ya later Lene."

"Later luv, Jon I mean." Selene smiled and blushed.

He smiled sadly back at her, and it almost broke her heart. But it had been the right thing, the pressure had been too much, and as hard as this was, it already felt better and lighter. She felt like she could finally get air into her lungs again. Time would tell, but for the first time in over a week she felt like she could breathe. She turned and walked out the door and headed to work.

Jon leaned back on the sofa and sighed. Somehow this had to work out, for better or worse. Although, if they stayed together, in the end, it meant another two years apart. A week here was all he had needed to know that home in Halifax was where he needed to be; he couldn't stay here. Elysia flashed into his mind, meeting her the day before he had left to go west, and the kiss they had shared had been warm company on many a cold night. He shook his head. *Enough of that, keep your focus*, he admonished himself. The months of isolation in the

163

camp and all the other visions and all, he needed to be home, stable, surrounded by his friends again. There had been times when he had felt like someone was playing with his mind, like he couldn't control his own thoughts. He needed that heart grounding, and the prospect of starting over here again, with no one else around, was overwhelming. It wasn't that Selene wasn't enough on her own, or that he didn't want to be with her and stay with her, but he just couldn't face it emotionally. He just didn't feel strong enough right now. He had no idea what the next ten days would bring, but he knew he would have to tell her, and soon. Torturous thoughts rolled around and around until he couldn't stand it anymore.

He launched himself off the sofa and grabbed his shorts and towel and headed for an early eve run and swim. *Clear out the cobwebs.*

Selene was feeling a bit less tearful when she came back several hours later. She had stopped to grab some wine earlier before the shop had closed. Work had been busy enough that she hadn't had time to think much. She was a little nervous about seeing Jon, wondering for a moment if he would be in, or if he would have gone out exploring. It was late, she reminded herself, and he didn't know anyone else here.

He was sitting at the computer watching a film as she returned. He smiled in greeting and she offered some wine, which he declined, raising his glass of beer.

"How did your swim go?" Selene asked as she sat across from him in the smaller chair.

"Good good. Had a good long run too, out and around the headland. Nice place."

"Jon?" Selene cleared her throat. "I need to tell you something."

Jon sat up, paused the film and turned to face her. "What's up?"

He looked mildly panicked, as what had transpired earlier had been hard enough, he had no idea what to expect next.

"I slept with someone else, before Christmas. It just kind of happened. I'm sorry I let us down. It was just hard being so far away and not being able to even talk to you. I just felt so isolated and alone. It was so much harder to make friends here starting in an upper year." Selene let the words fall out in a rush of a breath. "I just wanted to tell you so there was nothing between us."

Jon was silent for a while, then stood and walked around the room. "Ok. I get it. It's been a hard year for both of us. I know more about isolation that I care to admit Selene."

"You aren't angry with me?" Selene asked, surprised.

"No," he said as he turned his body away from her slightly. It hurt. But anger wasn't what he felt. "I understand. And if we're being honest, I slept with one of the teachers at the spring break. Same sort of thing. We were both just lonely."

Selene felt a bit of anger rise. She had tortured herself over this for months, and even more so since he had arrived. And now this?

"Would you have told me if I hadn't said anything?" she asked.

"No, I wouldn't have. What would be the point in hurting you?"

"Oh so we're even, is that what you're saying?"

"You're mad at *me*?" Jon said incredulously.

"I can accept that you shagged someone else Jon, believe it or not. I totally get that, even if I don't like it either. We have both felt the isolation and the shitty major lack of being able to talk to each other, or to write even. I'm not so okay that I have tormented myself for months over it feeling like shit, and here you are all casual about it all! I can't believe that you wouldn't have said anything."

"I mean it Selene, why would I hurt you with a one night thing with someone I will never see again? We were both so lonely and so isolated, you here and me there and no way to reach out to each other. I kept seeing you with these other college guys, man, when I think of the things I used to imagine. It was awful."

Selene stood and reached for his hand, feeling her anger begin to dissipate. "It wasn't anyone here, it was while I was in Ireland, not that it matters really. I'm sorry. I understand Jon, I do. I guess I just felt really bad about it and how to tell you, and I guess I'm not sure that I could have carried the guilt and not told you, even if it meant hurting you. I just don't want anything like that between us." She met his gaze. "Let's let it be water under the bridge then, both sides."

Jon nodded and embraced her. Another big step away from each other had ended with a step closer together again, with the air clear between them now. "Drink?" Jon asked, lifting the wine bottle to refill her glass. Selene nodded and snuggled up next to him on the sofa.

"What are you watching?"

"Dracula." Jon grinned. Selene rolled her eyes, sank back into the sofa and grinned back. *If he only knew.* They spent the rest of the late hours watching the film, and eventually falling asleep on the sofa together.

twenty

The dream had come back, and she wasn't sure what had been after her this time. She looked over at Jon, who was snoring beside her. She inhaled deeply and tried to slow her heart rate. She could feel the sadness between them now. As Jon slept beside her, it seeped out of his pores. But she felt easier and lighter than she had in the weeks leading up to his arrival. It was all out on the table, nothing stood between them now. She snuggled back into his shoulder and let herself drift off again.

When they woke again the sun was a little higher in the sky. Selene rose and set the kettle and began to make some coffee. She wasn't working today, so it might be good to get out and actually see some of the countryside. She could hear Jon rummaging around and eventually getting into the shower. She wondered what would happen now over the next ten days together. Time to start again. They hadn't even talked about the possibility of him staying with her in the UK and working and teaching here while she studied.

"Mmmm smells good in here. There's definitely something about the aroma of fresh coffee. All they had on the site was freeze dried crap. I actually stopped drinking it after a while, it all tasted like sludge in the end."

Selene smiled at him and nodded. Coffee was a vital part of the morning as far as she was concerned, although she was pretty partial to an Irish in the eves. "What do you feel like doing today? Fancy a run around the coast or up into Bath or Stonehenge?"

"Stonehenge sounds cool. Be good to walk around and get some air, exercise and all. Could be doing with some ancient magic, and maybe a bit of history right about now." Jon smiled at her.

Selene looked up and met his eyes, he looked so sad. She placed her cup down and went over to embrace him.

"It'll be ok. We are just starting again. It's the right thing to do right now. It's too much pressure on both of us to just pick up where we left off. I don't know what we thought we would do, but this is easier."

"Is it?" Jon asked.

Selene nodded. "Just give it a bit of time."

"It's the one thing we seem to be short on Lene."

Selene didn't reply. She turned and grabbed her mug again and sipped the steaming black brew. She let the statement hang in the air between them and breathed through the pressure she felt building again. It had to be one day at a time. The love was there, they just needed to find their feet again together.

"We love each other, but we need to get to know each other again. Just let it happen." She leaned forward and kissed him on the forehead and rose to go and shower.

Jon leaned back in the chair. *Time.* He still hadn't told her he was going back for good. That news would have to wait. *After all, it might not matter now in the long run anyway.*

They gathered up their things and jumped into the car and sped off towards Stonehenge. The millennia old stone structure filled Selene with an enormous sense of awe every time she saw it. Although she had driven by it many times, this would be her first time to actually walk around the stones.

The day was beautiful. Hot coffee, croissants, sunshine and good humour. With the pressure of trying to pick up where they had left off gone, the natural ease and true friendship between them had resurfaced. The drive to Salisbury was full of stories and sharing and general chatter, as well as comfortable silences.

They stopped in Salisbury for a pub lunch and made their way through the cathedral, and by mid afternoon they parked up at Stonehenge. Several busloads of tourists were departing as many more flooded through to take their place.

Selene was instantly aware that this was no ordinary place. She could feel an electric buzz through her entire body. The entire midsection of her spine beat like a drum, desperate to be free and alive. Unusually it wasn't pain that she felt, just an intense need for release, almost like she could take flight. Her body wanted to fly, and the urge was almost overpowering. The energy felt similar to the sensation she felt when Adam touched her, light and alive, like plugging into the entire universe.

Jon had been quite silent himself, as they wandered around the perimeter of the stones. He seemed to be almost a world away, softly humming to himself as he walked.

"Penny for your thoughts?" Selene whispered smiling up at him.

"Pretty powerful place, isn't it." Jon said and continued to hum. Selene regarded him with interest, remaining silent, sensing he wanted to say more.

"It feels like when the Aurora Borealis was present. The energy was palpable, completely overpowering. Awesome," Jon said. "I spent so many nights in silence and in total awe out there."

They walked on in silence for a while longer before stopping to rest on one of the smaller stones.

"Jon!"

A voice shouted from the other side of the circle. Jon turned and looked up, shading his eyes.

"Ryan?" he called back and leapt to his feet. The two met halfway and embraced like old friends.

"You're the last person I thought I would see here! How've ye been matey?" Ryan said.

"Same here! Small world mate!" Jon laughed. "Come meet my.... girl Selene."

He stumbled a little over girlfriend, it didn't feel right to say it, but neither did anything else. Ryan appeared not to notice.

"Hey Selene, lovely to meet you," Ryan said and smiled at her as they shook hands. Selene grinned up and shook his hand. He wasn't as tall as Jon, but was very muscular, with short strawberry blond hair and twinkly green eyes full of mirth. She could easily see why these two had become friends.

"Ryan and I met at Brighton when I came over to a term here a few years ago," Jon said. "So Ryan, you still playing rugby then, mate?"

"Yep. Two full seasons now with the Irish. Brilliant," Ryan said. "Been teaching in London as well, but I'm getting a bit citied out now. Time to start thinking of going south soon, a little less city and a bit more sea and outdoor life."

"I get ya." Jon said. "I just did a year out in the boonies, northern Canada. No phones, no computers, completely shut into the village for the winter. It was pretty wild."

"Wow, that sounds really mad! Bet that was quite tough though being isolated like that." Ryan said. "Did you go too Selene?"

"No, I was in Bournemouth studying." Selene smiled. Ryan's energy was so engaging, it was impossible not to like him.

"Man, that would have to be the worst! Oh, I mean being so far apart and all!" Ryan laughed as he caught her expression. "Bournemouth is cool though."

"And being in an alcohol free zone, yeah, it just about killed me!" Jon laughed. "Mind you, saying that, with little else to do but survive the winter, if alcohol had been on tap I might not have survived it anyway!"

"True on both counts mate. I don't think I could have done it either way. So what are you up to now then? You looking for work here in Bournemouth?"

"No. Not at the moment." Jon said, consciously avoiding Selene's gaze. "I've already been away from family and friends for a year, I kind of need to regroup and find my feet again. It was a pretty intense experience. I'm heading back in about a week to find some teaching work in Halifax."

Selene was staring almost open mouthed at Jon. All this time and he hadn't said a word. Maybe he was ok about not being together anymore after all. Maybe her leaving him to come here had shaken the foundation of their relationship more deeply than she had thought. Maybe that is what he had actually wanted in the long run, to go their separate ways. Her heart had ached enough through the year, never mind over the last few days. Now this. He was going home and had no intention of coming back. She looked up and met his eyes as he watched her, taking in her reaction silently.

"Cool man. Well, good that you came over to hang out, next time you come you need to let me know so we can spend some time together," Ryan said not missing a beat, nor sensing the growing tension between Jon and Selene. "You never know Selene, I could end up teaching down your way. If you're still there I'll get in touch."

"That would be lovely, Ryan."

"Look I gotta run, the group I'm with seem to have disappeared already. So great to meet you, Selene. I'll be in touch." Ryan grabbed her up in a big bear hug and swung her around, and she giggled in surprise. Then he did the same to Jon, both laughing.

"See ya, man."

"Later!" Ryan called as he headed over the site to find his friends.

Selene wasn't in the mood to pick a fight, so she slowly began to continue the walk around the stones, leaving Jon to trail silently behind her. So he wasn't staying. Another two years apart. Well, at least there would now be email, skype or phone calls, maybe even snail mail this time round, she stopped and stared up at the sky. It couldn't be as bad as the last year had been. But they hadn't had nearly enough time together to try to meet in the middle distance. Their relationship was far from solid ground at the moment, and she had no idea how the hell they were going to cope once they were a thousand miles apart again.

"Selene," Jon said softly, closing the distance between them. "I'm sorry that all came out that way with Ryan. I wasn't prepared, and it caught me off guard. We should have had that conversation first, but the last few days have really thrown me. Us. I don't know what to think."

174

He ran his hand through his hair, turning her to face him.

"I don't know what to say, Jon. We are so far from ok right now, and you are going home. You are staying home. You are leaving me."

"Well, technically, you left me to come here." Jon said softly. "I am not leaving you. Ok well physically distance wise ok, but not in my heart. I love you Selene. I want us to be together."

"Then why don't you stay?" Selene pleaded.

This was so hard. He had been so lost and so alone, and he knew he couldn't face another year of alone, even with Selene, he wouldn't know anyone, and it would really be starting over again. He just wasn't able for it, not at the moment anyway.

"Last year took a lot out of me Selene. You said you thought you were strong, well so did I. I thought I could pretty much handle anything life threw at me. But being alone up there.... it was a different kind of alone. It was me against the elements and the unknown. Me against the universe, and surprisingly, me against myself a lot of the time. I want to say I've come out stronger for it, and perhaps maybe in time, I might come to feel that way, but right now, all I want and all I need is to be surrounded by my friends and family and people who love me. I can't cope with more isolation."

"So I don't count then."

"It's not that..."

She hadn't realised how deeply she had set her heart on Jon coming to be with her, and her heart felt ripped in two. She moved to turn away but Jon caught her and pulled her close.

"My God I love you Selene," he said, tears falling openly down his face. "I love you so much it hurts to breathe at times. But I can't stay. And I don't know how to make you understand that. I need you, but I need my feet on the solid ground of home more. I don't know what else to say to make this better, and to not hurt you."

Selene felt the sob release, and she couldn't hold back any longer. She knew he was right. It was unfair of her to have left him, then expect him to uproot and move to be with her. A years worth of loneliness poured out of her, and she held onto Jon, and they cried together.

"I *can't* come home," she said when the sobs finally abated. She reached into her bag and handed Jon a tissue before drying her own eyes and blowing her nose. "I *need* to be here. There is no other place to study anywhere near Halifax."

"I know." Jon looked up at the sky in frustration. "I know. And I wouldn't ask you to give up your studies and come home. You know that."

"So where do we go from here?"

"I don't know," he said helplessly. "I just feel a bit overwhelmed. Too many decisions and too little time."

Selene nodded. She glanced around the stones and back up at the sky, which was now full of the deepening red and orange hues of sunset. *Beautiful.* She let the silence hang between them for a while, and just stared at the sunset.

"I can't think anymore," she said and looked up at him. "I just feel a bit numb."

"Yeah." Jon agreed. He looked up at her again, and around at the sun-fire-lit and darkening stones. "Look, it's getting late. Shall we make our way back towards Bournemouth, maybe grab a drink on the way?"

"Yeah, sounds good. I could use a little something to settle me nerves," she made a face, and Jon laughed out loud.

"A wee tipple then lassie?" Jon said in his best Scottish accent.

"Aye. That'd be the way of it."

"Come wench, else I'll be throwing ye o'er me shoulder." Jon said huskily, making a move to grab her.

Selene shrieked and ran, Jon in full pursuit. The heaviness lifted, the two then walked hand in hand back to the car, both relieved to have taken another step closer together, no matter what the future brought.

twenty-one

Too quickly, the days blended between work and hanging out by the beach - when they were out of bed that was. The days that had followed the Stonehenge talk had been full of fun and real joy at being together. They had made it home that night and had made love for the first time, *properly* made love, like people who were truly in love instead of strangers. They hadn't spent much time out of bed since. They had talked about everything, her experiences in Ireland (not Ciaran so much as meeting Anna Jane, vampires, and her travels) and his experiences with the vision quests and sweat lodges, and the lonely and dark times. They were so much closer than they had ever been, and she truly did understand why he felt the call to be home, and to feel the grass under his feet again.

The phone was ringing and Selene had to reach over the back seat to grab it.

"Hello?"

"Selene! It's me, Ev!"

"Hey babe, what's been going on? It's so good to hear from you! How's Edinburgh?"

"Ach ye know. All speed and nay dribble."

"Was I supposed to understand any of that?"

"Nay, just a little nonsense t'is all."

"Ah, got your full on Scot accent coming through loud and clear girl. Wow!"

"Yeah, it's been a lot o fun being home, but some not so good times too. Can ye talk?"

"I'm in the car with Jon. We're on our way up to London. He's leaving tomorrow morning."

"Oh no, that seems so soon luv. I wish I'd had the chance to meet him while he was here. Things have just been a bit crazy up here, and there was no getting away. Listen, I should be home tomorrow night, give me a ring when you can, will you?"

"Sure, will do. How's your Mum getting on, any improvement?"

The line fell silent for a while before Ev answered. "No, not really. Actually Selene," the line was quiet a while longer, and Selene could hear Ev's breath catch, "they've given her a few weeks."

179

"What? Oh Ev! That's awful. My God. What happened?"

"Well, they say the cancer has spread just about everywhere, and it's spread into her liver or something and now heart failure is starting. They don't know what they can do."

Selene could hear Ev crying through the phone. "God I wish I was closer. I'm so sorry, Ev. That must be so hard. Do you want me to come up?"

"No, no, you need to work, and for all we know it could be months not weeks. I just wanted to talk to someone."

"Well, keep talking, luvy. I'm right here," Selene said, wiping the tears from her own eyes. Jon placed his hand over her leg and gave it a little squeeze in support.

"No, no. Never mind that. You spend this time with Jon and we can catch up properly tomorrow night, ok?"

"Ok. Are you sure you will be ok hun. Stupid bloody thing to say, but you know what I mean." Selene smiled down the phone.

"I do. And thanks. Listen, catch you tomorrow, then," Ev said.

"Alrighty mate. Speak then." Selene ended the call. "God that is such shit." She said to Jon.

"What's happened?"

"Ev's mum has been ill all year, and it got diagnosed as some kind of rare cancer. They are super medical types and have done mega doses of chemo, but it's just made her sicker if you ask Ev. Now they say that it's spread, and her body is shutting down basically, and it could be a matter of weeks."

"That's awful Selene." Jon reached for her hand with his free one. "I'm really sorry to hear that."

Selene reached back into her bag and grabbed some tissue. This was definitely turning out to be the week of tears, *and more to come.* They were already close to the airport, and his flight was first thing in the morning. She turned her head to gaze out the window. How fast had the last few weeks gone?

A blink of an eye.

Five am came early, way too early as far as Jon was concerned. He reached over and set the sleeper alarm, and gently nudged Selene. He flicked the telly on so that he would be sure to not fall back to sleep. They had ordered in and spent most of the previous night together in the hotel room, in bed. He couldn't believe it would be another four or five months before they would see each other again. At least this time he would be home, and they would be able to talk freely and write over email, surely that would make it easier than the last year had been. He was already looking forward to hanging out with James, and singing with the old band (if they would have him back). He would miss her, but it still felt like the right thing to be doing.

Selene listened quietly to his breathing. She knew he was awake, and wondered if he was feeling sad or happy to be leaving. She knew he was excited to be going home, but she hoped that he felt as deeply as she did about staying together. It would be another hard year.

"Kiss for your thoughts?" she said, turning herself

over to face him.

He didn't reply, he pulled her closer and kissed her. She could feel everything pouring out of him, sadness, pleasure, excitement, loneliness, fear, and all that he held back, deep inside. He felt talked out, and now, in the last moments, he wanted to be inside of her, so deeply inside that a part of him would always be a part of her. Selene cried out as he pushed deeper into her, pulling him closer to her as he did so. She didn't want to let go. She too wanted to find a way to remain like this, physically part of each other as much as they were emotionally. They made love with slow deliberate tenderness, mesmerising each moment and each sensation.

Time was disappearing before them.

"I love you Selene. Remember me tonight." Jon nuzzled her neck.

Selene nodded and lowered her gaze, meeting his lips with hers. She held his lips silently, unable to hold back the tears as they fell between them.

"Soon enough, my love, soon enough," Jon kissed her one last time, tasting the salt of her tears, before turning to enter the security queues. "Speak to you tonight."

Selene nodded and turned to go, she couldn't watch anymore, and she wasn't sure how much longer she could hold back threatening torrent of tears.

twenty-two

Selene watched as the coffin vanished behind the rose coloured curtain. She didn't know what was going to happen next. She had never been to a funeral service like it. It was full of the normal tears, masses of grief, and few words. There were gentle expressions of kindness, and the greetings of people who had not seen each other for many years.

In her own limited experience there was a wake, a mass, then a burial. But here was she sat at a crematorium, and she had no idea what would happen next. Would they cremate the body now, behind the hideous rose curtain, as the family sat waiting? She really didn't know, and it unnerved her. She thought about what she would choose, a burial or pyre. She didn't know. It felt a bit morbid to think about it - and selfish, considering her friend's grief. She looked to Ev to follow her lead, but she could see her friend buried in her own grief, staring hard at the wall. Morten fidgeted restlessly beside her, not knowing how to comfort her. Once the curtain had closed, a few more words were said, then everyone rose and filed outside. Within moments, the close family stood together, a little apart from the rest of the mourners, and lanterns were lit. With a few more words of love and goodbye, the lanterns were released into the late afternoon sky, and everyone stood still until they vanished over the horizon. It was really quite beautiful and uplifting.

Selene made her way back to her hotel, sending a text to Ev to let her know she would be back at the reception in an hour or so. She needed a time to decompress. So much emotional strain over the last few weeks, she was exhausted. She noted that of all of her friends, she and Morten were the only ones to have made it. College wouldn't start for another three weeks yet, *where was everyone?* she wondered . Ev had always had a lot of good friends.

Dropping her bags into the room, she splashed her face and downed some juice, then sent a quick text message to Jon and AJ. Sitting for a few minutes to gather her thoughts, she then turned back to make her

184

way to the reception.

Ev looked very tearful when she arrived, and they held each other for a long time. It was a huge loss, despite the fact that she and her mother hadn't been all that close over the years, it had only been recently that their relationship had repaired and they were becoming so much closer. Selene couldn't imagine what it would be like to lose her mother, they had always been so tight. Her father used to laugh and say they were thick as thieves. She knew that her father would be making the journey long before any of them, and she didn't look forward to that day either.

"Listen," Ev said, "I have to say goodbye to everyone here, it might take another hour or so, then I will go back with me Da, and settle him in for the night. He'll be wanting some space to himself I imagine. Morten will leave first thing I think, to get back home. When are you off?"

"I can stay until after five I think. The flight is at half six. I'll be here if you need me, luv." Selene hugged her hard. "Why doesn't Morten come back to the hotel with me while you do family stuff? He seems a bit on edge, and it's really private time, isn't it?"

Ev nodded and waved to Morten. "Do ye want to go back to the hotel with Selene, I can catch up with ye later on, when things are a bit more settled like."

Morten smiled and looked relieved. He wasn't happy to be here at all, and was only here for Ev. "Yes I will Ev. I'll be waiting for you." He kissed her on the cheek and nodded at Selene.

Selene reached over and hugged her again, and waved goodbye. It was going to be a long hard night for all of them.

It was nearing nine o'clock when Ev finally turned up, Morten and Selene still sat in the hotel bar, both involved in their own books, chilling out. Ev looked awful. Selene rose and grabbed her in a huge hug before sitting her down beside Morten. She then went to the bar and ordered a triple baileys.

"Here, drink up." Selene handed her the glass.

"Thanks mate, could do with the bottle really." Ev smiled weakly.

"How's everyone at home?" Morten asked kindly.

"Still breathing. It's been such a long day. I'm relieved its over actually." Ev squeezed his hand. "Thanks for being here. I really appreciate you coming. You too Selene."

Selene smiled and relaxed back into the chair. "How you feeling?"

Ev eyed her with pure exhaustion. "Probably like I look."

"Yep. Do you guys want to crash here? We can make up the sofa for me and you guys can crash in the bed instead of having to go back to your folks." Selene offered.

"Sounds good to me," Morten said. "I'm knackered too. What do you think, Ev?"

"Anything would be better than going back there

tonight." Ev sighed. "Yes please, thanks Selene."

"Right then," said Morten. "I'm going to hit it. I'll make up the sofa bed for you Selene." He bent to kiss Ev on the cheek. "See you in a bit."

He grabbed the key from Selene and disappeared down the long hallway. Ev looked up at Selene and began to cry. Selene rose and sat down next to her, gathering her up in her arms, saying nothing. When the torrent had spent itself, Ev looked up at her. "I think Morten and I are going to finish."

Selene met her eyes in shock. "Why? What's happened?"

"I don't know. Nothing feels right at the moment. He can't do anything right, and I am always angry and fed up. I just feel really crowded. And he has been so unsupportive this summer with how ill my Mum was. All he wanted to do was go on holiday and party together. It drove me nuts, and all we've done really is fight all summer over the phone."

"It's such an emotional time Ev. Are you sure? You've been under such huge pressure with all of this."

"I know." Ev finished her drink and signalled the bartender for another.

"Well, whatever you decide, I'm here for you." Selene said giving her shoulders a squeeze.

"Thanks, mate. I know it, I really do. Thanks for coming all the way up, it means a lot."

Selene smiled and relaxed into the sofa again. "It seems like a cool city. Be good to come back sometime, when its not related to something so sad."

"Yeah, Edinburgh is quite a special place, really. So much history. And it's gorgeous. I do love it here. I like the south with its beaches and all, but there is something about this place that gets under your skin. There's a real vibe, magic-like, it's hard to put into words."

Selene stood up and stretched. "Fancy one for the road so to speak?"

"Yeah, go on then." Ev grinned. "I'm starting to feel pleasantly numb."

Selene waved the bartender over, ordering another round. She hoped Ev would be ok. It would take some time to grieve, and college might be just the distraction she would need. She thought about Jon. It had been two weeks, and many phone calls, and as usual, it felt awful to be apart. But it already felt better than the last year, when they had no communication at all.

"So, what's the story with Jon, then?" Ev asked, reading her mind, as Selene handed her a drink.

"Well, we broke up a few days after he arrived."

Ev's eyebrows shot up.

"Then we just spent time being together as friends, which was good as it took the pressure off. After a year of not talking or writing or anything it was impossible to just pickup where we had left off. I don't know what we were both thinking. I guess we thought well, love will carry us through and we can just be the same as we were, but we weren't. It was like being with a stranger, and I felt shy being naked with him even. It was all overwhelming and weird. It was like I couldn't remember what came before, our years together had vanished under a haze. I just can't explain it."

Selene drank then and was quiet for a moment. "I told him about Ciaran in Ireland, and apparently he had slept with someone too, so we both forgave and now let it go. And then we had a few deep and meaningfuls, especially after our trip to Stonehenge. Then we got back together and here we are, a couple thousand miles apart yet again."

"So long story short, then, why did he leave?"

"He felt like he couldn't handle starting again after being so isolated. It really affected him. I mean I was alone too, but in a place where I had a job and a group of people and basic communication. He had none of that, and he was overwhelmed by it. I think he just needs to ground himself and make sense of his experiences before he can move forwards."

"Yeah, I guess I can see that." Ev said softly. "I kind of feel lost at sea at the moment, and I feel like I can't connect to anyone right now."

Selene snuggled in closer and hugged her. "It will be a while yet, just take it easy, Ev. One day at a time. Morten is big enough to sort himself out. Ask him for some space, he'll give it."

"Yeah. I know. I suppose I feel like I need more than that. I feel like I just need time out on my own to make sense of it all. I guess time will tell huh."

"Maybe. Come on, it's well past midnight. We can all have a lay in tomorrow and take it easy before Morten's flight."

Selene rose and reached for Ev's hand to pull her up.

189

They nodded their goodnights to the barman and headed to their room, both in dire need of deep sleep and good dreams.

twenty-three

Selene was feeling quite buoyant and ready to start the year off as she approached the college gates. She had passed all of the last set of exams and was feeling much more confident and settled. The college was buzzing with energy. Students were everywhere, and she couldn't wait to catch up with her friends. Her schedule was pretty full on, but she already knew that most of her classes were shared with Ev again, and that pleased her. Freshers week was already in full swing, and this year she would help Ev host with another house full of their year.

It felt great to be in the upper years this time round. Kristoff and Paddy and many of the clinic year had all graduated and moved on, so it was a whole new batch of students and clinicians.

"Hey Selene!" Adam called out as he stepped through the library door towards her.

"Hi Adam! How was your summer?"

"Very good, very good. Yours?" Adam asked as he embraced her and kissed her cheek in greeting.

"Good. Lots of work hours but some good times with Jon."

"Has he stayed, then?"

"No. He ended up going back. He found it too hard to think about starting again, he missed his friends and family too much last year." Selene shrugged.

"Sorry to hear that. It's got to be tough." Adam said kindly.

"Yeah. But at least this time we have communications!" Selene tried to be upbeat.

"You heading to the pub later?"

"For sure! First Monday night back. Can't miss that!" Selene grinned.

Students. Any day was party day. Adam chuckled. "Ok then, I will be seeing you later on."

Selene waved goodbye and continued up the stairs to her lecture, hoping to catch Ev up on the way. It was good. Everything felt better than it had in a long time, and she felt that this new academic year held some changes, excitement and many new friends. She finally felt grounded and was starting to think of this as home.

Claude entered the library with a tray of large goblets and a decanter of wine. He placed them all down on the small side table then proceeded to offer each a glass.

"Welcome, my dear friends," Lilith said raising her glass. "Mahalath, Igrat, and Naamah. It has been some time since we have come together to enjoy one another's company. Thank you all for coming."

"With pleasure, Lilith. It is such a lovely place, I am grateful for the invitation." Mahalath said. Naamah nodded in agreement with her.

"Yes," said Igrat. "It has been millennia Lilith. Whatever intrigues are you building, my friend, that has called us out of our quiet lives?"

"Ever the enquirer, Igrat, and ever so smart." Lilith grinned coolly at her friend.

"There is a reason I have called you together. You are my friends, my consorts, my confidantes. We have worked through many thousands of years together to help each other when we could. Between us we are all extremely powerful women. Queens in our own rights, sorcery, seduction, ancient knowledge and wisdom is ours. And I need it now to enact a Labyrinth, in order to get to the bottom of something."

"Sounds like a very intriguing mystery, Lilith. Do tell us more," said Mahalath, turning away to stare out at the volcano in the distance, sipping her wine.

"Well, not so long ago, one of my lamiae came to me,

193

and informed me that there was a new creature. Someone who could possibly be a child of an eternal." Lilith paused for effect as her guests all turned to look at her. "Yes, I thought that would catch your attention. Gamaliel and I had a little chat and we thought that perhaps, since we knew where to find the girl, we would play the Labyrinth, and try to isolate her, in order to see what else we could gain from it, if more knowledge would then be forthcoming."

"How exciting!" said Igrat gleefully. "A proper intrigue, just like the old days!"

"Yes, but what will we gain from this?" asked Naamah. "Other than a way to pass time, of course?"

"Well," said Lilith, measuring her words, "if we can find out if she is truly a mix of eternal and immortal, then a precedent is set. Surely there is some benefit to our kind against those damned celestials. Surely some good may come of this?"

Mahalath nodded. "Perhaps, perhaps not. But in the end, it does not matter. It has brought us back together, and given us a focus. What do you need, Lilith? Whatever it is, count me in."

"Well, we will need an incantation to enact the Labyrinth, and encircle the girl placing her in play, so to speak."

"Done," said Igrat. "What else?"

"I will ask Sariel for more information.' Lilith said, and again, her words caught the attention of those present. This was serious indeed, for Lilith had not called on Sariel in millennia.

"Yes," she said, "this carries the risk of letting the celestials know we are up to something, but I feel that he may hold the key, if she is indeed what this lamiae has claimed. And any head start we can gain, the better."

Mahalath smiled at that. "Wonderful! We will begin working through the incantation for the Labyrinth immediately. Come sisters, we will rest until nightfall and gather our thoughts. Then we shall reconvene with Lilith here and proceed. It is a fortunate moon, we have no time to waste. You know what we will need for tonight, Lilith?'

Lilith smiled and nodded at Claude. The women bowed slightly as they took their leave, following Claude to their rooms on the upper floors. Lilith was delighted. It was all coming together quite nicely.

Several hours later, the women reconvened on the far side of the large terrace where a large circle of black charcoal had been set out on the stone tiles. The moon was round and waxing to almost full, a fortunate moon indeed. Claude had prepared five enormous pillar candles and had set them in a pentagram within the charcoal circle. In the very centre of this precise configuration, a small fire of incense was already burning, giving deep sensual and atmospheric air to the surroundings.

Lilith waved the others through, and they formed a small circle around the flames. Lilith looked to Mahalath, one of her most trusted and powerful sorceresses and waited.

Mahalath stepped forward and stared into the flame

before her. Her voice had a surreal timbre as she started
the incantation.

Borne of Lilith
sired by demons
we
call on the sun
to complete our circle
we
call on the moon
to cloak us in shadow
and raise our power as one

She waved her hands over the flames, pressing
towards the directions of the winds.

Come to us
we lay the Labyrinth
we plant your vibrant
seeds
layer by layer
circle by circle
we beckon to you raise
grow lush and bountiful
through dreams and waking states
bind the child of ancients
as we control the gates

Mahalath stepped back and lit the five candles that lay
waiting around them, and as a circle, they stepped right

five times to open the gates and bind the spell.

Lilith stepped away first, releasing the bind that held the four together. Claude was at the ready with their wine, and they moved towards the large outdoor sofa to relax.

"That was perfect Mahalath. I knew I could rely on your expertise. That spell is well bound, and everything will now come to fruition," Lilith said with a dark smile.

Mahalath nodded and accepted her praise with modesty. "It feels good to feel the use of our power once again. It has been too long."

There was an agreement all around the table, and all took the time now to relax and enjoy, hoping that the fruits of the spell would soon become evident.

twenty-four

Jon glanced up from his paper and sipped his coffee. He replaced the cup on the table, suppressing the pang of guilt as Elysia entered the Athenaeum Café and smiled at him. *Just a new friend.* He flash-backed to the passionate kiss they had shared before he had left for the west, not a week after Selene had left for the UK. His body reverberated with it, and he had to shake it off before he felt himself harden with the energy of it. *Just a friend,* he repeated with admonishment, trying hard to banish the memory.

"Hello Jon," Elysia said, and her voice washed over him silkily as she bent to kiss his cheek. "How are things?"

"Good, thanks, good."

He smiled back at her, feeling a bit of unexpected tingling in his body. She was as gorgeous as he remembered from their first meeting. His body also remembered their kiss, which had taken his breath away at the time. "It was great to see you the other night. I didn't realise you were still working in the area."

"Yes, great music wasn't it? I love live bands!"

Jon smiled, "You'll have to come and see us play sometime. Can I grab you a cuppa something?"

"Sure, double shot cappuccino would be wonderful, thank you."

Elysia shook her coat off and settled onto the plush cream coloured sofa next to him. Jon sprang up and made his way to the counter. His heart was pounding. He should have sat at one of the tables rather than the sofa. *God if I don't get a grip I'll be sweating in a minute.* She was stunning. More than stunning. The thought of touching her skin alone nearly drove him mad. If he hadn't known any better, he would have sworn she was one of Aphrodite's daughters in the flesh. That thought alone unsettled him, the un-reconciled visions from the outpost still haunting his thoughts. He felt suspicious all of a sudden, like she was a spy....*Stop being so ridiculous! What the hell is wrong with you? Now you really are acting crazy.* But the niggling feeling remained, no matter how deeply he shoved it away. Perhaps it was the edge of guilt creeping in, for spending time with Elysia and not thinking of the time away from Selene. But he couldn't

199

seem to help himself.

Elysia checked herself in her hand mirror. She knew she looked good, now she just needed to reel him in, slowly, one step at a time. *So far so good*. They had shared a rather passionate kiss last time they had met, and she fully intended a repeat of that experience and more. Her instructions were very clear, she was to ensure that Jon never laid eyes on Selene again. And with how gorgeous and kind Jon had turned out to be, she fully intended that to be the case. She could see several other demons hanging out in the bar, Sitri included. She knew that he was impatient, but this was not a game to be won on physicality alone, she needed to get inside Jon's heart, and that had yet to happen. She had worked hard the last several months to become close friends with Beth, and with a few of Jon's friendship circle. Slowly but surely, she was becoming one with his life in all the ways that mattered, with the one exception - being his. *Soon*, she smiled at Sitri, as he stirred restlessly across the bar. *Soon*.

Jon rejoined her in moments with the promise that their drinks would arrive shortly.

"Are you hungry? We can order something to snack on or lunch if you want?"

"Yes," she said. "Maybe in a little while, let's just catch up, it's been far too long." Elysia settled herself closer to him on the sofa and gazed steadily into Jon's eyes. She smiled slightly as she watched his eyes dilate and his posture relax.

Merope woke in a sweat. Breathing heavily she reached over and switched the small bedside lamp on. Her eyes wild from running, it took her a moment to fully collect herself and realise she was safe. She had clearly seen Elysia's face, grinning darkly at her as she ran from the King's room. It hadn't been the first time that she had known he slept with other women, but she hadn't expected to find her friend and his own cousin in their bed. The overt sexuality, the rawness of the exchange between them gripped her even now. But in her last backward glance, in this dream, it had been Jon, Selene's boyfriend, with her in the bed with Elysia, not her first husband. She didn't know how that would be possible, over three thousand years had passed since she had left that life.

Yet, it had been incredibly lucid. Confused and disturbed, she rose silently and reached for her robe. Making her way into the lounge, she opened the curtains to see the moon, and poured herself a single malt. Sitting on the soft chair she relaxed and gazed out over the garden. It was time to return to Europe. She would tell Nikolas in the morning. They needed to be closer to Selene - things were shifting in the skies and somewhere down below, and she needed to know her daughter was safe.

twenty-five

Lilith looked up as Sariel appeared by the edge of the long
veranda that overlooked the volcano. So much time had
passed between them, but he would always be her child,
even despite the role he had been chosen to fulfil, and his
role in thwarting her many many times in the past. She
took him in quietly as he approached. He hadn't aged a
day. He still looked as youthful and beautiful as he had a
thousand years before. His hair was longer, blond and
flowing straight to his shoulders, his skin a deep olive,

and his deep green eyes steady, holding her in his gaze. A human would have mistaken him for a surfer, so laid back and relaxed he appeared to be.

"Mamma," Sariel said, as he leaned in and kissed her on both cheeks. "It's been a while."

Lilith smiled and waved at Claude in dismissal. "Yes it has my child. Where has life been taking you, all this time?" she said, making him feel a bit like an errant child.

"Here and there when I can," he said. "Mostly to South America otherwise.' Lilith met his gaze again in surprise. He was being deliberately vague. *So he is still working with the other side. Interesting.*

"I have something I want to discuss with you, Sariel. It has come..."

"Before you ask, I will tell you again that I cannot always be of help to you, Mamma. The things you desire to know are often not for you to know. I cannot control the information, even when it is I who seeks it, either for you or for anyone else."

Lilith raised her eyebrows. She had always assumed that when the celestials asked for information through Sariel, who had been cast an enlightener in his earlier days and spirited away from her, that they would get what they asked for. It had never occurred to her that they might not. *Yes, very interesting, indeed.*

"I want to know if there are any prophecies involving a child being born of an immortal and an angel," she said. "A child of an eternal."

Sariel stared at her in frank disbelief. "Where has this idea come from Mamma? Nothing like that has ever

203

happened. Between angels and humans maybe before the time of Noah, but not an immortal."

"I am curious," she said. "Nothing more. There have been some interesting developments, and I want to know if I may be able to use them to my advantage."

"I do not have the answer you seek, but there are some who might. All I can say is that I will ask. You are not asking with a pure heart, Mamma, and this is never the right foundation of query. This is all I will say for now."

"Oh but my query is pure my son, as is my heart. You have never really appreciated that, though I had thought you might as you matured." Lilith stared at him. "Goodbye, then Sariel. Edom keep you safe."

"There are things that keep me safe of which you have no knowledge, Mamma. These many thousand years between us have been immense."

Lilith grinned. "In peace then my son. In peace," she crossed towards the door and reached up to kiss his cheeks, but he vanished into the ether.

"May your queries be met with helpful information," she said silently before stepping through the doorway into Eden house.

twenty-six

Six weeks had passed since Jon's departure. The phone
calls were becoming more strained and communication
online more sparse again. The distance wasn't doing
them any favours, nor was the fact that he was back in
the thick of it, playing on stage and gaining a growing
mob of young groupies. Hard as she tried, Selene was
finding it really difficult, much harder than when he had
been safely tucked away on the outpost. A break was
coming up in another week, and perhaps it was time for a

surprise visit. She couldn't really afford it, but it seemed a case of desperate times calling for desperate measures.

Something was niggling at her, thought she couldn't put her finger on it. She just had a feeling there was something else at work. She kept having odd dreams, none of which made sense. In these dreams the same characters always appeared, always from ancient times. Her mother was there, and a king and lots of servants bustling about. And there was a very beautiful dark skinned woman, who kept appearing and smiling at her, then walking away.

Her instinct was that the mysterious woman was no friend, and couldn't be trusted. She had another crazy dream where she walked in on the same woman having rather wild sex with a man wearing a crown. It was similar to the weird dream she had had when she had fallen asleep in Kristoff's arms last year. *Who wears a crown when you have sex?* The woman had looked her right in the eye and grinned at her, and the dream had ended. It was disturbing. Something told her that this woman knew her or of her somehow. Something was definitely going on over there, and no one was telling her anything, not even her closest friends.

She had to convince Jon that coming out and working here for the next two years was the best thing to keep them together. They could go anywhere once she had graduated. It seemed such a reasonable plan, as being broke and three thousand miles apart for the next two years seemed almost impossible. She knew he had landed a good job at a local high school though, and that would be a huge stumbling block. He wasn't the traveller, she was. He came from a long line of stable family types. She emailed Sacha and let her in on the plan. She would fly out next week and stay the first night at Sacha and Derry's and then turn up at the gig the following night and surprise Jon. Perfect.

Selene packed everything up, locked the flat, and headed out on foot to the bus station, choosing not to drive this time as it was far cheaper and easier to National Express it. Once aboard she closed her eyes and tried to envision the surprise. How would he take it? Would he be happy to see her? Would she be interrupting someone else? Something was still chirping at her in the back of her mind. It was unsettling, but she forced the bad thoughts away and focused on the lyrics playing in her headset as the bus droned on.

Arriving just in time to get through security, she was called aside by the flight attendant, who asked her if she would mind giving up her seat for another passenger who needed to be in economy with other family, would she mind an upgrade? Certainly! First class, home with style, things were looking up!

Selene wandered onto the plane and found her seat, settling in well and graciously accepting the glass of champagne offered to her. The anxiety of earlier in the day began to lift, and she began to enjoy the thought of being home again. Suddenly something bumped her shoulder, shaking her out of her reverie and nearly causing her to drop her glass.

"A thousand pardons. Sorry to crash into you!" a

deeply sexy and accented, and confusingly familiar voice spoke from above her. 'I lost my grip on the bag and did not want it to fall onto you!'

Selene looked up to see one of the most impossibly attractive men she had ever seen. Absolutely flawless. Perfect olive skin on a beautifully shaped face, large eyes the colour of an endless dark starry sky, hair soft, straight and black as night falling to his shoulders. Very broad shoulders at that, on a perfectly proportioned man. Something about him was achingly familiar, but she couldn't actually put two thoughts together to place him. *He's god-like.* All she could do was smile, momentarily unable to speak.

He grinned down at her, seeming to enjoy her momentary lapse. "I think I am in the seat next to you, Miss?"

"What? Oh yes, s-sorry. Of course," Selene shifted herself sideways so he could pass. "Selene. My name is Selene."

She was still a bit flustered, but being able to remember her name seemed reassuring and normal, and her pulse began to slow down. *You sound like an idiot!*

"Ah, a beautiful name for a beautiful woman," he said, with such genuineness that she looked up and met his eyes. "It means the moon, or in your case, the moon goddess. Where are you from, Selene?"

Selene smiled, blushing a little at his compliment. "I was born in Greece, on the actual Mount Olympus believe it or not."

A funny expression fluttered across his face, but he

208

recovered himself swiftly. Selene looked at him more closely, his eyes were rare, so deep in colour, like sapphires, but with little starry like light flecks in them. They were so dark in their blueness that she couldn't distinguish an iris at all, it was like there wasn't one. She suddenly had a déjà-vu sensation of wanting to fall deeply into them. They were so familiar......

His smile broadened.

"Do you not remember me Selene?" he settled himself into the seat.

Selene looked up at him in surprise. Ios. She had a momentary flashback to the masquerade ball in Dublin last year. Could this be the same man? She remembered him alright, she had dreamed about him for months after their meeting. She remembered his protectiveness and his kindness. How could she have not remembered those eyes?

"I do! Ios. I'm afraid your mask kept you well hidden! I truly didn't recognise you! I'm so sorry."

He smiled at her and swiftly continued with their previous conversation before she had a chance to ask any questions about that night. "So your mother gave birth to you on the mountain, then?"

"I think so, my dad was a warden at the National Park there, so they were up visiting the cabin where they met, and I came early."

"I think I've been up there. There's an unusual land formation there in the mountainside, like a crater."

"Yes, that's the place. Mamma never used to go near it."

209

Ios sat back in the airline seat and sipped at the champagne. *Interesting.* A similar disturbance in the threads of time had occurred recently, and this is what had drawn him to Nova Scotia. He had quietly kept an eye on Selene since that chance meeting in Dublin and knew that she had planned this trip home. He had purchased the extra seat in first class to ensure that they would be seated together so that he might try to gain some insight into her life and the connection with Merope. He had watched the demon spy fall from the sky over three thousand years ago, like a comet, bursting into flames as he fell, and hitting Merope at speed it had knocked her from her place in the Heavens. He had also watched as a mysterious celestial wind picked up, blowing her through the threads of time to where she had landed, three thousand years hence on the same Mount Olympus. Landing from the Heavens at speed had left the enormous crater in the mountain that Selene now described, unaware of its true history. He had been there when Merope had landed, he had followed her through time, but he hadn't been the only one. Gabriel had been there too.

"Do you know the story of Merope and the Heavenly Sisters?" he asked, knowing he was throwing caution to the winds, hoping that she might reveal her own mother's name.

"Oh yes, ad nauseum. My mother's name is Merope." Selene smiled. "It isn't a common name, and everyone and their dog used to recite the story after she had been introduced."

The champagne glass in his hand snapped at its base as Selene spoke, making her jump. Fortunately he caught it with his other hand, recovering quickly. "Sorry, these flimsy glasses."

The stewardess, who had barely taken her eyes off him, fluttered about apologising, and instantly replaced the broken glass with a new full one.

Settling in once again Ios gently began to ask more leading questions about her life. "And you have always lived on Mount Olympus?"

"We lived at the foot of it, until I was sixteen, then we moved to Canada, and my father opened a Greek restaurant there."

"Really, where is that then?"

"Toronto. They really liked the city and they had lots of family there. There is a large Greek community there as well."

"Ah. It has been many years since I have been to Canada, and this is my first trip to Halifax. Apparently the best time of year to visit, so I am told."

"Oh yes," she said. "The leaves are turning for the autumn season, and it's like walking through endless forests of living fire. It's rather spectacular in places actually. You should try to make your way up towards Cape Breton if you can, it can be breathtaking. And, they have the only single malt distillery in North America, if you're into your whiskey that is."

Ios smiled at her use of language to describe the changing of the seasons. It had been a very long time since he had even noticed such things, if ever. Forests of fire. Well, that did sit well and did pique his interest. So far, this trip had proved worthy of his time, and being stuck on an airplane, and he had yet to even arrive in Canada. Whatever waited on the other end, he now had no doubt, it involved this beautiful daughter of Merope, his old nymph friend. There could be none other than her, and Selene, despite her rather unusual eyes and tall stature, was indeed the very image of Merope, just as he had remembered her.

"Where are you staying in town then, Ios?" Selene asked as the stewardess replenished their glasses.

"The Athenaeum."

"I haven't heard of that place. Perhaps it's on the old library site, they were completing a building of some sort then, I didn't know it was going to be a hotel."

"Yes, it's a rather upmarket boutique type hotel I think."

Of course it would be. She sat in first class by the grace of God, but he had paid for his seat, and judging by his clothing, and his sense of culture and language, she didn't think he was short of a few bob. They relaxed into comfortable silence and Selene reached into her bag for her book, Like Water for Chocolate, and began to read. They sat in companionable silence for a long while, and Selene drifted off to sleep.

When she woke, she realised that she was leaning on his shoulder, and sat abruptly up.

"I am so sorry, why didn't you wake me?"

"Why would I wake a sleeping goddess?"

Selene blushed. "I really am sorry, I guess it was all the

212

champagne."

"Selene, I simply cannot have a beautiful woman like yourself apologise for using me as a pillow to rest your head. Believe me, I have enjoyed every moment."

Almost crimson at this point, Selene couldn't help but laugh, the mirth in his eyes was as blatant as his flirtatious words. His eyes were so unusual, she looked deeply into them again before he averted them ever so slightly. He really was the most beautiful man she had ever seen. She remembered how drawn to him she had been when they had first met, and today was no different. She felt like she would almost follow him anywhere, like no one else existed. She didn't understand why she felt that way, when she was going home to see Jon.

"Would you meet me for a drink in town sometime, Selene?"

"I would love to, Ios, but I am visiting my boyfriend as a surprise. He doesn't know I'm coming. I really don't know how much time I will have."

"Well, here is my card. If you have time for a coffee or a drink, please ring. I mean to ask in friendship, I understand your situation perfectly."

"Thank you, Ios. I will."

The plane had landed, and as they gathered their things they said a final goodbye. Selene gave him a piece of paper with her telephone number in the UK.

"If you make it to the UK sometime again."

Ios embraced her lightly and kissed her softly on the cheeks.

"Keep well, my moon goddess friend. I am looking

forward to meeting again soon."

Ios nodded his head slightly and departed, leaving Selene smiling as she watched him walk away. Her skin was on fire again with his touch. She shook herself back to reality and glanced down at the unusual card. It was entirely black with embossed red print, solely containing his mobile number, not even his name. It was a Greek country code, which was interesting. She slid it into her laptop bag so as not to lose it, and disembarked, returning her thoughts to Jon and hoping he would be happy to see her.

twenty-seven

Jon wandered around the bungalow lost in thought.
Selene was already in the sauna. Her arrival had thrown
him completely. The gig had gone really well, and they
had played several encores. It had been their first night
on stage performing together again since his return home.
He hadn't even known Selene was there until they broke
midway through. Between sets she had jumped out of
the smoky haze and surprised him. And surprised he
really truly had been. Elysia had been waiting in the

wings for him as well, and at first had looked away, but then something seemed to change her mind.

They had been seeing quite a lot of each other over the preceding weeks, and Jon had asked her to come and hang out. Elysia had been quite possessive, refusing to acknowledge Selene beyond a cold hello. And Selene's reaction to her had been nothing short of bizarre, as if seeing Elysia was like she was seeing a ghost. He had finally had to pull Elysia aside, and remind her that Selene was still his girlfriend. She had gone off with Beth then, which had upset Selene more than he had anticipated.

He sensed that she felt left out of his life, like she didn't belong there anymore. She had cried. He just couldn't seem to keep a thought in his head let alone think straight when Elysia was around. It wasn't like him at all. He felt like his life had suddenly become shrouded in mist, and he just couldn't see the way through. His nerves jangled, raising sweat from every pore.

Without even realising it, he had gathered together the sage herbs given to him by one of the elders of the tribe. He had already laid them out on the iron pan, ready to light. He reached for the matches above the stove and struck one. Suddenly the whole room filled with the smoke of the dry leaves. Heavenly. He stood over the smoke and inhaled deeply, feeling the tension drain from his body for the first time since Selene had arrived. Somehow everything felt clearer, like the brain fog that had clung to him for weeks since their last parting had vanished. He felt like he had been freed from an endless turning maze. Like a labyrinth from which he couldn't escape. He turned and walked back through the deepening smoky haze and down the hall to the sauna door. He inhaled sharply as both the blast of heat and the sudden realisation of her complete nakedness hit him at once.

"It's hot...I-I didn't bring a suit...." Selene mumbled.

"Indeedy," Jon smiled and wiggled his eyebrows. "It. Most. Certainly. Is."

Selene burst out laughing, the eggshells beneath her feet swiftly disappearing, all tensions between them broken. Jon dropped his clothing at the door, and in seconds stood in front of her naked himself.

"Now *this,* is more like it," he said gruffly, pulling her off the seat and into his arms, kissing her hard. His whole body wanted her, more than he had anticipated, so many weeks had passed, and the sexual electricity with Elysia mixed with the absence of Selene had left its mark. She moaned, the sudden heat rising within her, her skin feeling the slash of the heated wood against her back as he spun her around. He held her fast, lifting her onto his thighs, her back against the burning wall, and thrust into her.

Selene cried out in release, tears flowing from her eyes. And just like that, they were home. Home in a way that the lost suddenly wake into, finding all that they had been searching for had been there all the time, right in front of them.

The rest of the night was a blur of dancing naked in the kitchen, lovemaking and laughter. Reunited, in every sense of the word. Finally falling into a deep peaceful exhausted lovers sleep in the early hours of morning, Selene sighed with contentment. A long year apart had clarified one thing for sure. They belonged together.

Jon rolled over and wrapped himself around Selene. It felt strange to have her here in his bed. She had never been at this house with him. He had found it too hard to live in town after having been out in the barren wilderness for so many months. He needed a refuge from it all, a place to find peace, a place where he could sit outside under the stars, a place where he could light a fire and rest. It had taken him far longer to settle in again than he had expected, and trying to manage a new teaching job full time, the band, and a long distance relationship had proved more stressful than he had anticipated too. Then there was the powerful connection with Elysia. It had proven overwhelming.

The time apart had been hard the first year, and this year was proving to be no different. It was easier to just not think about her when she wasn't here, and that was also proving to be his undoing, as he spent more and more time with Elysia. He had the companionship, if not the physical relationship. The last few years had been all about Selene. He loved her, she really was the only woman he had ever considered spending the rest of his life with. But she was so elusive, so driven. He never felt that he was her first choice in anything. He just wasn't sure anymore. Several days had passed with them being together, isolating themselves with the urgent need to reconnect, but his mind hadn't come to any sort of peace at all. And it didn't feel good, that these thoughts were even playing on his mind in the first place. He felt a similar emotional distance between them, and a lack of control of his thoughts, as he had when he was alone out west. He consciously blocked them out, and turned his thoughts to her naked body beside him.

"So what's your day going to be like then?" Selene asked as she stretched out beside him, then snuggled in closer. It was already quite cold at night, and the fire had lost its embers hours ago. She knew that he would be at work most of the day again, and she had already made plans with Sacha and Derry for lunch.

"Same as the last few, I think. Work then head to the gym," he said. "It's a band rehearsal night tonight though, fancy coming?"

"Yeah, I might if that is ok? Seeing as I am on a plane first thing tomorrow morning."

Jon squeezed her closer. "You don't mind? It's our last chance before the gig next week."

Selene smiled and shook her head. The time had passed in a blink of an eye, and she was due back already.

He knew that he could reasonably skip the rehearsal tonight, but he didn't want to. He wanted life to be back to normal. No more surprises. No more chaos. He knew, too, that she would be expecting him to come to hers for Christmas, but that wasn't going to happen, not this year. This year was a home year, home with his family and friends, not travel. He was still feeling so ungrounded. He chose again to just not even broach the

219

subject of it, lest they end in a fight before she left. Better to leave it for another time he reassured himself. *Coward,* his conscience shouted at him. He kissed her head and rose from the bed, throwing himself into the shower. It would be a long day and an even longer night.

Sacha was waiting for her as Selene entered the little vegan bistro on the corner of Salter and Hollis.

"Hey babes how's things?" she asked, standing to embrace Selene.

"Hey luv," said Selene responded. "Ok I guess. It's been a bit of a weird week."

"We haven't seen hide nor hair of you two, been making up for lost time then?"

"I guess so, it's been nice, just hanging out together and all, but I kind of also feel like he doesn't want me to spend time with any of our friends as a couple. It's been a bit weird. I mean, we haven't even seen Beth or James since the gig."

Sacha sat back a bit in the chair and thought for a moment. "And then there's that hideous harpie Elysia."

Selene cringed. "Please don't say that name. I don't even know her really and I hate her. I mean, real hate, proper strong anti her feelings. She was a proper cow to me when we were at the gig, and being all over Jon like that really pissed me off."

"Yeah. Like she had rights. She has been a real hanger on this year. She and Beth get on famously being all artsy and all, but no one else has really taken that much

220

interest. It's like she appeared from nowhere, and now she is everywhere."

"Yes," said Derry, walking up to the table and joining right in as though she'd been part of the entire conversation. "Like a bad smell dahling, you know the type! Hey Selene, so glad we had time to properly catch up! Sorry to be late! It's been so awful with you gone! We miss you!"

Selene laughed, and embraced her friend. "Thanks hun, I appreciate your saying that, and I miss you guys too, loads!"

"Well, Jon hasn't been out much," Derry said, surfing back onto the wave of the previous subject without missing a beat. "And when he is out, she isn't far behind, whether it's with Beth or with himself. It isn't right."

"True. But the question is, what do we do about it? I mean you go home tomorrow and there you are, thousands of miles away again. And Jon is a good guy and all, but she is constantly in his face, begging for his attention. Wily ways that one, wily ways, I don't trust her - and I *could* throw her!'

Selene grinned. "I know. I don't know what to do either, other than to hope that we make it until Christmas, and hopefully he will come out and stay for a week or so over the break."

Sacha and Derry exchanged looks and Selene had an uneasy feeling.

"What?"

"He hasn't told you?" Derry asked.

"Told me what?"

"He said he was going back to Antigonish to be with his family for Christmas, that they were having like a family reunion type thing, a week long celebration."

As Selene sat there, tears came before she had thought to control the rising emotions within. His mother had never been her greatest fan, but they had been together for over three years and had always thought to be married one day. She couldn't believe Jon hadn't even mentioned it to her, a big family thing like that. Why did she feel so isolated?

"Wow. That's a bit shit,' Sacha squeezed Selene's hand. "I don't know what to say, Selene."

"That makes two of us." Selene sniffed and dried her tears with the tissue Derry had given her. "I guess time will truly tell whether or not we make it as a couple then. If he isn't coming and I can't come back unless he pays, who knows when we will see each other next. This is such shit. I hate this."

The friends sat in silence for a moment, taking time to order some drinks and lunch, and get on with their meal. When the waitress left, Derry leaned in and said, "Well, we have a little surprise for you."

"Please let it be good news!"Selene said.

Sacha squeezed Derry's hand and smiled. "We are going to be married soon!"

"What?" Selene jumped up and hugged them both. "That is the best news ever!! I am so happy for you both! When, where?"

"Well, we will need to make that decision," said Derry.

"Somewhere like Hawaii if that is possible!' Sacha said

dreamily.

"And elope with a friend or two as witnesses."

"Wow! That is amazing! I am so happy for you, really truly," Selene said. "That really is the best news ever. I won't be able to be there most likely, but please send loads of pictures?"

"Of course we will, hun. It will be very small and quaint, and when we have a party to celebrate afterwards, your presence will be expected." Derry said, leaning back as the waitress finally arrived with their food.

Selene's phone buzzed with a message, and she leaned to read it. It was from Ev.

"Oh dear."

"What's up?" Sacha asked between mouthfuls.

'My friend Ev just texted to let me know she just split with her boyfriend Morten. They've been together for around three years too. Sorry, I'll just text her back, and I can ring her later to see if she is ok."

Selene texted quickly saying she was sorry and hoped she was ok, and that she would be back on the bus from Heathrow, by tomorrow nighttime and the two could meet up and commiserate. Ev replied via the text to saying she would be waiting at the bus station for her when she arrived.

Selene had already decided to not bring up Christmas at all. It seemed easier to not fight when she was leaving in a few hours. The band practice had been fun, and she had enjoyed the antics of the guys and listening to all of the new songs as they rehearsed and messed around. All in all it had been a good night, and it was nice to be out

223

with each other having fun. She knew the alarm would kick in any moment, and felt a deep sense of déjà-vu as she lay there listening to him breathe beside her. Her heart pounded anxiously, part of her fearing what would come next and the whole leaving scene again.

The future between them was unknown, but then so was any future, all they could do was make a choice to remain together and keep holding the space, come what may. It had been the right thing to come, her intuition had been dead on, and she knew now that Elysia would be one to keep a close eye on from abroad, through Derry and Sacha. At least they were on her side as far as that was concerned. The commitment remained the same between them, to keep in contact as much as possible, and to stay together. She couldn't ask for anything more. The little hope she had for their future together had to be enough.

twenty-eight

Ios looked up from his espresso as Elysia walked into the
Athenaeum café. She hadn't seen him yet, but he
followed her every move with interest. It had been a
very, *very* long time since he had seen her, almost three
thousand years in linear time, but more like a century in
his travels. She was ever such a dark witch.
Manipulative. Cunning. Still, she wouldn't have had the
power to arrive through time on her own, someone was
up to something. His curiosity was piqued. He had

known something was afoot, something big enough to shift people through time. It was what had drawn him here from his business dealings in London. The threads of time were altering, ever so subtly, but enough that someone like him, who regularly travelled, had seen the lights flickering where they shouldn't. The first big one was when Merope was knocked from the sky all those centuries ago. Someone had pulled her through time then, and it hadn't been him. He had been following the celestial developments ever since, trying to uncover the bigger picture - what the end game was and who was playing. And he hadn't been the only one searching for her.

The angel had gotten there first, and Ios had kept silent, not wanting to involve himself with the Heavenly Spheres. He smiled as he thought of the many secrets he was keeping. It made the art of Chaos a very strategic pleasure. He might not be able to travel back in time to change the future, rather in that role, he was more of an observer, but he was certainly able to play a long hand in altering futures from each present day. He had always had a long vision and a good grasp of strategy.

His attention suddenly returned to the matter at hand. Elysia still carried herself with the same arrogant pride and self-serving attitude, he could see it in her movements. She swanned around this afternoon not unlike the cat that caught the canary. Her self-satisfied smile met his eyes, and vanished into an expression of shock.

"My Lord, whatever brings you through this time?"

she asked, lowering her gaze and shrinking into a slight curtsy. A slight panic rising in her eyes.

"Elysia. It has been some time child. Tell me how it is I find you here?" Ios was pleased to see her cower a little in his presence. He was not an *entirely* evil creature, but he was powerful in this world, and he was not to be trifled with on any level, and she knew it.

"I was sent here to distract someone, and force the end of a relationship."

"Why here, in this time? And who are these characters whose lives you are messing with?"

The tone of his voice implied he already knew, and would brook no lies or insolence on her part. Elysia shuddered and sat as he waved her into the seat across from him.

"Jonathan Bryce and Selene Kostantakos."

Hearing her say Selene's name rocked him, another piece of the puzzle falling into place, but Ios guarded his expression carefully. "When did this happen? Judging from your expression earlier, you seem to have been successful."

"Not yet, but shortly, yes I think it is happening. In the next few weeks, Selene will no longer be a factor in his life."

"So what do you gain from this, Elysia?" Ios leaned forward to face her squarely.

"My freedom. Forever. I will be free to live a life without being directed, bought or sold, by anyone but me. A new and mortal life, in a new century, all of it."

Ios sat back in his seat with a sigh. That was a high-risk bargain with a high price based on someone else's life and fate. She must have known that she would succeed. He just couldn't work out who was behind it. "Who."

"Who?" Elysia repeated trying to sound casual.

"Who brought you here Elysia. I want to know who is behind this charade."

The tone of his voice made her pale.

"Truly, my Lord Ios, I was given instructions only by a lower demon and sent through, I know nought else. I swear it." Elysia was shaking under his stare. She knew that answer wouldn't be good enough, but she really didn't know what the ultimate master plan was. And as for whom she was playing her role in it, she daren't say. "It was an offer I could not refuse."

Elysia had burnt every bridge once the King had taken her, and she had had nowhere left to turn. The appearance of Lilith and Sitri had been nothing short of a miracle, and this was her only choice short of being sold into slavery or burned to death for her sorcery. She had taken it and never looked back, and she had no intention of returning to that time.

"If this is true, then I will hold you responsible should anything happen to Selene. I will be watching you, Elysia. I don't care what you get up to, but I will have the truth from you eventually, and believe me," he paused as he leaned closer to her, his dark eyes boring into her wide and fearful ones, "the longer you wait, the higher the cost will be to you."

Ios stood then walked out of the café, leaving Elysia shaken and cold, her eyes boring into his back in terror.

twenty-nine

Selene had felt much more positive about things between herself and Jon since her return to Halifax, despite the hole in her bank account, and despite the lack of Christmas discussion. It had seemed easier to not bring it up, as she didn't want to leave on a bad note or fight about it. And she wasn't ready to admit Elysia was a real problem, not yet. It was easier to ignore the clouds, for the time being anyway.

Their calls had been far more regular and almost fun at times, and they had managed to skype a few times as well, which was even better, if not a little weird. Selene was feeling much lighter and happier and beginning to look forward to the Christmas season, even though she knew they would be apart again. She finally felt secure that she and Jon were going to be ok, and that it was just making it through the time in between seeing each other that would be tough. At least he would be working now, and he would have the money and the holiday times to come over, or fly her home to him. It all felt good.

But as the weeks passed, again, more gigs meant less time, and teaching meant being up and gone early as well. Exams and assignments were creeping up, as were the night shifts at the pub. The calls became shorter and more sparse, and on one in particular, he casually mentioned Elysia and a fun gig they had both gone to together. Selene lost the plot. How could he? After the way she had treated Selene when she had been home, hanging all over Jon like she owned him. He had protested that he was allowed to have friends with similar interests, and that they weren't proper friends, more acquaintance like, but Selene was no dummy. She knew that woman had her claws in, and she wanted them out. The call had ended badly, really badly, and Selene had cried herself to sleep.

James opened the door and greeted Jon with a big smile and a quick hug. "Hey buddy, glad you could make it.

Got a great crowd here tonight. What did you bring with you?"

Jon laughed and stepped inside. "Me, cook?"

He handed the big cake that was obviously deli-made and several bottles of wine to James and shrugged his coat off and slung it on the hook by the light.

"Figured as much." James stepped back into the hallway leading to the large open living room. It was a gorgeous old house, just outside of Point Pleasant Park. Beth was a decorator and interior designer, and her taste was truly impeccable. Being that it was Christmas season, the décor had been muted into silvers and whites with colours splashed here and there via small bell lights. It had the feel of a real winter wonderland, and the roaring open fire completed the picture.

"Hey Jon!" Beth said as she walked into his arms for a loving embrace. "How's things? I feel like I haven't seen you for months. How's Selene?"

"Yah, good, fine. Studying and that," Jon said. James glanced sideways at him and knew by the tone of his friend's voice, that all was not rosy in paradise. He decided not to say anything.

"You remember Viv and Hugh from the pub, and Gilly and Cas, and of course, you know Elysia." Beth made some general introductions. "You know the boys already, and Sacha and Derry should be along shortly."

Jon met Elysia's eyes and smiled. His skin tingled again, and he had to think of cold running water to shift the direction his thoughts were going in. He was glad she'd come, but it felt a bit awkward after the argument

231

he and Selene had just had.

"Hello Jon," Elysia crossed the room and reached up to kiss his cheek.

"Elysia, can I get you something to drink?" he asked, noting her empty glass. She nodded and he turned and led her towards the table, which was overflowing with exotic punches and mixed cocktails. "Where to start?" he laughed, shaking his head. *Leave it to James, any bloody excuse really.*

"I would like to try the green one," Elysia said, handing Jon her glass. He filled two up and handed one back to her.

"Did you enjoy the gig the other night?" he asked as they moved toward the sofa and sat down together.

"Yes, it was fab! I loved the guitarist. It's not often you hear that kind of Spanish guitar within a rock context."

Jon smiled, now this was a conversation that he would never have with Selene that's for sure. "Yeah, he was great wasn't he? Amazing style."

Derry and Sacha turned up just then, and Sacha sent a few daggers Elysia's way. Derry just clocked them and moved on with a disapproving smile, but both seemed totally unimpressed that she was there, and annoyed that Jon was sat with her and so engaged in conversation. They had known Jon and Selene as a couple from the start, and were particularly close with Selene. Jon realised that it would be a hard night for secrets, especially as Elysia had been welcomed by his friends so easily. It had taken Selene a long time to get to know James and Beth,

232

and many of his other friends. She just had so many different things going on all the time. But with Elysia it was different, he couldn't put his finger on what it was, but she just fit.

The night turned to games, the drink was flowing freely, and good times were had all around. It was well after three in the morning before things started to wind down. It had been snowing heavily, and the roads were treacherous. Fortunately Jon had thought ahead and had prepared to crash upstairs, but Elysia had a long walk home.

Elysia made sure that Sacha and Derry had gone before making her first real move.

"There are no taxis! It's over two hours wait." Elysia groaned in frustration.

"Let's walk. Come on, I'll take you back. I can walk back from yours or catch a cab when one comes available." Jon said.

"Thank you, Jon. I wasn't looking forward to that walk alone. That's very kind."

It took every ounce of control she had to play it down, knowing that this was the break she had been waiting for, this was her chance to finally win him over.

They wrapped up against the wind and snow. When they said their goodbyes, James grinned at Jon, nudging him in the chest. "Don't worry mate, I won't be expecting you back, but you know where the key is anyway."

Jon raised his eyebrows at him in mock whatever-do-you-mean, and laughed. He fully intended to return at some point. He was still with Selene, and he didn't want to ruin what was there and what was worth saving. He nodded at Elysia and they walked out and down the already snow covered steps. They walked quickly, but even so, it was a good and cold thirty minutes later that they arrived at her house on Dresden Row.

Elysia opened the door and switched the lights on, stepping into the foyer and shaking her coat off. She hung it up by the inner door and reached for Jon's as he held it out for her. "I am fr-r-rozen!" She shivered and laughed, utterly grateful for the modern invention of central heating.

"Yeah, it's a hot toddy night for sure!" Jon said.

"Hot toddy?"

"Hot whiskey or hot buttered rum, take your pick," Jon said with a smile.

"Well, I have both if you feel up to making something up," Elysia said with a sly smile. *Perfect.* "You know where the kitchen is, the alcohol is just on the side by the French doors."

Jon smiled and walked past her into the kitchen. He wasn't anxious to head back out anytime soon. Elysia quickly used the bathroom, and checked herself out. *Yes. No time like the present.* Sitri suddenly appeared in the mirror with her.

"It's now or never my friend. Let's get this done, shall we?" Elysia said coolly to the demon standing beside her. "Lilith shall have her victory, and I shall have mine. It is time. Yes. It is time."

Sitri nodded with a satisfied grin and vanished.

Elysia lay stretched out across the flat top edge of the

sofa completely naked, her legs draped over the far side. Jon froze where he stood, whiskey in hand, as he returned from her kitchen. He had already had too much to drink, and for a moment he thought his eyes were dreaming it. She was breathtaking. In his mind he had already touched her in places he would never have dared. And yet, her she was, glorious, her dark skin shimmering in the tiny sparkling bell lights above, her image erotically reflected by the mirror behind her. He couldn't see anyone, feel anyone, be anywhere but here, with her. His brain couldn't register a life before her. His desire for her was all consuming. He could feel his body hardening below, and he bowed under the pressure of it. He slowly placed the glasses on the table before him, and moved closer.

"What do you want me to do?" he asked, still drinking her in as she lay there.

"I am yours, come and seek me."

She slowly stretched one of her legs out, sliding it down the side of the sofa.

Jon bent and took a drink from the glass and slowly swished it around in his mouth. He moved towards the far end of the sofa, and ran his hand slowly from her foot, to her ankle, tracing the curves of her leg to her inner thigh. Missing her tantalizingly naked mons, he traced the line of her fleshy but toned belly and leaning forward slightly followed the outline of her breast, then returned to her thigh. Suddenly sliding his hands under her thighs and grasping her hips with both hands he fell to his knees and buried his face inside her.

Elysia gasped at his boldly erotic move, and the sensation it inspired. She hadn't expected it of him, and her own desire rose quickly. She was as soft as velvet, and as his tongue began to unfurl the little petals, leaching the wetness from within with each stroke. Elysia moaned and began to arch her back, her hands massaging her full breasts and pinching her nipples.

Glancing up, Jon could see her mirrored reflection and the bliss in her expression. He continued to drink her in as he disrobed himself, stopping only for the moment it took to remove his shirt. He then pulled her forward and off the sofa, and stood her in front of the long mirror that now faced them on the wall, holding her tightly and forward facing. He nuzzled and kissed her neck as his hands caressed her breast and pulsing clit. He could tell she was high, she was struggling to stand, but he held her fast, watching them together in the mirror as desire began to break through their control. He swiftly threw her forward over his hands, and hanging onto her pelvis he thrust into her with short sharp bursts, then just as quickly falling to the floor, he rolled her over to face him and plunged long and deep as his lips joined hers. Unbridled at last she arched and came hard, biting into his shoulder with shocking force. Jon finally lost control and filled her with everything he had inside to give, collapsing in the last thrust onto her sweat soaked body.

They lay still for ages, just breathing and feeling the slow descent of their heart rates from frenzied to peace. Elysia rose first, and took Jon's hand, leading him to her bedroom, where they both fell into bed wrapped in arms

236

and fell asleep.

Jon woke with a start as the midday sun shone brightly into his eyes. Disoriented, he had no idea where he was for a moment. He sat up and looked around, knowing then what he didn't want to know, that he was at Elysia's home. In *her* bed. Little details of their passionate night together began to course through his veins, and despite his protesting head, his body perked up with the memory.

"Good morning."

Elysia entered the room, large mugs of coffee in hand. She was still completely naked, and Jon lost all track of thought again as he reached for the cup she offered. *This cannot be happening.* He sipped the steamy froth, watching her as she walked around the bed and placed her mug on the night table. She met his gaze, then slowly crawled over the bed and pulling the sheet back, sat astride him, planting him deeply within her in one movement. Jon gasped spilling the coffee before he could set it aside. She grabbed his hair and kissed him deeply as she rocked back and forth over him. He reached for her clit and rolled it between his thumb and forefinger. She was so wet, he could feel the moisture dripping between their legs onto the sheets underneath.

"God, I'm going to cum," Jon shouted as he released, grabbing hold of her body and forcing himself deeper into her. Elysia just smiled and held him as his breath caught up.

"What are you doing to me?" Jon asked as he regained conscious thought. He pulled her closer and they lay

237

back against the pillows together, reaching for their coffees. Elysia held the silence, and Jon let his mind wander. The last three and a half years of his life had been all about Selene. His woman. The one he was meant to marry and be with. But all of a sudden, he couldn't see her. He couldn't see their lives together anymore. Nothing made sense anymore.

"I need to go," he sat up abruptly and set the mug down. "I need to sort my head out, Elysia. This isn't fair on you or on Selene. I don't know which way is up. And last night, well," he paused and ran his hand through his hair, "it was incredible. But I don't know where to go from here."

"It's ok," Elysia shrugged casually. "Take some time. But you know that from the first moment we met, there has been something between us, Jon. Perhaps the time is now to look towards a different future."

Elysia rose and reached for her robe. "I want to be with you, and all I can see is that she wants a career in a foreign country."

Jon sighed with frustration and annoyance at himself. "This shouldn't have happened while I was still with her though, can you see that? I'm *not that guy*."

Elysia strode across the room and placed her hands on his shoulders, looking deeply into his eyes. "I know who you are. I know what kind of man you are. I will be here. I want you here with me, and I want all of you. I am no mistress."

Jon smiled at that. No, she certainly was not the mistress type. Elysia was all consuming or nothing. "I'll speak to you later."

He bent and kissed her on the lips. He left the room and grabbed his clothing from the other side of the sofa where he had peeled it off last night. Dressing quickly he grabbed the keys and phone and headed out the door. There was only one way to solve this one, and James had better be home. A serious issue was now afoot, and the hoops would serve as a good brain sweep.

thirty

James opened the door, took one look at Jon's face, and his jaw hit the floor. "No way. Tell me you didn't. Holy shit, you did. Come on in buddy."

"Game. Need game. Come on let's go."

It was all Jon could muster at this point. James shouted up to Beth that he would be back in a couple hours, grabbed his trainers and the ball and closed the door behind him.

Jon was silent as they walked down to the court, which was mercifully unmanned.

"What the fuck, man? What is going on?" James was beginning to worry. Jon's face was like thunder, anger, confusion, self-hatred, loss, love. It was all there.

"I slept with her."

"No shit Sherlock. It's written all over that guilty face of yours. What happened?"

"I took her home, went to make her a hot toddy in the kitchen, and she was lying on the sofa naked when I came back.."

James dropped the ball, completely speechless. He couldn't believe it. *Damn that girl plays hardball.* He knew that she was after Jon, of course, anyone could see that. Still. *Sweet moves. No time wasting there.* Jon grabbed the ball out from under him, and for the next half hour they shot hard and fast, engrossed in competition as a way of clearing the decks.

Tired out and soaked in sweat, Jon finally spoke.

"Selene and I had an argument, a big one last night before I went to yours for dinner. It was all about Elysia funnily enough. Here I was defending her saying that we were just acquaintances really, not even proper friends yet. And that wasn't actually the truth either, but I felt so defensive all of a sudden. I feel like total shit man."

"Was it good?"

Jon whacked James with the ball, hard. "What do you think?"

"I think you're in trouble. How do you feel about her?"

"I don't know yet. I mean, when I'm with her I can't see or think of anyone else. It's all consuming you know?

241

It's like being drugged. But is it real? It's all so new, and I barely know her. The last few years have been all about Selene, and building a life with her. And now she's gone, living in the UK for another few years, and I don't want to go. What does that mean? That I don't love her enough to go, or to wait for her? We just keep hitting obstacle after obstacle. What does that mean?"

James didn't answer right away. Thinking on it, he dribbled the ball between hands, then shot a hoop.

"Personally, I think it means you're done. But you are the only one who can answer that. Where Beth goes, I go. No question. You and Selene have barely lasted a year apart, and there are two more to go. What if she doesn't want to come back? What if she chooses to stay in Europe?"

Jon winced, he hadn't even considered that. He caught the ball as it slid through the hoop. Bouncing it as he walked back and forth, he stopped and looked at James.

"Yeah. I think that's it. I mean I love her, but we've really hit a cross roads here. I don't want to live there, I want to be here with my friends and family. I love teaching. My life is here."

James faked left and grabbed the ball from Jon, dribbled past him and leapt up to score another point. "I guess that's that then."

"Pint?" Jon said smiling. "Winner buys."

James laughed. "Yah, go on then, your mind isn't here anyway. You're no competition at all!"

Jon whacked him again with the ball, as they headed

242

out to the Grad House pub. The smell of Elysia caught him off guard, stopping him in his tracks as they entered. That rare mix of sandalwood, frankincense and orange; all heady, ancient and sweet at the same time. She wasn't here, but this is where they had first met. How could it be that her smell would be here? He realised that he really wanted to see her, his body burned with the memory of her touch. He could feel himself hardening. He looked around again to be sure, and shook his head. *Cold shower cold water. I'm going crazy, slowly but surely.* James already had the two pints on the bar by the time Jon reached him.

"Cheers big ears." James raised his glass to Jon. Memories from their time in Brighton together met with the clinking of glasses.

"So what now?" James asked, leaning up against the bar.

"I need to think things through a bit, and I need to talk to Selene."

James drank deeply. He didn't envy Jon at all. Crossroads in relationships were hard work. Heart wrecking work. That phone call could go in any direction, and none of them looked good. "When will you see Elysia again?"

"Dunno. I need space man. But after last night it doesn't feel right to not talk to her."

"So, let it go, and see how the day pans out. First things first. You need to talk to Selene."

"Yeah. Yeah. That first." Jon sighed and sank further into his pint. "Right then. Time to face the music."

243

Swallowing the last of his pint, he saluted James and walked back to the house to make the call.

The phone was ringing, waking Selene from a troubled dream that fled before her. It was half past one, and she staggered into the lounge, flicking on the light as she entered. She grabbed the handset, her voice thick with sleep.

"Hello?"

"Selene."

The voice was serene. *Jon.*

Selene felt a jolt in her heart at the sound of his voice. He sounded terrible. After the argument the other night, they still hadn't really talked things through.

"I need to say something, please don't interrupt. I've thought a lot about what you said the other night. And I love you, I really do. But I can't do this anymore. This coming and going, this limbo, it's killing me. I need to be here, fully here, and I just can't keep doing this my-heart-is-over-there-and-the-rest-of-me-is-here-thing-anymore. My work, my family and my friends are all here. It's been a hard year apart, and this one is worse. Being so isolated last year really took a toll on me. I need to be in a place where things are stable, and real. I know that is hard for you to understand. Maybe if you come back, but at this point I don't even see that happening. Selene, we need to move on in our present lives, and being like this is killing both of us. You know what I'm saying is true. You know we can't keep this up. I love you more than I have ever

244

loved anyone, you know that too. But I can't live like this anymore. It's just time to let go."

Selene felt the ending burn through her skin, the doors of her heart opening and then slamming shut in front of her like a film, the butterflies fleeing in all directions. She felt sick.

By the time he had finished his monologue, all she could muster was, "I understand. I love you. Goodbye."

And he was gone. That was it. Nothing more was said. Selene sat quietly in the chair for a long time. Tears flowed down her cheeks, but she couldn't actually cry, she couldn't actually properly breathe. In the recesses of her mind she could see the mist and smell the sage that invigorated every dreamtime vision she had about Jon. In true Brit style, she rose and flicked the kettle on, settling in for a long night of restorative tea drinking. This wasn't her first heartbreak, it was just the deepest. She already knew that she would survive it, eventually. It would simply be a matter of time, and plenty of distraction. She felt helpless.

She had woken one day knowing that this work with her hands and her heart was her calling. She had had to leave everyone and everything behind and follow that call. This work was not a career or a job. And if that was true, then perhaps letting him go was meant to be, even after almost four years together. She could feel her rational brain kicking in, and swiftly shut it down. Selene set her tea aside untouched and reached over for the whiskey bottle. She was going to need something a little stronger. She poured herself a long one straight up, and downed it.

Taking a deep breath between tears,
she poured again, flicked some music on, and lay back on
the sofa.

Kristian appeared and surveyed the scene in front of him.
This wasn't normal Selene behaviour, something had
happened. He looked down at her with love as she slept
on the sofa, covered in used tissues, her empty glass and
the empty bottle. He gathered the blankets from her
room and gently placed them over her. He wandered
back into the kitchen and filled the empty glass with
water, then placed it on the table beside. He could feel
the pain as it radiated untethered from her heart, and it
saddened him. He could feel the sadness around
thoughts of Jon, and he instinctively knew it had ended.
He closed the lights and with a last look at her, raised his
left palm and vanished.

thirty-one

Someone was banging at the door. It seemed so far away. But it kept happening. She realised that her duvet was over her, and not remembering how that had happened, she reached for the water and downed it in one. She wondered vaguely how many more days she could do this. Sleep, drink, go to the shop, sleep, drink. Awake all night and asleep all day. She dragged herself off of the sofa and made her way to the flat door, then down the stairs to the main entrance.

Opening the door, Ev stood there exasperated.

"Thank God! I've been trying to reach you for like ever Selene. What the hell?" she broke off at the sight of Selene. "Jesus, you look like the wreck of the Hesperus!"

"Um, yeah," Selene said, as she turned and retraced her steps up to the flat.

"It's like *Tuesday* girl, what the hell has happened? I've been texting and ringing!"

"Jon and I split up." Selene said mechanically, but with the shocked expression on Ev's face, the damn finally broke, and the sobbing overtook her.

"He broke up with you over the phone?" Ev was incredulous. "What a bloody coward."

Selene laughed humourlessly from the floor. She slowly gathered herself back up and went to the bathroom to wash up. "Can you stay for a while? I need a shower."

"Yes. I'll make us some lunch shall I? When did you eat last?"

Selene groaned in response and turned the shower on and stepped inside, grateful for the hot deluge as it hit her cold skin. She stood under the pouring heat for as long as she could, then stepped out to get dried and dressed.

Ev had made some soup and toast, and more tea. Selene sat down across from her at the small table. "Finished the whiskey, heh."

Selene smiled sheepishly. "Yeah. Tea wasn't cutting it."

"What the heck happened? I thought you really nailed it back together when you went home a few weeks ago. What changed?"

"I don't know. I mean, I told you about that woman I

248

had the dreams about, and she was there and very attached to Jon. We had a huge fight the other night about her. And then he rings me after midnight the next night, and tells me he can't go on like this and that it's over for him, us."

"Just like that?" Ev slumped back into the chair, considering things for a moment. "He slept with her."

Selene looked up sharply. "What?"

"He *must* have shagged her. I mean he is in love with you, you have been his universe like forever. And then *bam*, 180 degree turn around in a few weeks? She must have got him really drunk...."

Tears began to flow again. "Do you really think so?"

"I don't know what to believe, but he had to have a reason for this sudden '*epiphany*' Lene."

Selene nodded. It would certainly explain a lot.

"Right then. Over is over," she reached for her phone and deleted his number in one final press. "Done. Temptation removed."

"Good girl. This is gonna be hard, but you'll get through it, hun. We'll go out and drink and dance and just shake it all loose. Then it's just time, I'm afraid."

"Thanks Ev. I have to break it to my parents at some point. But that can wait. It feels good to just be here and not feel any pressure to be honest. I feel a bit relieved. It's not the decision I would have made, but it does just crack the pressure valve of constant missing and aching, and wondering what he was doing all the time."

"And your phone bills will be way cheaper!"

"Ah yeah, I *knew* there had to be a bright side." Selene

249

smiled at her friend. *Thank God for good girlfriends.*

"So what's next then?"

"I dunno. Finish the term, work like a demon over Christmas hols, then back to college in January." Selene shrugged. "The normal life of a student I suppose."

Ev eyed her warily. "You are the least normal student I have ever met. Something interesting is bound to happen. What about that guy? The one you met again on the airplane? You exchanged numbers this time didn't you?"

"It's a little soon to be thinking rationally Ev. Jon and I broke up like forty-eight hours ago!"

"Who said *rational?* What's wrong with a little rebound sex with someone as hot as that?"

Selene doubled over laughing. Ios wasn't old, but he was very cultured and mature, she couldn't see him being remotely interested in her.

"Look, just consider that it might be a healthy thing when you're ready to move on, ok?" Ev rose and grabbed the plates, sticking them back into the tiny kitchen. "Never mind all the gooseberries at college that would love to get the hands on you given the opportunity!"

"Ok. Ok!" Selene laughed half-heartedly.

"Back to college tomorrow? Enough with the mourning and drowning in drink. Time for that over the weekend. You can't afford to get behind."

"Ok boss. I will be there bright eyed and bushy tailed." Selene knew it would be good to get her head busy again, and let the pain continue to wash through her until it eased. Even now it rose and fell like the tides.

Her phone started ringing and her stomach clenched. She had left it in the kitchen, and the ring was so faint, no wonder it had been easy to ignore it the last few days. Part of her didn't want to answer it. Ev left the room to tidy up the kitchen. She caught it on the last ring, an unfamiliar London number.

"Hello?"

"Selene?"

His voice hit her like an electric charge.

"Ios?"

"Yes. Selene, hello. I am in London for a few days for work," he said. "Can I come and take you out for a meal?"

"You do realise that you are at least two hours north of here, Ios?"

Ev stuck her head around the corner and made a face.

"Yes yes, no worries. I have things to do here, but I could come Thursday, late afternoon? Say around three o'clock maybe? I will stay at the Park Inn. Meet me there?"

"How could I refuse? It will be lovely to see you."

"Ok, I will see you then!" And he was gone. That fast. Selene could scarcely believe the timing. It was bizarre.

"That was him wasn't it!" Ev hopped up and down. "I told you he was into you!"

"Well, the timing of that call was something else, I'll give him that. I wonder what he's up to. It just seems a little too coincidental don't you think?"

"The words *gift* and *horse* and *mouth* come to mind. Dinner out with a gorgeous fella post-heart-break? You're

251

right, *how could you refuse?*" Ev mimicked the last few words of the phone call and Selene tossed the throw pillow at her from across the room.

"Speaking of hot fellas, when is your super hot brother coming down for another visit? My lonely little self could use some company too ye know!"

Selene rose and hugged Ev tightly. "Thanks a million. You're such a great friend Ev, I really don't know what I would do without you. I will ask Maty when he is coming next, promise!"

Selene surveyed the state of the flat and knew she had better get it cleaned up and sorted out. The next few days she would focus on college work to keep herself from crying, and then Thursday, she'd go out and enjoy a night away from it all.

thirty-two

Thursday afternoon Selene left college early to shower and dress for her dinner with Ios. She had no idea what to wear, being that she was in total student mode. Her room look like a tornado had hit, but she eventually chose a slim fit pair of black trousers and heeled boots, with a turquoise and indigo silk top to set off her eyes. Simple silver jewellery, a few bangles, no rings. Light make up set to cover up crying eyes, and she was ready to fly.

Ios was waiting in the lobby when she arrived. She felt she could melt into the floor just looking at him. The women behind the hotel reception could barely keep their eyes off him. He wore dark diesel jeans with a wide leather belt and expensive leather shoes. Under the brushed leather jacket, the soft pink of his shirt set off the light flecks in his otherwise dark eyes. The shirt was open at the neck, revealing just enough of a promise of the strength below. He was so simply, incredibly sexy.

Ios warmly embraced her and kissed her cheeks, then pulled her hand and led her outside to the waiting car.

"Where are we going?" Selene asked as she pulled the seatbelt across her chest. The car was totally lush, one of the new silver convertible jaguars. Selene sank back into the heated seat. It suited him, and it beat the purple Yugo hands down. She was quite relieved that she didn't have to find a way to fit him into it.

"Isle of Purbeck. I thought we would see some castles. What do you think?"

"I've never been there. Is it far?" Selene asked as he turned the car out of the lot.

"I'm not entirely sure," he said, affording her a sideways glance. "I haven't driven it myself, and it has been a very long time since I was there. One of the castles is a ruin, and I'm told that the other has been turned into a restaurant."

"Sounds good to me. Thanks for calling, it was a really welcome surprise."

Selene knew that though she did not know him well, but there was a sort of kindred connection between them. He had a kindness about him that made her feel safe.

"Delighted," he said with a smile. "I imagine you don't

get to do these kind of things while you are busy studying, and sometimes a break from the harsh realities the day to day is just what's needed."

Selene regarded him thoughtfully. *He couldn't know. Could he?* Her mother had called the night after Ios, saying that she had had a dream that something was terribly wrong, and Selene had told her then about Jon, and about Elysia and her own premonition about what was going on there. Her mother had sounded a bit strange, and the ways she spoke about Elysia was like she had known her, which was impossible. She had asked a lot of questions about what she looked like, and where she was from. She seemed to want Selene to wash her heart of both of them and be done with it, not even a word of encouragement to try to reconcile. *Let them go,* is all she had encouraged. It wasn't the response or advice she had expected, knowing how her mother had loved Jon.

It was a beautiful evening, the sun was just starting to make its final descent into darkness, and being early December, it would be completely dark within the hour. They crossed over the chain ferry and continued on through the dunes and farmlands. Half an hour later he pulled off into a laneway and drove into the castle grounds. It wasn't large and it wasn't the prettiest castle she had seen, although after her love affair with Arundel Castle on the east coast, it would be hard to compete. Arundel was her vision of Camelot, even if it was historically in the wrong place.

Ios opened her door and held his hand out to help her

rise from the low platform of the car. She took it gratefully and managed to stand up with something akin to grace.

"Come, let's have a walk around the grounds before we go in, it will be too dark when we have eaten." Ios kept her hand and led her down the far right side of the castle, where the path wound downhill towards the cliffs. It was so barren, being winter, everything was in deep repose and seemingly unprotected from the rawness of the elements, as the fierce wind blew up from the sea below.

The path opened onto a small sloping field, and they followed the stone staircase down towards an enormous stone globe. Selene gasped as she saw it, it was so unexpected, and a wondrous addition to such a beautiful walk around the grounds. Poetry was chiselled into the surrounding stone walls, barely readable at points due to the wearing of time and weather.

"It's amazing!" Selene exclaimed as she ran her hands over the words on the wall. "Virgil, Shakespeare....the sun the moon the stars....Ios, I'm beginning to think you're a romantic!"

Ios smiled, enjoying her pleasure at seeing something new and unusual. "Come," he said reaching for her hand again. "Its darkening now, and it's too cold to make the walk to the lighthouse and the caves, but we will return someday."

Selene nodded and followed Ios back up the staircase towards the restaurant entrance. Entering through the large main doors, they were greeted with a blast of heat from the roaring fire. The hostess waved them over to a small private table by the windows overlooking the sea. It was still light enough to see the coast on the other side. She gave them menus and took the drink order, reappearing shortly with a bottle of pinot noir.

"Thank you Ios. This is really lovely." Selene raised her glass to meet his.

"Delighted Selene, it is an unexpected turn of events that brings me to London, and it is my great pleasure to now find myself here with you," he said, looking directly into her eyes.

Selene was silent for a while, enjoying the light but intense flavours of the wine, the rather interesting and a bit bizarre décor of the castle, and the view. She was aware of his gaze resting on her, watching her as she took it all in. She met his eyes evenly again.

"'Why did you call?"

"I enjoyed our chance meeting Selene, why would I not call, given the opportunity to see you again?"

"I was just surprised to hear from you, that's all. I also get the feeling that you know something I don't, and that your being here isn't as innocent as you claim."

Ios threw his head back and laughed a deep hearty laugh. She couldn't help but smile and blush at her own boldness. Maybe he was being genuine, but she just couldn't figure him out. Did he want to be friends with her, or did he want more? He was very cultured and there was something definitely otherworldly about him. It excited her as much as it made her nervous. After everything that had happened this week, she just needed to know.

"So I am guilty until proven innocent then, beautiful Selene?" he said, his eyes still full of mirth. "However shall I pull that one off?"

"I'm sorry. I didn't mean to be rude. It's just been a hard week that's all, and your call was quite coincidental."

"Tell me then, what has happened that has been so hard?" Ios knew full well that Elysia had played her final card, and he had no doubt what the outcome had been. She was never one to gamble without a sure win, especially not with her own life at stake. She was as dangerous and as cunning as she was alluring. She also obviously had the aid of the demon realm. Jon hadn't stood a chance.

"Jon and I broke up a few days ago." Selene said.

Ios reached out for her hand, as she looked away and reached for her glass with the other one, and drank deeply. The waitress appeared to clear their plates and asked if they needed anything else.

"Yes, two espresso and a bottle of ouzo." Ios replied without taking his eyes from Selene. They gazed at each other in silence until the waitress returned. Ios opened the ouzo and poured two long shots into the tiny old glasses she had placed on the table. "Drink."

Selene slowly sipped at the ouzo, feeling the heat penetrate through her body one cell at a time. It was an incredible sensation, one she hadn't felt before, despite having grown up with it as a common drink. *Ouzo with Ios, a special kind of drink with a special kind of man.*

She smiled inside, but he caught the glow and smiled

258

back.

"Better," he said, satisfied. "Your heart is far too precious to be wasted on someone who will not know what he has lost."

"Thank you," Selene whispered, mutinous tears rolling down her cheeks. *Dammit*. She reached for a tissue to wipe them away, but he was already there, gently catching each one with the sweep of his hand.

"It's alright, don't hold back for me. I know a little about broken hearts," he said, still holding her hand across the table. He poured again for both of them, and they relaxed back into an easy silence and sipped the ouzo.

After a time, Ios waved the waitress over, and paid the bill.

"Let's go, we still have another castle to see, and the night is glowing with stars for us."

Selene smiled and stood up. She felt a little off balance, the ouzo was strong, and she could feel it making its way through her veins. It was quite sensual, if not a bit dizzying. She followed Ios out to the car, and sat comfortably in the seat as he made his way to the other side.

thirty-three

"Is this one far?"

"No, it should be on our way back, the ferry is finished now, so we need to take the road back through Corfe. It's a ruin now, but I think you'll like it. If you can bear the cold that is."

Selene laughed. It wasn't actually that cold. It was a crisp enough night, and there would be a frost, but it wasn't cold like in the Canadian winter. And even there she rarely felt the intensity of the cold like others. Her mother was the same. She guessed he must be used to much more Mediterranean style climates. She relaxed back into the heated seat while he drove through the town and up through small and windy roads. Minutes later he pulled off on the side of the road. There was a small pub across from them on the right, and then on her left she could see the towering keep. He was already out of the car and opening her door. Grasping her hand gently, he pulled her up and out.

She followed him around the car to the foot of the bridge. They walked over to the middle and stood admiring the huge tower and the surrounding ruin. The moon was clear and bright, the thickening Milky Way of stars crossing the sky behind the tower illuminated the night sky with breathtaking beauty. Selene shivered slightly. The air around them was cold, but she was wrapped up pretty warmly in her winter coat. It was more like the sensation of electricity, and Selene could almost feel goosebumps on her arms from his touch.

"Timewalk with me," Ios said casually, taking her hand in his.

And in the time it took for her to glance up at him, they were there, a thousand years before, on a bridge with the odd person passing in and out of the south bailey of the glorious castle before them, which only moments ago had been ruins. Selene couldn't believe her eyes. She could barely take it all in, it was beautiful. The towering keep in its full glory left her speechless. The stars were even more glorious, with no little light pollution to pale them from the bridge. Ios looked down at her and nudged her forward slightly.

"Come, let's have a look inside."

Selene nodded and followed his lead. They crossed over the end of the bridge and entered through the gates. Hand in hand they walked through, weaving their way towards the entry. Huge torches lit up the cobbled path, and the inner square. However, just as they made a move to step inside, a voice called out with accusation.

"What black magik is this?"

Ios and Selene turned to see a middle aged man glaring at them, staff in hand, pointing to their odd appearance, he must have seen them appear on the bridge. Before any more attention could be spent on them, Ios glanced at Selene and smiled, pulling her closer towards him..... and in the blink of an eye, they were returned to their time.

"How did you do that?" Selene asked with admiration. "That was incredible." Although she wasn't sure that she wasn't just a little drunk at this point, and maybe had imagined the entire experience.

"You can do this," Ios said, testing his theory. "Timewalking is in your blood Selene. Didn't you know?"

Selene regarded Ios intently. "No. I've never done anything like that before."

Ios returned her gaze with equal weight. "Really? *Think.*"

Selene took a deep breath and let her mind wander over the year. So much had happened. She had no recollection of having time travelled anywhere. Before arriving here, her entire life had been university and Jon. Her body contracted at the thought of his name, and she brushed it off quickly before the tears had a chance to reform. Kristoff. Yes!

"I had an interesting night with a friend I hung out with one night. We smoked a bit of pot and fell asleep.....I thought it was the pot.....but maybe...it was so real. I was with him in another time. I held him in my arms, like a child, but he wasn't my child. I had four sons, this was the best friend of the one I was closest to. I was older, and it was Egypt or Greece - I was a Queen...I saw the King shagging his cousin who was oddly enough, named Elysia, then I woke up."

"Yes, see. You *can* timewalk. Interesting though, not only a timewalk, but reliving your mother's past--"

"What?"

Ios didn't respond, so she demanded again, "What did you just say?"

"Nothing, slip of the tongue, my lovely," he said. "Anyway, come, you have much to learn about your talents, and I am only here for the night. You really have no idea, do you? Let's go warm up in the pub there."

He walked slightly ahead of her, leaving her almost in shock. This was certainly unexpected. *Timewalk*. She had never encountered the expression, let alone contemplated the idea that she could do it. She followed him into the pub, where he ordered two Irish coffees before leading her to a small table near the fire. The pub was full of locals, noisily sharing stories and drinks. The bar maid couldn't take her eyes off them, Ios especially, as she hurried to make the coffee.

The atmosphere was thick and heady, almost electric. Now she *knew* what she had been sensing, the electricity

263

attached to the timewalk. It still followed them, like a marker in time showing where it had been slightly bent. The charge formed a little bubble around them, and while they were vaguely aware that people were glancing and some openly staring, their eyes rested solely on each other.

"Why did you show me that?" Selene finally broke the silence.

"I wanted this night to be special, especially after the week you have had."

It was a weak answer, but she chose not to challenge it. She was still feeling a little awed and charged. Selene's head was spinning, and she focused on the coffee, sipping it slowly, allowing the heat to bring her back and ground her a little.

"Explain."

"You have the ability to travel. The new agers in this time call it astral travel. Your *ruach* is the light body part of your soul, your *nefesh*. Your nefesh stays attached to your body while you live. But your ruach can travel through space and time. Most people who are able, can do it when they sleep. Some are more advanced, and can do it at any time, awake or asleep, and can consciously choose where they are going. This is a rare gift. Incredibly rare actually, and not usually a human gift."

"Not a human gift? What do you mean *not human*?"

"It is a gift of some immortals to timewalk, to be able to sift through the threads in the multiversal bands of time. Like eternals, who you will know as angels or archangels, beings from the Heavenly Spheres. And

264

perhaps a rare witch or sorcerer, and demons...."

Selene remained silent. *Angels. Eternals. Immortals. Witches. Demons? Not human. I have definitely had too much to drink.* Did that make Ios not human? And if he wasn't human, what was he? It was too much to take in, but she knew he was telling her the truth, something inside had opened in her chest, and the space between her shoulder blades was fluttering madly. His eyes were wide and stared deeply and solidly into her own. Those eyes. If she hadn't just been in the castle at least a thousand years ago, there would be no way she would take his words seriously. But having actually walked through time with him, she could now feel the sensation in her body telling her it was true.

"I think it might have happened in Ireland last year too, I was listening to music in the pub, and suddenly I was back in time somehow," her head was starting to spin.

Looking into her eyes he could see her confusion was threatening to overwhelm her. "Come Selene." Ios rose and held out his hand. "It's late. Let's get you home."

Selene nodded and took the hand he offered. It was grounding, warm and stable and very comforting. They walked across the road and jumped in the car, driving in a comfortable silence with music playing quietly in the background, to her flat.

"Thank you for coming with me tonight. I enjoy your company Selene, and that is a rare thing for me." Ios took her hand and helped her out of the car. Selene smiled up at him with sleepy eyes.

"I think you are a rare man Ios. Or not man? I cannot figure you out for the life of me, but I am happy being with you, it just feels good, and I like it."

Ios embraced her and held her for a long while. But he made no other move to either kiss her or give her any indication of his feelings towards her. He finally bent and kissed the top of her head, released her and stood back, looking into her eyes.

"You have *many* gifts, my dearest Selene, and time will bring them out. You are more special than you can ever imagine. There may be those who try to hurt you, but I swear that I will be one who will always be here to protect you. Be true to yourself, and you should be safe."

Ios stepped back and turned towards the car, giving her a reassuring smile before sinking into the seat. Selene smiled back, feeling a little dazed and confused. She waved, turning and opening the door to the flat, and heading upstairs to her own space. *He just swore to protect me. Protect me from what? Or who?*

She was too tired and confused to think anymore. The ouzo and whiskey was hitting its mark. She dropped her kit on the floor, and fell into bed. Not even bothering to wash up, she was asleep in minutes.

Ios returned the car to the hotel and thanked them for their service. Walking around the corner into the darkness of the car park, he simply vanished, reappearing in his large flat in Knightsbridge. He was still a little shocked that Selene had no idea that she wasn't human, that she was a *creature,* not unlike him. She was not a demon, however, and where she fell on the scale of who was who was what, remained yet to be discovered.

thirty-four

Sariel appeared without warning by Lilith's side, causing her to drop her goblet of wine as a result. She turned to face him, slightly breathless as she did so, her heart still beating rapidly.

"Really Sariel!" she said crossly. "A bit of warning or distance would be most welcome!"

Sariel grinned and leaned down to kiss her cheeks before seating himself on the large chaise in the library.

"You have news?" Lilith asked hopefully.

"I do. I am not sure what use it will be to you, or to be truthful, I am not sure whether I should share what I have learned Lilith, Mamma. I was not clear on what you were after when you asked me to seek information about your curse."

Lilith remained silent and walked to the large windows, staring darkly at the fiery glow of the volcano. She glanced back through the threads of time, feeling slightly overwhelmed by the newness and the potential of possibilities that lay ahead. He had found something meaningful, she could feel it in her blood as surely as she could feel the rage inside of her building. She held fast to the steel rail before her, then turned to face Sariel with burning eyes, her flaming red hair flowing with electricity from her shoulders and encircling her face and body. Her skin shone with a soft eerie glow, and she stood to her full height. The result was fairly menacing and overpowering, and Sariel almost knelt in trepidation as a response. It was the first time he had ever felt the depth and breadth of her power, and his entire being knew terror deep within.

"Here me now, *my child*," she hissed. Sariel could have sworn he saw flames lick the sides of her mouth. "I have had many faces through the sands of our times. I've drifted pure and alive, vital with the energy, the potential of the universe. All that is, all that once was, all that will come to pass. I have been, I am and I will become. I am the maiden Adamah, I am the wife of Adam. I am the Leviathan, the cursed beast of Eden, who tempted Eve with the first taste of knowledge. I have eaten from the tree of knowledge and lived to tell the truth, and to *share* these truths. I have spoken His secret name. I have warred with Gabriel on Holy ground, and I did not surrender. I have flown with eagles and screeched like owls. I have slept with demons, and procreated with the devil, Sammael, your father. I am wife of Asmodai, the King of all Evils. I am the Queen of Sheba and Zemargad, and I am the consort of the One, when your Shekinah is in exile. I am the unbridled sexuality of all women. I am the maiden and I am the crone. I am the circle of life as you know it to be. *I am free will.* I am the taste of what can be, I am the taste of your freedom, of what lies in the deepest darkest most vibrant part of your heart and soul. I am your dreams, I am all of your desires. So do not tell me who I am, or what I am not. Do not tell me what I deserve to know or not know. Do not tell me what I can and cannot do. *I AM.* And in living and creating, I have the power to become who I am meant to be. I have everything I need to become. I will meet my eternal soul on judgement day. It is only then, that I shall bow with grace to Him who created me, and say thank you. For the greatest gift is the one most elusive. And stupid useless humanity has always missed this message, lost in their soft and malleable ways. The key lies within me, and I need to unlock this now. I am, and I will be. And you, *my son*, son of Sammael, *will do my bidding.*"

She turned and left the room, leaving Sariel standing open mouthed in shock. He knew now, that he had no choice but to deliver the message in its entirety. The prophecy Pfiron had relayed had the potential to change the world as they knew it. And he was terrified.

He let himself fall into the chaise and tried to catch his

breath. He looked up sharply as Claude entered the room, carrying a large goblet of wine. Claude remained expressionless and loyal as always to Lilith, as he held it forward for Sariel to grasp.

"Thank you Claude. You are most thoughtful."

Sariel met his eyes for a fleeting moment, before Claude looked away and nodded, turning and leaving the room. Sariel wasn't sure how long he sat there for, but Claude had returned at least three times to refill his goblet. He rose and thought to seek Lilith, however Claude shook his head and motioned for him to follow. He was shown to a luxurious room on the upper floor, with a huge balcony overlooking the endless stream of firelight from the lava flow in the crater beyond.

"Madame does not wish to be disturbed tonight. She will meet with you at the break of day. You are to relax and make yourself at home, son of Lilith. Might I suggest, that you take some time in the spa tubs overlooking the crater?" Claude held his arm out towards the window, revealing the steaming tubs.

"Thank you Claude. I think I will." Sariel replied. Claude departed and Sariel sighed deeply. He really was caught between a rock and a hard place. He feared what his mother was capable of, if her past involvements and history had any bearing. The prophecy was wholly unexpected. He had never imagined in his wildest dreams that the birth of a child of an angel and an immortal would amount to anything much. But it had, and it most certainly did, and the implications were potentially enormous. He had no idea how long that prophecy had lain hidden amongst the old texts, nor how Pfiron had come to find it.

But tonight, he would rest. He would retire his mind and his soul, and rest. He shed his clothing and reached for the heavy robe Claude had left on the enormous bed. *Yes. Rest, in the proverbial calm before the storm.*

Lilith paced heavily across her room. She could see Sariel as he made his way down towards the spa tubs and shed his robe. She was still riding the wave of rage from the torrent of history as it had fallen from her lips. Her heart rate was still ragged and her breath light and rapid. Incensed, but also exhausted from the feeling of being dragged backwards through the beginning of time, through all she had thought she had come to terms with, all she had come to peace with. The facets of her own life like the reflective faces of the diamonds she now wore, each revealing a different time, a different Lilith, a different challenge, a different call to rise.

All that I am. I am. She thought angrily. The surge of rage had surprised her. She had not so deeply considered Gabriel, nor the Garden in as many years. It remained a deep wound, even now. Gabriel had forever borne the brunt of her hatred for his role in distancing her from all she had loved - and forcing her hand. Then he had become her plaything, an amusement, for Gamaliel and herself to remind themselves that they too still had a role to play in the larger schema of the universe, while time ticked so.slowly.by. While they waited for eternity to come to its potential. They had played many practical jokes, and some perhaps not so practical. They had played with the only commodity they had, *time*. But they had yet to get the better of him. Gabriel had remained as always, untouchable. Hatred ran like electricity through the darkness of her blood. She had loved him back then, in his unmistakeable, irreplaceable self. His beauty, his radiance, his wisdom, kindness and gentleness. His power. And then she had hated him, for his rejection of her. Their eternal existence, it seemed, could be as exhausting as it was renewing at times.

She dressed herself in her most sensual attire and signalled Claude. Tonight she needed release. It had been some time since she had gone hunting late into the night, and she could feel her blood lust mating with the hatred that still burned like fire through her veins.

She would deal with Sariel later.

thirty-five

And Friday hit with a bang.

There was a pop quiz in physiology and biomechanics and technique all in one day. And hungover at that. Selene wasn't sure the hangover was from the time travel or from the enormous amount of wine, ouzo and Irish coffee they had consumed. She was too tired to care. She managed to promise Ev a complete rundown Saturday afternoon, get through the day, and grab an hour's kip before heading out to the pub for her shift. It was the week before Christmas break, and she was working the entire weekend, and from the following week, straight through the holidays.

Waking late Saturday morning, she could hear someone at the door downstairs. Groaning and pulling herself from the bed, she stumbled down the stairs and opened the door.

"Miss Kostantakos?" the man asked.

"Yes, how can I help you?" Selene asked, her brain still in service mode from work.

"I have a gift for you from Lord Ios."

The man handed Selene an enormous bouquet of white roses, and a black coloured box with a big red bow. The box had small holes around all of the edges.

Lord Ios? Well, that explained a lot.

Selene reached out and took the two items and placed them beside her on the floor. She thanked him, and closing the door, gathered the things up and trudged back upstairs.

The dozen white roses were immense, and not at all like the ones you buy in a supermarket, for those had no smell. These, however, were bursting with such a delicious scent it made her a little heady. As she placed the bouquet and box down on the table, intending to find a vase, she heard a small little sound coming from the box. A miao! She stood very quietly for a moment, and the sound came again. She removed the ribbon and lifted the top, to see the teeniest cutest little white kitten looking up at her. It had one black paw, and pale blue eyes. She gathered the kitten up in her arms and snuggled it. She was speechless. Unbelievable. She would never

275

have considered a pet, but as a gift, it was perfect. She was instantly in love with the tiny thing. It looked up at her with its sweet blue eyes and miaowed again.

"Hello little sweetie!" Selene cooed at the miaowing kitten.

It climbed up her arm and sat on her shoulder. Sweet! *Oh my, better get dressed and get some food for this kitty.* She placed the kitten back down in the box and laid it on her bed. She grabbed an old t-shirt to make it more cosy in the box.

"I'm going to jump in the shower and then we'll get you sorted with food and a bed little snowball."

The kitten miaowed again, snuggled into the shirt and promptly fell asleep. Selene turned the radio on low so it wouldn't be scared in the silence and jumped into the shower.

"I'm coming!"

Selene shouted as she grabbed the towel and raced down the stairs. Ev stood tapping her foot impatiently, but grinned as she saw the state of Selene as she opened the door.

"Late night girly?" she laughed as she followed Selene up to the flat.

"Ugh. Hungover and exhausted all day Friday and then yes, late night at work at the Boar. But check *this* little guy out!"

"Wow!" Ev exclaimed, gathering the little kitten into her arms. "Where did he come from? He's *so* cute!"

"*Lord* Ios, and the flowers too." Selene said as she waved her hand towards the window.

276

"No way!" Ev sat down with the kitten still asleep in her lap. "So things went well then the other night? Did you......"

"Nothing nada. Perfect gentleman."

"Well, that's a little disappointing..."

Selene laughed. It was a little confusing, but not disappointing. It was too soon. *Way too soon.*

"It's ok, really. We talked a lot and I loved just hanging out with him, he's so different."

"Different?"

"Mature?"

Ev burst out laughing and woke the kitten. "Just how old is this guy Lene?"

"I have no idea. He must be at least ten years on me though, maybe a little more?"

"Well, whatever. He is super hot and has money and treats you with some respect. That I can dig."

Selene smiled and reached out for the kitten, and snuggled him closer under the nape of her neck. It was super cute with the little black paw. It took a minute to think where she had put Ios' card, she needed to ring and thank him sooner than later.

"Are you out tonight then?"

"No, thought I would take it easy and do some reading, maybe watch a film. Why?"

"I have to work, thought maybe you would be up for some kitten sitting? I feel so bad leaving him all alone for so many hours."

"Sure, I can watch a film here until you get back." Ev stood up and bent to pet the kitten again, who miaowed and purred at the same time in response. "I have a key, so I'll pop back around eight or so."

"Thanks babe." Selene returned the kitten to its little box and it fell asleep again. She searched for her bag and found her iPad. Sure enough, in the case was his card.

"Hello?"

"Ios, it's Selene."

"Hello Selene! How are things down south?"

"Great thanks, you're still in London then?"

"I am. Plenty to keep me busy for the time being. I might even stay for the New Year celebrations."

"Ah that will be fun up there! Listen, your lovely gifts have arrived and I just wanted to say thank you and I love little Snow! He's the cutest ever!"

"Snow?" she heard Ios pause. "Ah the kitten. Yes appropriate name, I am sure he will love it."

He could tell she was truly smitten, and already loved the little beast. That was a good sign, it would be far easier to track her movements with the help of a familiar. Witches tricks. Another gift of time.

"If I *am* here for New Years Eve, would you like to meet me in London?"

"I'm supposed to be working, but I can see if I can get out of it. My mother is arriving New Years Day, and my brother Mathios was going to collect her and bring her down to stay with me for a couple of weeks. Mathios lives in Notting Hill. It would be fun to all meet up, if that would be ok with you?"

"I didn't know you had a brother. That would be fine with me Selene. Ring me when you know and I can make

278

some plans. It will be lovely to see you again."

"Yes, I would really like that Ios, thanks. I will call when I know for sure. Talk to you soon."

They said their goodbyes and rang off. Selene grabbed her dosh and headed out the door to find supplies for the cat.

Merope woke to find herself still sat in the chair in the early hours of morning. So many dreams and premonition-like visions, it had been a rather sleepless few months. The skies had cleared to leave an almost warm beam of light surrounding her. If she didn't know better she would have thought Raphael was close by, she sat up straighter suddenly.

"Raphael?" she called out under her breath, not wanting to wake Nikolas.

"It's funny how you always seem to know when it's me." Raphael suddenly appeared beside her with warm smile.

"Yes well, it has been some time, hasn't it, but your warmth is unmistakable. Like the embrace of a long lost friend, even if you aren't visible at times." Merope stood up to receive him.

"What's wrong?" she asked as she took in the expression on his face.

"Kristian came to me the other day--"

"Is Selene alright?"

"Yes, I think so, for the moment. You are aware that Jon has ended their relationship, and that he has begun a

279

new one with someone known to us from the past. This appears to be tactical, Merope. Elysia has had help, we actually think she was enlisted to complete this as a mission or some sort of exchange. There is something else too. A demon named Ios has also suddenly appeared in Selene's circle of friends, and this too is a puzzle."

"Ios?" Merope paced around the room. "I haven't seen him in millennia. How is it that he has come to know my daughter?"

"I do not know, but they have seen each other, and are friends. Merope," Raphael paused mid sentence, not sure how to put the words together. "Ios has taken her timewalking. He has also taught her to recognise that she is also able to do it. Although she has not done so consciously or purposefully on her own yet."

Merope stared open-mouthed in shock. She set herself down on the chaise by the open window. She could see the stunning Ios in her minds eye. Selene would certainly find him very attractive. "How can this be? I mean I always knew she would have special gifts being that she may be both eternal and immortal. But it's all happening too fast!"

"I know, and I am concerned. Tell me what you know of Ios, Merope."

"He's a demon. Lord of Chaos is his other title. Although in all the years I knew him, he was never anything but kind and protective towards me, and my sisters. I do not think he would ever harm Selene. If anything, he would chose to protect her I am sure of it. Of all the years I knew him, I knew little about him really.

I was a young child compared to my life now."

"Lord of Chaos!" Raphael was pacing, a bit frantic. He knew exactly who Ios was now, and that the threads of time could open up completely and swallow him up. He would be impossible to track if he didn't want to be found, and if he took Selene with him, he could think of nothing worse. "It's a rare thing for a demon to attach to a human without intention. But he obviously knows who Selene is, and perhaps he knows who she really is as well. Merope, this demon has many qualities and abilities, he is very powerful in the demon world, and not on the Heavenly side. I do not think we can be so trusting. He has been entangled with Lilith forever, and we do know she holds a deep grudge against Gabriel. Selene would be in very grave danger indeed if Lilith ever found her."

Merope rose, feeling helpless. Entering the kitchen she switched on the kettle and began to prepare the cafetiere and breakfast. Nikolas would wake soon enough, if he wasn't awake already. Her premonition dream was one sign, this was another, it was time to move closer to Selene and be more of a presence in her life. Who would want to play with her heart like that? Who would want to hurt her like that? Mind you, demons weren't particularly interested in human emotions. What did they want with her daughter? And, what did they know about Selene that she did not? Try as she might, she simply could not see the bigger picture.

"I don't know what to think Raphael. But as long as Kristian and Osian are close to her, she will be safe won't she?"

"I can no longer guarantee that. When Ios took Selene back into time, they crossed over a thousand years in an instant. It took Kristian completely off guard. He was set to track them when they reappeared again beside him. But it takes more than that to track someone travelling through time Merope, you can't just latch on for a ride. Ios would have sensed his presence if he had been any closer. Angels live in the threads of time, not on them, and most of the guardians cannot travel through them, never mind the dimensional aspect that Ios is capable of. He--"

"What do I need to do? Tell me what to do! Should I talk to Selene and tell her what I know, who she is, who her father is?"

"No." came the simple answer from behind them, and both Raphael and Merope swirled around to face Nikolas as he walked into the room. "No. It would completely shatter her. Her heart has just been well and truly broken by Jon. Let time and ability reveal itself in the time it was intended. Right now we need to pay attention to the signs, and keep a close eye, but anything else would be an over reaction, and might give a heads up to those who are after her. We have no idea what they know or don't know, but they want her for a reason. We need to know that first."

"Nikolas is right," Raphael said with a sigh of relief. "How I do wish we could call on Gabriel, he has such clarity of vision."

"It's not time for that either," Nikolas said. "It would draw too much attention to us right now. Merope, can you reach this Ios character?"

"I have no idea how to reach him Niko, I knew him three thousand years ago, and even then, he appeared and disappeared, we never called for him."

"He must have had a familiar with you if he appeared like that to you, can you think of anything animal wise or jewellery that was around you at the time?" Raphael asked.

"He gave us each a white kitten with a single black paw. Seven of them, identical kittens, to each sister." Merope, eyes wide stared hard at Raphael. "A familiar?"

"It's a way of a witch or demon to watch over you without needing to be present. They can be any shape or kind of animal, or be present in a piece of jewellery. They act as spies, guardians or slaves really. Your kittens were just that, a way for Ios to be in communication with you without needing to be present."

Merope sat at the table and tried to digest this information. She had always been fond of Ios, he had been full of practical jokes as they were growing up, and then later a good friend with lots of friendly respite when needed after her disastrous marriage to King Sisyphus. She had always trusted him, despite knowing even then, that he was not human. Being a nymph she never worried about that aspect, and often had felt safer and more alive with her fellow creatures. She laughed out loud suddenly as a memory hit her, and Nikolas and Raphael looked at her with confusion.

"I was just remembering that that damned cat used to go into these hissy fits at times. I could never suss out what caused it, as usually it was really calm and placid, weirdly for a cat actually. But I do remember once when Gabriel arrived suddenly, but hadn't appeared visually yet, the cat went crazy hissing and its fur all at end. It wasn't until I saw Gabriel that I made the connection. The cat knew before I did that someone was there, and I soon began to learn to feel the charge in the atmosphere and its shift when someone was coming and going."

"Yes that would make sense. The familiar would have seen or at least sensed what you could not, being that they are lower demons themselves."

"Has Selene mentioned any new pets, or even Ios?" asked Nikolas.

"No, not yet anyway. She mentioned Elysia as she had a dream about her being with Jon, but funnily enough, like my vision, hers was also in my old time. We need to move Niko." Merope said suddenly, turning to Nikolas with pleading eyes.

"I know my love, but it isn't that simple. We need to have earthly means of supporting ourselves remember?" Nikolas laughed, placing his hand on her shoulder. "Let's go and find a house there, somewhere far enough but near enough, and scout for a restaurant location. I will not sell up here until we are established there, if at all. We can have a good manager here and give a small portion of ownership so that they treat it well, and I can travel between the two when needed."

"Niko you are a love!" Merope leapt up into his arms.

"I knew what I was getting into when I agreed to all this, although I never would have imagined love would be such a part of the bargain, and I do love you my little sea nymph."

Merope grinned and found her feet. "Thank you my love, I am ever grateful that it is you here with me." *My anchor, where Gabriel is my wings.* She felt very grateful for all of it.

"I think the best plan would be for Merope to go and stay with Selene for two weeks. At the end of that I shall join you, and we will travel to where ever you like and seek a new home."

"Good. We will see if Ios has provided a familiar, and we can get an idea of who and what is around her." Raphael said. "For my part, I will listen to what is happening in the Spheres and beyond our veils. It is the most I can do at this moment. Something will surface soon, it has to. If Lilith is behind it we will find out. Now as Selene's abilities are beginning to reveal themselves, no thanks to Ios, we must be on guard."

Merope embraced Raphael and Nikolas nodded, Raphael raised his left hand and the mandala glowed, taking him with it.

thirty-six

New Year's Eve. Selene gathered up her belongings and exited through the turnstile at Paddington. It was an easy trip, nice and quick from Bournemouth, straight to the city in under two hours. Snow kitty was settled with her elderly neighbour for a few days, despite being rather grumpy about it for a kitten. Just long enough to have too many memories flood the gates of her mind. No matter what she played on her iPod, or what games she tried to occupy herself with, memories flooded her senses and had filled her with tears. Everything had been so abrupt. *The end. Over the phone. Asshat.* The grief was still quite raw, and time with friends and studying had helped to keep the dam from exploding, that was yet to come. Ios appearing again had been a gift. Someone she could focus on, someone real, someone that kept her forward facing, and enticed her with new and exciting things.

She searched around for Mathios as she wandered through the busy open area, making her way towards the cookie shop, but couldn't see him in the throng of revellers, some of whom had obviously started the night way early. Finally, she saw a tall, curly dark head that looked familiar and she shouted out to catch his attention. Mathios turned and seeing her, and waved back, pushing through the crowd to reach her.

"Little sis!" he laughed and grabbed her up into a sweeping embrace. "How's studying going? Life in the south? Where's Ev?"

"All good Maty. All good. Ev is already here, she'll meet up with us later on, I just have to let her know where. You look really well, what's happened? Someone started to feed you again?" Selene laughed and punched him on the arm. "Ohh and fit too! There must be a girl involved!"

"Ha very funny. Well if you must know, there was, but it didn't last. *Next*!" he shouted to no one in particular and dramatically snapped his fingers.

"Well there's a bevy of gorgeous fit gals down south who would be most delighted to spend time with you, big brother, if you are feeling lonely. Actually, I can think of one in particular who is quite sweet on you!"

Selene smiled and curled herself under his strong

287

loving arm.

He was only an hour and a half away but worked such long hours they barely saw each other. She missed him terribly, and being with him also made her miss Jon. Her heart creased a little at the thought, and she let her mind wander, and wonder if he was ok and if he was with Elysia. She hadn't spoken to any of her friends from Halifax for ages, part of her just didn't want to know.

"Earth to Lene!" Mathios waved a hand by her face. "Where'd ya go? Lost you there for a moment."

"Was just thinking of Jon. Missing him. Being around you makes me miss being around someone who cares about me, I guess."

"Aww Lene, it's not all that bad. Come on. Mamma will arrive stupid early tomorrow and everything will come to rights. She will make you eat, do your laundry....it will be like a little holiday in your own house, and all the love with it."

Mathios stopped walking and embraced her gently. "I know it's been hard, but it will get easier. I promise."

"Thanks Maty, I know. Just time right? I mean I guess I find it hard to just cut off almost four years together after one short phone call."

"*Arhithi.*" Mathios stated in their mother tongue. "He's a dick and a coward. I can't believe he did that over the phone either, but I guess you are far away, and if you are going to end things then spending a grand on airfare wouldn't be that appealing to me either to be fair."

Selene whacked Mathios hard in the shoulder. "OW! I'm not saying that you weren't worth it, but I can see that

288

side! As for time, that is the biggest part, the rest is distraction I think. Speaking of which... let's go dump our stuff and get jazzed up, then we can meet up with your friend and see where the night takes us. Most of my friends will be hanging at the Athenaeum at Hyde Park, then heading out from there."

"Athenaeum? That place seems to be popping up everywhere! There is a new one in Halifax too. How odd. We Greeks seem to be getting around these days." Selene said. "Ok then, I'll text Ev and ask her to meet us there."

Mathios smiled and popped open the large umbrella as they stepped out from the rail station into the rain. He was delighted that her friend Ev would be coming out with them tonight. He had had a crush on her since they had met, and this would be the night of nights to make magic happen, if it was going to happen at all. He was also very curious about this Ios she kept talking about, and wondered what his agenda was with his sister. He must have known about the break up, and suddenly appearing in London again so soon was interesting too. *Ever the big brother.* They stopped into a small café for a quick bite to eat, then crossed back over to the station and took the tube to his home in Notting Hill.

Selene followed Mathios into the main room and dropped her bag beside the large sofa before plunking herself down. She stretched out and placed both arms behind her head.

"So then, what gives? Tell me about the girl."

Mathios laughed as he hung their coats up on the small hat rack. "She came, she conquered, she left. Not much to tell."

"Conquered huh. She obviously had some impact Maty, look at this place, its clean, you are like fit, and you were on time to meet me. Seriously, you look better than I have seen you look in a long time."

Mathios threw Selene a dirty look before heading to the kitchen to find the Ouzo. Selene sat up with a smile, remembering her evening with Ios.

"So you like Ouzo now do you?" Mathios said as he placed the small glasses on the coffee table.

"Didn't I always?" Selene asked as she sipped it slowly and relaxed back into the sofa.

"Not really, no." Mathios answered her. "So why the sudden change?"

"When Ios took me out to see the castles, we had dinner at one of them, and we shared a bottle before heading to the second castle." Selene paused, blushing slightly at the memory. "It was the week Jon and I split up, and it seemed to warm me in places that had only been frozen since. Everything just felt easier, more alive again."

"A *bottle*, were you still standing?" Mathios looked mildly alarmed.

"We didn't finish the bottle, but it was a good few long drinks of an evening. I really enjoy spending time with him, Mathios, he is so different. He isn't like anyone I have ever met. I don't know what to make of him or how to take him to be honest. He never even tried to kiss me, he was a perfect gentleman the entire evening. Actually, come to think of it, he's been that man since we met in Dublin."

Mathios sat back and regarded her closely. He had never heard if Ios until recently, but conversations with Merope had enlightened him considerably, and it was obvious that Selene had no idea who or what he was. He wasn't human, Mathios knew he was a demon, but not what kind of demon, or if he posed a threat. Osian and Kristian, were really wary, especially since the timewalk gig. Losing her in time had really wigged them out. Where Ios fit into the otherworldly remained a mystery that Merope hadn't wanted to solve for him- she had left so much unsaid. But here he sat, talking about this unknown element, and he already knew his sister was falling in love with him. And that could not be good on any level.

"Maybe he's just playing it cool, he knows you've just had your heart broken."

"Maybe. Truthfully, I was really surprised to hear from him. He is wealthy, well travelled, very mature, thoughtful, gorgeous--"

"Good catch then sis!" he said trying to hide his disquiet. "Maybe he's just too old for you?"

Selene hit him with her pillow. "Very funny. I just don't see what he sees in me if anything. He might just want a new friend, who knows."

She sat up and downed the last of the Ouzo and rose. "I'm going to shower and beautify myself, when are we due out?"

"Another hour or so before we have to make a move. I'll change but I'm ready when you are."

thirty-seven

Sariel was woken at dawn and summoned to the library. He rose slowly and dressed himself before making his way down to meet Lilith. Her demeanour had calmed slightly from the night before. She was more relaxed, sated by her intense hunt through the night. She wore a soft fitted white gown, that highlighted the new flush of her skin, her hair was still wet and pulled back from her face. She motioned to him to be seated, and Claude brought them steaming cups of coffee before departing.

"Good morning Mamma." Sariel reached down to kiss her cheeks.

"I trust you slept well Sariel." Lilith relied a little coolly. "What say you this morning then, Son."

Sariel sipped his coffee and met her eyes as he sat across from her.

"I will relay what I know."

Lilith merely smiled.

Sariel sat back and took a deep breath. This was the part he hated most, the utter invasion of his body and senses. After several thousand years, he had never gotten used to it, nor surrendered to it, even though he had no hope of ever controlling it. The shadow quickly gripped him in its thrall, and his body became enshrined by cold blue fire. Eyes rolling back deeply into his head, an ethereal voice spoke from somewhere deep within:

When the Holy sky falls into the Heavenly sea
Immortal and eternal blood shall mix
By true love drawn forth a new race
The fallen shall be unfallen
Hidden by loving arms
Lethe and Demon will enthral
Within the liminal space between worlds
Shall be
But one daughter to save them all

Entombed deep within corporea prima luna
Her virgin womb doth hide
By passionate ritual she shall endure

And crystalise His Holy stone of life
By silver knife
Holy semen and bitter water
Blood and fire unite

The dream is made for only one to see
Beyond the grave and beyond the tree
Where the temptress Leviathan her primal decree
Coerced Adam and Eve
Heavenly Cherubim and Principalities
Sacred guard secret therein lies the key

Banish be the curse of all
One life will forfeit another
One daughter shall be taken too soon
And eternity lost again to its mother
By the blood of the moon
Ripe shall become the demon womb
One moment in time for all creation
And all shall fall into shadow

The prophecy ended as quickly as it had begun. The blue flame vanished and Sariel collapsed into a heap. Lilith leapt up to catch him and Claude ran to her side. They placed him on the chaise and waited for him to come around. It was several hours later when he finally opened his eyes and recovered his senses.

"Worth waiting for Mamma?" Sariel asked drily as he nodded to Claude and accepted the glass of water he offered.

"Is it always like this when you are called on Sariel?" Lilith asked with concern. "When a prophecy is delivered through you?"

"Yes." he replied shortly. "It will be a few days before I am back to full strength again now. Don't ask me to do that again."

"I've seen many prophecies over the years, and every one is different. All these many years, and I didn't know it was like that for you. But I am very grateful for what you have shared with me. I need time to think and to decipher what it all means."

"It means that our world will change should you pursue any course of action relating to the prophecy and the birth of that child."

Lilith regarded him warily and chose to remain silent. She needed time to absorb the meaning of the prophecy, and to decide on the best course of action. The first part of the plan- to isolate the girl had been enacted- and it would soon come to fruition. If she proved to be the child of the eternal and the immortal, then life as they know it would change indeed. And as far as Lilith was concerned there was only one way to find out. The blood lust still fresh from the night before, she grinned and made her way back up to her rooms, leaving Sariel to rest in the good hands of her manservant Claude.

thirty-eight

Two hours later the pair walked through the main doors of the Athenaeum Hotel at Hyde Park. Selene looked stunning in a Ted Baker silver backless mini dress and knee high stiletto black boots, which she had borrowed from Ev. Mathios was equally well-dressed, in a tailored navy suit and silver shirt, open at the neck.

Ios was waiting for them, already friendly with the people waiting for Mathios at the bar. His head turned and his face gave away the mix of desire and joy when he saw Selene. He fought to recover himself before briefly meeting Mathios' eyes, then turning his attention to Selene.

"Selene, you are beautiful," he said, taking her hand and kissing it. "Hello, you must be Mathios." Ios gently released Selene's hand, holding his own out in greeting.

Mathios took it and looked Ios in the eye. He knew straight away that this creature was definitely a demon, but gave nothing away. "Please, meet my friend, Seere," said Ios, gesturing to the tall blond man at his side.

"Hello Selene, Mathios." Seere was similar in height to Ios, but in colouring the exact opposite- tanned skin and dirty blond mad hair, with wide green eyes. Selene could almost picture him with a cowboy hat, which made her smile and almost chuckle out loud. They made such unlikely friends, and that made Selene like Ios even more.

Mathios turned to greet his friends and then returned to introduce Selene around.

"Selene, these are some of my best mates here in the UK, Mikail, Una, Fredrik, Rups, Sarah, Ben, Seb, and Dean."

"Hi all!" Selene said with a smile. "Great to finally meet you. I was beginning to think Maty really only had Ben and Mikail as friends! It's good to know the rest of you aren't imaginary!" she laughed as Mathios swotted her on the arm.

"Come Selene, let's get some drinks for you two," Mikail said.

Selene stepped forward and thought for a minute. It would be a long night better had stick to one sort of drink.

"A glass of red please, pinot if they have it. Thanks Mikail."

She looked over her shoulder at Ios, who was deep in conversation with his friend Seere. He looked up and met her eyes and winked. She blushed and turned back to the bar. She wondered what his game really was, but whatever it was, it was working. She knew that she was into him, and playing it cool was not really something she was terribly good at. Her heart still had the raw ache from the break up, but the time they had already spent apart was blunting the edge somewhat. *Thank God for small mercies.*

In terms of Ios, *(Lord* Ios thank you very much) she would follow his lead, and not set a foot forward till she knew where the ground lay. She was not going to allow this new year to begin with any sadness, tonight, she was going to shake off the past and all memories of Jon, and see the new year in with style. She looked around the bar, but no sign of Ev yet. Having Ev here would make this night a hundred times better, and with Mathios being single, maybe sparks would fly again. She knew that they liked each other, it was just time and the right opportunity.

Ios was already beside her before she turned from the bar again.

"Selene," he whispered in her ear. "It's lovely to see you again so soon. How wonderful you could make it up for the New Year celebrations. It's always such fun to leap across the crack in time as the bell tolls. I shall enjoy it even more being with you."

Selene's eyes widened and she looked up at him. His eyes were full of mirth. *Oh my, girl, you are so in trouble.*

Mathios was watching the two from the end of the bar where he stood talking with Ben. Ben looked at him, then back at Ios and Selene. "Older brother having a bit of a protective moment?"

Mathios looked at Ben and smiled. "Yes as a matter of fact. What's your take on this guy?"

"Seems nice enough, genuine. Bought the first round, always a good sign. Generous. Excessively good looking which always puts *anyone* off really."

"I hear *that*," Mathios laughed and the two raised their glasses. "Must be a Greek thing, then heh."

"Ugh should have known. Bloody Greeks!" Ben laughed. "His friend doesn't look Greek though, more like a cowboy western gone wrong."

It took a lot of control for Mathios to not spew his drink through his nose, let alone across the bar. Swallowing hard and fast he laughed heartily and raised his glass again.

"This is going to be a very interesting night my friend!"

Ben grinned and downed the rest of his pint, leaning forward to order another round. It would be an interesting night indeed. He looked up and saw a rather beautiful blond heading towards them. He nudged Mathios and tilted his head towards her.

Mathios smiled and gathered his courage. Downing the rest of his pint, he looked at Ben and said, "Watch this."

He made his way through the crowded bar towards her. Ev looked as beautiful as he remembered her to be. Her dress was stunning, she too wore a mini dress style, but in a deep indigo, with silver beading through the neck and waist. It wrapped closely around her neck, leaving her shoulders bare. She wasn't as tall as Selene, but was as slim and very athletic.

He felt a little anxious as he approached her, but he took a deep breath, and reached out and grasped her by the waist. He twirled her quickly around and into his arms, so they were face to face.

"I've a bet going that I can't steal a kiss from a woman as gorgeous as you." he whispered into her ear. "Come on Ev, give us a chance?"

Ev recovered herself and began to laugh, throwing her head back slightly with a grin.

"Well then, Maty," she said seductively, looking deeply into his eyes. "How could a girl refuse an offer like that?"

She leaned closer to him and reaching up, touching his face, laid one on, taking the opportunity to kiss him thoroughly and deeply, in a way she had only ever dreamed of. Bet or not, she really didn't care, she had loved him since the day she had met him, and this was her chance to let him know. Mathios' eyes widened with her kiss, then he relaxed, returning it with an equal measure of heat and desire. He was almost breathless as they parted, and stared smiling silently into each other's eyes.

"Oh get over it Mathios!" Ben shouted laughing. "That

was such a set up!"

"Get a room!" Mikail chimed in, and Selene suddenly looked up to catch the end of the kiss that had set the night on fire for everyone.

Wow. That was good, unexpected, but good.

Ev righted herself and turned to face everyone, blushing from head to foot, even more so as she caught Selene's surprised expression.

"Ev!" Selene made her way through to her best mate and gathered her up in a huge hug. "I am so happy you made it! *Nice* entrance by the way."

"I know! Sorry about that, Maty started it!" Ev said, still blushing.

"True, guilty as charged," Mathios said with a smile, keeping his arm around Ev's waist. "Can I get you a drink, Ev. Selene can introduce you to everyone?"

"Thanks Maty, G&T for me please."

"That was a kiss and a half girl! Well done! And Mathios started it? I am super happy for you!! Come. Meet Ios, he's here too."

Selene took Ev by the hand and introduced her to everyone as they made their way towards the end of the bar, to where Ios and Seere stood.

"Ios, Seere, this is my dearest friend Ev." Selene said as she gently nudged Ev ahead of her. She could tell from Ev's stunned expression that she was slightly awed by Ios too. He was rather different than any of the guys they had dated. It wasn't just his looks, it was his *presence.*

Ev gave Selene a look that spoke a thousand words and Selene giggled in response.

302

"What's so funny?" Ios asked innocently.

"Nothing Ios, nothing at all, just girl stuff." Selene felt a little silly saying it, but it was true. There was no way she was going to come clean about that look, that was for sure.

Ios smiled. "So what kind of name is Ev?"

Ev groaned. "My proper name is Evangeline Mary Jones. Welsh father and Scottish mother. Please don't call me that. Ev is fine, really truly!"

Ios laughed and nodded. "It's a beautiful name and it suits you. But I will call you Ev if that is your desire."

Ev tilted her her head a little to take all of him in again. "Yes, Ios, that is my desire." she repeated the words softly entranced. "Although, it sounds so different when you say it..." her words trailing off into silence.

Mathios returned with their drinks and relaxed into the side of the bar as they chatted. "So what's next on the agenda then?"

"I have tickets to the Guanabara party. Or we could crawl next door and do the Hard Rock." Ios suggested. "Or both." Guanabara was a hip Brazilian-inspired restaurant and nightclub on Parker Street.

The lads looked up and smiled. The general consensus was early doors and dinner at Guanabarra, and then see the new year in at the Hard Rock. Being with Ios guaranteed entrance to both with no hassles, and everyone was delighted to join in and see where the night would lead them. The atmosphere was light and happy, charged with a heady mix of joy, playfulness, and desire. Everyone had their own personal agendas to bring with them into the coming new year, and each in their own way, had already found the unravelling of the early eve much to their pleasure.

thirty-nine

They gathered their things and headed out towards the
Guanabarra for dinner, and a few good dances. The line
up was already half way around the block, but Ios showed
something to the bouncer, and they were all waved
through. Following him up and around the corner and up
the many stairs, they were led to the far side of the bar,
where a private table had been set up for them. Drinks
and food ordered, everyone relaxed, swaying to the Latin
rhythms as they pulsed through their bodies. It certainly
didn't feel like London in the dead of winter. The disco

ball reflected every colour imaginable, lighting up the darkened room, and in the centre of the circular dance floor several professional dancers led the way in beautiful sensual Latin style.

"It's all very *coupley* out there, never mind that I cannot dance to save my life!" Selene shouted in Ev's ear.

Ev nodded in agreement and smiled. Tonight she was definitely not going to be alone. Mathios had barely left her side the whole evening- it was bliss. She had noticed that Ios was always within reach of Selene, but he was careful not to crowd her. She wondered what his gig was with her. *Did he want to get together with her or was he really just being a friend?* He was so hard to read. Ev had found it really hard to really gaze into his eyes, they seemed so blue they were black, but seemed to have little flecks of silver through them.

Mathios gently tugged her arm to catch her attention. "Come dance with me Ev."

He didn't wait for an answer, and led her away from Selene to join the others on the dance floor. It was heaving out there now, and Selene laughed, feeling reassured that Ev wouldn't have to pull any dance moves at all, as there was barely room to breathe.

Selene became aware of Ios standing behind her, and he slid his arm around her waist, pulling her closer to speak in her ear. "Are you enjoying yourself Selene?"

Selene looked up and back at him and smiled a yes. She looked back to the dance floor and felt her body sway against his slightly. He took it in stride and responded in kind. She turned and they held each other in a soft

306

embrace and swayed to the rhythm. They danced for a few songs without talking, just looking into each other's eyes and smiling. Selene felt him suddenly tense, he pulled her closer then released her, spinning her around and tight to his side, but slightly behind. She looked up at him in surprise and then forward to follow his gaze.

A stunning, sexy and rather vivacious woman with large green eyes and long hair the many shades of fire, was approaching them. Selene wasn't sure that this wasn't the most beautiful woman she had ever seen in her life. Her features were exquisite, as was her flawless light olive coloured skin. Her dress was embroidered diamante red silk, with a plunging neckline, the large diamond necklace framed by her great cleavage and delicate chin. She obviously knew Ios and approached with purpose.

"*Habib alby*! What a pleasant surprise to see you tonight."

Her voice was silky, sexy, and deep, but held an edge to it. "Why ever didn't you say you would be here?" she reached up and kissed Ios on both cheeks.

"Lilith. Enchanted as ever to see you. I wouldn't have thought this would be your scene." Ios smiled back at her. If he was shocked to see her he held his emotions tightly in check. "Please let me introduce you to my new friend Lene."

Selene raised her eyebrows and looked sharply up at Ios as he introduced her using her nickname, one that only her closest of friends had ever used with her. There had to be a reason for it, so she kept quiet and turned to Lilith and smiled.

"Hello."

Lilith took her in-every inch of her-- it was maddeningly uncomfortable, she had the feeling that she was being inhaled with her eyes. It made her shiver, and Ios gently squeezed her side in response.

Lilith held her hand out to Selene. "Charmed little one."

As Selene met her hand with her own, she suddenly felt a searing pain across her palm. Ios tried to stop it, but had realised too late what Lilith was up to. Selene withdrew quickly, and caught sight of the blood seeping through.

"Ow! What the hell?"

"Oh my dear, I am so sorry. My nails seem to get away with me at times, they are so-very-long. Did I cut you.... *deeply*?"

There was no apology in Lilith's voice as it seemed to lean into her, in fact it felt like acid was pouring through her every cell, like she had meant to finish her sentence with deeply *enough*. Selene looked on in shock as Lilith lifted the hand that had cut her, and licked the blood from her nail, staring seductively into Ios' eyes as she did so.

"You cannot hide anything from me my darling. Too much time has crossed between us. Lifetimes. I know who she is now, and immortal and eternal can only mean one thing. The truth is out. Mark my words."

She licked the nail again and held it close to his face, his nostrils flaring instinctively at the smell of Selene's blood, as Lilith wrapped her arm around his neck. "Tell me you don't want it. Tell me you don't want her, all of her."

Her voice was low and gravelly, her seductress charm weaving its magic. Her hand slowly drifted down over his chest towards his belt.

"She tastes like....*eternal life*."

Ios looked down at her and snarled. Lilith laughed and stepped away.

Selene had never seen Ios look so deadly or so frighteningly powerful. He was furious, his eyes were black and his body rigid, he stood in front of Selene to shield her from any sudden movements that Lilith might make.

"Get out of here Lilith, before I do something we will both regret."

Lilith laughed and leaned in towards him again, holding his chin firmly in her grip, and kissing him lightly on his mouth.

"Love like this is not possible Ios. You need to tell her."

She turned to Selene and said, "I will be seeing you soon little one."

With that, she turned on her heel and walked through the crowd, which parted as easily as the red sea must have done in days gone by.

Mathios had seen everything from the jam-packed dance floor, but no matter how hard he tried, the way back to Selene had been blocked. He and Ev had tried every direction, but as long as the lady in red had been with Selene and Ios, there was no getting anywhere close.

Finally she departed, and within moments the tension lifted and they were able to start making their way through with ease.

"What the hell was that about and who the hell was that?" Selene demanded, facing Ios. She was completely unwound, her palm was still smarting and bleeding from where that woman had sliced her open and drank her blood! "Don't even think of trying to get out of this one Ios. I want the truth."

Ios was at a loss for words, he was still too furious to respond. He handed her a handkerchief, to stem the flow of blood from her hand. Then he pulled her close to him and held her, comforting her and calming her as much as he could without words, his own body pulsing with anger as hers coursed with pure adrenaline. He looked around and caught sight of Mathios and Ev as they continued to push their way through the crowd. Mathios didn't look happy.

"Let's get out of here. Time to go to the Hard Rock, I *promise* I will explain everything there."

"Seere, did you know she was here?" Ios growled angrily as his friend appeared by his shoulder.

"No way, man. I clocked her just as she reached you, and it was too late to warn you or to distract her. Sorry Ios, she was pretty amped up, there was no getting anywhere near you."

Mathios looked at Selene, and saw she was holding her hand. "What happened? I saw that woman here and the look on your face. Ios looked like he was going to strangle her barehanded. What is going on?"

310

"I don't know Maty, one minute she was shaking my hand, the next, she cut me and drank my blood off her hand! How fucked up is that?"

Mathios glared at Ios. "You have some explaining to do," he said leaning in to his ear to ensure he wasn't overheard. "*Demon.*"

Ios looked at Mathios and nodded. If he seemed surprised that Mathios knew he wasn't human, he didn't show it. "Let's get out of here. I want to get Selene as far away from Lilith as is physically possible."

If it were possible, Mathios paled further and stepped back.

"Good God," he said under his breath. *Time to call in the reinforcements.*

Lilith. This was bad, bad news indeed. If Lilith knew about Selene, hunting season was open, and it would be very difficult to protect her. He could see Kristian and Osian faintly in the background, and made a move to speak with them, stopping only when Kristian shook his head and they vanished. So they knew then, that was good. Mathios knew they would not interfere unless Selene was in danger, and they had not, so he took a deep breath and began to gather their friends together.

311

forty

Within a short period of time, everyone who wanted to move on was back together and headed out to the Hard Rock. Seere vanished with his arm around a mysterious tall dark haired man, saying he might catch them up later. Selene was feeling a bit dizzy and tired, but held onto Ios as they walked. Two taxis were waiting for them outside, and whisked them quickly back towards Hyde Park.

Huddled in the cab, Ios finally spoke.

"Are you alright Selene?"

She nodded slightly and looked up at him, her eyes still wild with curiosity and confusion.

"I am so sorry, I had no idea she would do such a thing. Lilith is unpredictable at the best of times, but this was most unexpected."

"Who is she, Ios?"

Mathios looked at Ios and waited for an answer, when it wasn't forthcoming, he replied.

"She is a demon of the underworld. Not just a demon, but like the mother of all demons."

Selene met his eyes, she had no idea how or why Mathios would even know that, but she already knew it to be true.

"A demon of the underworld?" Ev cracked up. She was more than a little tipsy. "Man, I knew tonight would be full of surprises. Can we just stick with the kissing type surprises please? I really like those."

After a moment of intense silence, Ios spoke. "Look, she's gone. I will tell you what I know, I promise. Tonight, let's just try to enjoy what we have left of the year, shall we?" Ios still looked tense under a feigned good humour.

"Agreed, as long as you are sure she is gone for the time being," Mathios said through slightly gritted teeth.

Their friends in the other cab woot wooted and hooted in response, and everyone let the night's tension ease and refill with merriment.

"I am sure." Ios said, forcing a grin on his face.

Outside the Hard Rock they met up with their friends in the other cab, and their troubled moods were, for the moment, swept away. Again, Ios was able to walk them all in past a long line of would-be celebrants at the curb.

313

Inside, Ios took Selene aside for a moment and looked deeply into her eyes. "Are you alright Selene. You haven't said a word."

"It's a lot to take in Ios. Suddenly I am aware of a whole other world again, which now seems to include *you*. Vampires and demons in Dublin was one thing, but this is *my* life. And suddenly I am aware that you all seem to know something about me that I do not. What did she mean immortal and eternal? It has to do with how I can timewalk doesn't it?"

Ios ran his hand through his hair. This was definitely not a conversation that he wanted to be having here and now. "Selene, she is very powerful, and I don't know what she is after, and why she said that. Please, I know this is hard, but please, let's leave this talk for tonight and leap across into this new year with some joy, rather than this shadow she has cast. Please?"

Selene reached up and touched his face. "Kiss me," she said, looking into his eyes.

Ios looked surprised, but he lowered his head and with his hands held her close. His mind raced with Lilith's arrival, and his need to protect Selene. His mind hadn't crossed from protector to lover. He touched her lips with his, holding for a mere moment, and withdrew. Selene pushed him away in frustration, turned and walked towards Ev. Linking arms with her without a backward glance.

"What was that all about?" Ev asked Selene as they made their way to the ladies.

"Ugh! I have no idea. I just don't know what to make

of him. The more time I spend with him the more I like him and the more attracted I am to him. But he seems to hold me at arms length. I don't get it. I just asked him to kiss me. You saw it. I mean, what the hell?"

Ev rolled her eyes. "Men. Stupid beasts. I saw it. I don't get it either girl. He hasn't been anywhere but with you all night, like a bodyguard or something. And what was with that chick in the red outfit? Did you say she tasted your blood, like she cut you?"

"I don't need a fucking bodyguard!" Selene swore. "Yeah she did, with her ultra assassin length sharp nails. It freakn' hurt Ev. Then she sucked the blood off her nail. It was utterly disgusting. Then she came on to Ios big time. I've never seen him go cold and furious like that. It really unnerved me, but she didn't blink an eyeball."

"Do you think she's an ex or something?"

Selene paled. *No*. She hadn't even considered that idea. Her wide eyes revealed her raw emotions, and tears started to form. "Sorry Ev, it's just freaked me out a bit. God, I hope she isn't an ex. That's just creepy."

"Shhh now, come on. Enough of the scary demon monster talk now. We have ten minutes left of this hideous year. Let's go get a really fun drink, and spend the next ten minutes the way we began tonight. Let's go find out fun!"

"Ok", Selene sniffled and looked in the mirror. She cleaned her hand off and wiped it clear of any remaining blood, then checked her make-up. "Ready. Let's go then, deep breath."

Holding hands they made their way upstairs to the

315

main bar where the guys stood waiting for them. Ios still looked worried, but his face relaxed when he saw them approach.

"Tequilas all around please bartender!" Ev shouted above the din. The bartender nodded and started pouring them out. Mathios handed out glasses of champagne in preparation for the countdown, less than three minutes to go.

Ios reached for Selene's hand and gave it a small squeeze. She looked up and smiled weakly at him. She sipped the champagne and then placed it on the bar. She looked around and saw Sarah and Ben, Mikail and Rups smiling and laughing with Mathios. It was all so good. She loved to see him happy with such lovely friends. Dean, Fredrik and Una had stayed behind at the GuanaBarra, completely unaware of the incident with Lilith. The new year couldn't come fast enough. *Bring it on. Enough of this hard bloody heartbreaking year.*

Mathios returned to the bar and stood close to Ev, and reached for Selene's hand, but she wasn't there. Alarmed but unable to move, he began to join in the countdown, *five, four, three, two, one!*

Selene was first aware of the silence, and then the cold. Standing in the frosty cold night, she found herself with Ios, alone, next to Big Ben chiming the new year in. "Which new year would this be then Ios?" She asked in surprise, turning to look at him with a smile.

"1859, it's first new year," he said, "thought what you

316

hear chiming are quarter bells." He turned to face her and lifted her chin towards his. He slowly bent down and kissed her, softly at first, then more passionately and demanding as she responded. Selene felt her legs go, but he caught her up in his arms and held her close.

"I wanted to kiss you Selene, but not in the middle of a crowd. I wanted to have time with you, time alone with you. My existence is so complicated, and yours soon will be too. There are things happening that we cannot control, and right now, I feel the need to protect you over anything else. Can you understand?"

"No. I don't understand. I don't understand *any* of this nonsense. How can I when you won't explain it?" Selene felt so confused. "I don't understand. But I know I need some time, I'm not ready to be with anyone yet Ios, even if it's you."

"My beautiful Selene." Ios smiled at her and turned around, still holding her in his arms. Her phone was ringing, and she realised that they were back in the bar, as if they had never been gone. Mathios was reaching out for her hand, and she grasped his and held on.

He looked up with relief. He knew then, that Ios had taken her for a moment, but it had only been a moment. She was back safely, and he breathed a sigh of relief.

"Happy New Year bro." Selene found her feet and hugged Mathios tightly. Ev was next, and then the rest of their friends cheered and toasted them. Her phone began to ring again, and she stood aside and answered it.

"Sacha! Derry! Happy new year girls!" she shouted into the phone. She couldn't hear very well, so she made her way down into the hall where the toilets were to hear them better, but only just. There were crowds of people tucked everywhere.

"How's things over there then?" she asked.

"Same-o same-o. Too much damned snow and not enough alcohol in this damned town hahaha." Derry laughed. "Seriously, its been a tough fall term all around, I'm not sure I'll last at this teaching gig. Jon seems to like it, but we haven't seen much of him lately."

Selene's heart leapt at the mention of Jon's name. She hesitated, but asked anyway. "Is he ok?"

There was a moment of silence, then Sacha answered. "Selene, Jon married that Elysia bitch today."

The world began to spin again and Selene almost dropped the phone as she held her hand out to the wall, catching herself with the rail before she hit the ground. Demons, angels, eternals, immortals, vampires-- and this?

"What?"

"I'm so sorry hun, I wasn't sure if you knew or not. He proposed at Christmas and they married today at the park. The fucking park. Winter wedding and all that shit. We didn't go Selene. Sacha hasn't spoken to him since Christmas. God I'm so sorry Selene, I never should have said anything. I didn't mean to say anything."

Derry and Sacha broke into an argument on their end. Selene's stomach lurched.

"Gotta go, talk later and love you." she disconnected without waiting for a response. Within moments she ran for the toilet and vomited the entire days takings in one go. Tears flowed freely and she sat beside the toilet

318

sobbing and hugging her knees.

Married. She couldn't believe it. Icing on the cake of an insane night. A Christmas proposal meant he had broken up with her only two weeks before. Unbelievable. She couldn't take it in. And three weeks later he was married to someone that wasn't her. The door slammed forcefully shut inside her heart. It was a finality she hadn't been prepared for, nothing could have prepared her for that. Ev knocked lightly and opened the toilet door, took one look at her and knelt beside her.

"What happened Selene? Did that red dress demon witch find you again?"

"That was Sacha and Derry," Selene said. "Jon married Elysia today."

Her entire body felt wrung out and dry. She had nothing left. "Enough. Home. I need to go home now."

Ev helped her up off the floor and waited until she had cleaned herself up. She texted Mathios and asked him to sort a cab asap, as Selene had shocking news and needed to go home. Both Mathios and Ios were waiting outside for them when they emerged upstairs. Having already said their goodnights to the others, they swiftly departed. Ios insisted they go to his, as it would accommodate them all far more comfortably, so they swung by Mathios' to gather their clothes and necessities and headed towards Montpelier Square.

319

forty-one

The terraced house was as beautiful as it was enormous. Mathios looked at Ev in disbelief as they entered the large townhouse via the first floor. It was superbly decorated, very masculine, and very light oriented, with large mirrors and high ceilinged rooms. The fireplaces were already lit, and Seere appeared by the French patio doors with a cigar and whiskey in hand; the tall dark-haired man still by his side.

"Everything alright mate?"

He took in the energy of the group and looked at Ios.

"This is Eilif. We can vanish downstairs if you prefer, or somewhere else entirely."

"No that won't be necessary Seere. I could use *you* here actually though. I need to get Selene settled and we'll be back down. Will that be enough time?"

Seere caught his drift straight off and nodded. Mathios smiled in greeting and followed Ios through the main foyer to the staircase.

"Let's get you into your room Selene. There are five rooms upstairs, mine is the one here on the second floor, but there are three more upstairs, so take your pick." Ios led Selene to the room closest to his, and waved Mathios and Ev onwards. They left them momentarily as they headed further up into the house.

"Selene," Ios lifted her up into his arms and held her. Elysia, he knew, had won her freedom, and Selene was devastated.

"I want to stay close to you Ios. I don't want to do anything. I just don't want to be alone."

"Your brother might just kill me if I bring you into my room Selene." Ios smiled, trying to humour her a little and lighten her mood.

"I'm not a child Ios."

Looking into the paled blueness of her eyes he could clearly see the depth of hurt. It was like looking directly into her soul, and it caught him off guard. He felt something unleash in his heart, and it unnerved him. It was enough that he enjoyed her companionship, it was another thing entirely to care for her, and to possibly love her.

321

Love her.

The sensation resonated slowly around his body, pulsing through his blood. He turned and slowly walked back through the room and crossed the hallway to his. He continued to hold her as he pulled the duvet back, then gently placed her on the large bed. He reached down and unzipped the long black boots and placed them to the side. She smiled up at him, and still in her silver dress, she laid herself back against the pillow. He lifted the duvet and covered over her shoulders and kissed her on the forehead.

"I'll get you something to drink. Water or whiskey?"

"Both? And maybe a few crackers or something if you have it?"

Ios nodded and withdrew from the room. His head was still spinning with the sensation of feeling emotions for her. This was a rare thing for him, especially being that he wasn't human. Sex for demon kind was easy, emotionless, untangled. This on the other hand, was leading him somewhere he had never really been before, and every atom within him shook with the knowledge and recognition of it.

Mathios and Ev were already downstairs waiting when he returned.

"Ev, would you mind bringing Selene some water, whiskey and crackers, in that order? She is in my room rather than the guest room. At *her* request, Mathios." Ios looked at him in a way that was hard to read, neither smug nor defensive.

"Of course Ios. Where is everything?" Ev said,

turning to leave.

"Down the stairs and you will find the kitchen fully stocked. Help yourself. The whiskey is here though, so I'll pour a glass for her and leave it on the side. Can I offer anyone anything else to drink?"

Seere reappeared from nowhere and headed straight for the large built in bar by the patio door.

"Bartender at your service," he said smiling.

Ev looked from Mathios to Ios and shook her head. "Did he just appear, like out of thin air?"

Mathios nodded and turned to Seere. "Double Macallan please. Ev?"

"Baileys. Definitely. Double. Thank you."

She looked from one to the other and decided that it was pointless stating anything more obvious, so she descended to the kitchen to find what Selene had asked for.

"Was that necessary Seere?" Mathios said, annoyed as he handed him their drinks.

"What? She doesn't know? You appear to know, why would I assume she didn't know?" the demon grinned. "Come on, it's not like she passed out or nothing."

"It's not funny. It's been a hell of a night, if you pardon the expression, but first Lilith, then Jon being married. I mean how much more needs to happen here? Ios, what do you know about Jon, and do you know this Elysia?"

Ios sat back in the large revolver chair and sipped his whiskey. He ran his other hand through his hair and inhaled deeply as he drank.

"I do. Elysia is a black witch—black magik. I first came across her over three thousand years ago, in your mother's castle." Ios paused, not sure how much history Mathios knew about Merope. He had already calculated that Mathios knew he was not a true son of Merope, the maths didn't hold true with the timing of her fall. "She was a distant cousin to the King. She was as manipulative and cunning then as now, and had gotten herself into some deep troubles. I ran into her in Halifax a few months after I'd met Selene. I interrogated her about why she was there, and she said it was her mission to disconnect the two, Jon and Selene, to gain her final freedom. She would not however reveal who had instigated the plot, or what purpose it would serve. I threatened that I would return should some harm come to Selene. There must be a connection between Elysia and Lilith, how else would she have known who Selene was?"

Ios sat quietly lost in his own thoughts. "Lilith is up to something, there is a strategy, but I just can't see it yet."

Mathios was staring at Ios, his brain still stuck on the part about his step-mother Merope living in a castle three thousand years ago. He knew she had come from somewhere different, he remembered her falling out of the sky, and the appearance of the angel at her side over twenty years ago. His brain just couldn't seem to take it all in.

"Ios, are you telling me that Merope is three thousand years old, and she just landed from some time

324

warp?"

Ios looked steadily at Mathios, unsure of how to answer.

"Tell me what you *do* know Mathios."

"I was there when she landed on Mount Olympus, over twenty years ago. I was seven. There was an angel by her side, and my father helped them. A week later she came to live with us. Selene was born nine months later. I knew that she was not my father's child, and they were open with me and swore me to secrecy. Selene doesn't know. She doesn't know I know so much. I probably know more about her than she does herself."

Ios nodded looked at Seere. "On your blood oath my friend, swear to me that what you have learned in this house tonight goes no further, on pain of death." Ios was deadly serious as he met Seere's gaze.

"Of course Ios. Not even on pain of Lilith. I swear. It all makes sense now, why she is after Selene. Immortal and eternal, a rare find indeed."

"You are right of course," Ios continued, turning to look at Mathios, "We need to look to the bigger picture-what is Lilith after and why? What does it matter to her that Selene is immortal and eternal? What is the connection we are missing? At least we have confirmation now that it has been her behind these shenanigans all along. But what does she want from Selene? This is where I come unstuck, I am missing something vital." Ios drank deeply again, and refilled his glass, as Ev reappeared from upstairs.

"Selene is asleep. Will she be ok up there on her

own?" Ev looked at Ios and then at Seere. "I mean with people just appearing and all. People can't just *disappear* can they?"

Ios smiled. "No my lovely Evangeline, they cannot. This house is protected by many charms, no one can enter without my permission. She will be safe here, which is why I insisted we stay."

"Ios, I am in love with your house. I will come housesit whenever!' Ev said smiling. She downed the first lot, then poured herself another Baileys and snuggled in close to Mathios on the elegant cream coloured sofa. The house really was spectacular, there were mirrors everywhere, and the paintings on the walls drew her eye at every turn.

"Why do you have so many mirrors, Ios? Just curious."

"As you may have noticed Ev, I do not like surprises, and the light ensures that if someone makes it past the charms, there is nowhere to hide."

"Ah." Ev sipped her drink. "So what did I miss then, it's all very serious down here."

Mathios said, "We were talking about this evenings events, Lilith and the marriage of Jon."

"Bastard. I cannot believe he went and married her, after breaking Selene's heart with a cheap bastard phone call not even three weeks ago. What a total asshat." Ev said hotly.

Ios and Mathios laughed out loud, and Seere smiled.

"Asshat?" Mathios finally said. "Well that's a new

one."

"One of Selene's favourites, I can't believe you haven't heard her say it." Ev laughed. The mood lifted considerably in the room, and all seemed to breathe a sigh of relief. It had been a very intense night all around. Ev looked at Mathios, he looked exhausted.

"What time is your mum arriving in the morning?"

"Oh God. I forgot. She arrives on the red eye, six-thirty from Toronto. Holy hell," he glanced at his watch, it was just ticking past 4am. He groaned and sank back deeply into the sofa.

"No bother Mathios." Ios said. "I will collect her myself, I do not need to sleep as....." he caught himself then, "well, as *you* do."

"Not as humans do, you mean?"

Ios looked at her.

"Yes. We do not sleep as humans do Ev."

"And that makes you *what?*"

"He's a demon Ev. So is Seere," said Mathios.

"And Lilith for that matter, as you may remember from the cab ride.

"Uh ok. Well can anyone tell me what the hell that is supposed to mean? I mean, Selene has never really been the most normal person ever, but does that mean you and she are demons too?" Ev couldn't help the elevation in pitch as she felt the panic rise in her heart.

"No, Ev. I am human," said Mathios. "Merope, Selene's mum, isn't human, but she isn't a demon she's something else. Don't ask. And Selene, well, now we know for sure after Lilith's little escapade that she is both

327

immortal and eternal. But that is all we know now for sure. Selene doesn't know. I know you were probably raised to believe demons are bad and angels are good, but it just isn't that simple. Please don't freak out, things will come clear in time, and please don't tell Selene any of this just yet?"

Mathios reached for her hand as he finished his explanation, and to his great relief Ev grabbed hold and squeezed hard.

"I don't scare easily Maty, it's good to know and to be part of helping protect Selene. She is my best mate, and I would be devastated if anything should happen to her. I just don't understand why we are withholding any information from her. She already knows she is immortal and eternal, whatever that means. I just don't feel right about it."

Ios placed his drink on the side and leaned forward. "I think tonight has been overwhelming for Selene. At this point, dropping her entire family history on her might just be too much. I think we need to gather more information first, then we can see a way forward. Should Lilith come into contact with Selene, the less she knows the better, for her own protection at this point."

Ev looked at Mathios, who nodded in agreement. "That makes sense, for now. But don't expect me to hold out on her for long."

"Right then, it's settled. Everyone human off to bed." Ios stood and dismissed the group. "We will reconvene in the morning after I have collected Merope. Seere stay in the room opposite mine, and keep an eye for

Selene. It's unlikely she will wake, she is exhausted, but if she does, I do not want her to be afraid."

Seere nodded and waved good night, vanishing on sight, not bothering with pretending to use the stairs now that his secret was out.

"Awesome." Ev whispered.

Ios smiled and embraced her. "Look after this one, he is a good catch as you say, as are you beauty."

Ev blushed and took the hand Mathios offered. Together they climbed the stairs and bodies entwined, fell gratefully into bed, and into a long needed deep sleep.

Ios appeared upstairs and changed his clothing into something more casual. He leaned over and lightly kissed Selene on her forehead. Things had really taken a turn sideways. So much to work out, never mind these new things called feelings he now had for her. Demons didn't have feelings, they had sex. They were volatile, and unpredictable. This was completely new territory. He shook himself and focused on the day ahead. He was looking forward to seeing Merope, after all this time. It would be good to be able to relax into another time again. He already knew he had another quick stop to make before making it to the airport. He glanced at the clock, grabbed a light coat and vanished into the early morning hours.

Elysia was humming blissfully to herself in the kitchen, still in her wedding dress when Ios appeared in front of her, causing her to drop the glasses of champagne in her hands.

"By the goddess!" she exclaimed jumping back.

"Happy New Year, Elysia. I hear congratulations are in order." Ios said with a menacing smile, as he turned and crossed the room. He could hear Jon in the other room moving around.

"Everything ok in there my love--my wife?"

"Yes Jon, sorry," Elysia replied hurriedly. "I just tripped a bit on the carpet, don't worry, I'll be back in just a moment," her eyes wide with fear, she regarded Ios without moving an inch.

"How can I help you, my Lord?"

"You have a story to tell my child. I am all ears."

"I have no more information to give to you Lord Ios. I swear it."

"On the blood of your first child Elysia? Would you swear on that?" Ios hissed coldly, stepping closer with each word he uttered.

Elysia cowered and tears began to form in her eyes as she stared at him. No not now, it wasn't fair! Surely this was meant to be a happy ending for her. This fine man she had married, she had won. *She had won!* She had her freedom. "No Lord Ios, I would not. What do you need to know."

"Ah, I *thought* you would see things more clearly. Funny how memory works, isn't it?" Ios seethed. "Who sent you here."

"The lady Lilith sent me with one of her demons, Sitri to help me win Jon's heart. She wanted to separate Jon and Selene."

"Why?"

"Sir, I truly do not know, *that* I swear with my whole heart. I overheard her mention something about a seed and making sure that Selene was not with child. I also overheard something about a labyrinth. That is all I know," Elysia fell to her knees before him. "I promise you. Please."

Ios held himself in check and showed no reaction. The Labyrinth. Well, that made sense, as to why Jon had been sent away and how they had come to be parted. At least that part of the puzzle fell into place, but not the rest. The laying of a Labyrinth took quite a lot of strategy and cunning, there had to be an endgame for Lilith to have enacted such a complicated diversion .

"Why would she not want to let her have a child. What seed? None of this makes sense." Ios thought aloud. "Stand up child. I will leave you in peace, for now, but I will return. Until this mystery has been revealed, your part has not yet come to its end."

Elysia stood and gathered herself together. Ios was gone before she even lifted her head. She leant against the kitchen counter to steady herself, and tried to slow the shallow and rapid breaths. She closed her eyes and prayed silently to the goddess that this would be their last meeting, and that he would find what he needed to know from someone else.

forty-two

It was still pitch black and raining. Lovely London in the winter, Ios sighed. He appeared at Heathrow Airport, just in time to meet Merope's flight. They would hail a cab back to his in town, but first a light breakfast away from a house of sleepy ears.

He stood by the arrivals gate and waited patiently. He smiled as he watched her walk through the glass sliding doors, not a day had grown on her in all of the years he had known and not seen her.

"Merope."

She turned and gave him a surprised but happy smile as their eyes met.

"Ios?" she said, reaching for him to embrace as old friends. "My dear old friend, whatever are you doing here? Where is Mathios?"

"Ah, your lovely children are still tucked up in bed after a very long and intense night out. They are both at my house in the city. We have much to discuss before we return. It has been a rather enlightening night, and not all good. Is this all you have with you?" Ios asked, looking at her single suitcase. "Let's grab a quick breakfast in the airline lounge, we can talk there. Everything else will be closed this morning being new years day."

Merope smiled and followed him as he lifted her case and turned towards the lift. He slid his card through the security plate, the glass doors opened, and they left the frenetic pace of the airport behind them. The lounge was warm, with soft music playing, soft extended recliners awaited. The hostess greeted them and took their order, and they settled themselves into a private corner with a small table.

"So what has been happening over the last three thousand and twenty years with you, Ios?" Merope laughed. "How is it that you have come to know my daughter, and come to be here now?"

The hostess arrived and served the cafetiere and left the croissants on the table. She took the order for their hot breakfast, and quietly left them to their business and retreated to the bar.

"Three thousand years." Ios whistled quietly. "When you say it, suddenly it seems more real to me, knowing you were there too. It was by chance, but I saw you fall. I followed you through the threads, and I was there when you landed, but you were already not alone."

He looked deeply into her eyes with a serious expression.

Merope swallowed hard, so it was possible he knew the truth.

"I kept a casual eye on the threads over the years, and one day, a light slid through, and someone shot forward just as you had. Unusual, so I followed it up. I had already met Selene at a party the year before in Dublin, and there was no mistaking that she was your child Merope. It was too coincidental. We became friends, and I travelled with her overseas. But I didn't make the connection with the timeshift until a few weeks later when I bumped into Elysia at the Athenaeum café in town there. She told me she had bargained for her freedom, on completion of one further deed. She was to end the relationship between Jon and Selene. I travelled back this morning before meeting you to interrogate her again, and she confirmed that it was with Lilith whom she had struck this bargain."

"Well, *you* can slide back and forth, I cannot! It all makes so much more sense now, with the one missing piece being why? What is she after? What could she possibly want of Selene, and how did she even know about her?"

"That I do not know. Elysia also said Lilith had begun

a Labyrinth. This is quite serious, as once it has begun, it can take on a life of it's own."

"What does that mean Ios? I don't understand."

"A Labyrinth is a maze of sorts, but it is played out in real time and with real lives. It begins with a player, who doesn't know that they are being played, and then draws on those around them. It is a mental undoing, by making the player feel like they have no control over their lives. It begins with isolation, where friends and family become emotionally, if not physically, distant from the player. Then it becomes layered with obstacles and confusing circumstances. Then things like insomnia, or psychic tethering, interfering with dream sleep and the ruach. Then paranoia sets in, and the player begins to doubt themselves and their actions or choices. It basically drives them insane, and then the driver of the Labyrinth can control the player. And so on."

"Oh Ios, that is awful! What purpose would this serve? It's so cunning and devious!"

"I know. And it can take years to place properly. And fortunately for us, we have those years being demons," he said so knowingly, that Merope looked up. "Twenty years since I saw you land on Olympus, but it could have been a day. We have a warped sense of time. We will need to watch Selene quite carefully, and ensure that even if there seems a physical distance at times, that there is no emotional distance. The success of this depends on the emotional weakening. But we can defeat its onslaught by remaining vigilant and in constant contact."

Merope nodded. "We will be moving to the UK

shortly Ios. The children do not yet know, but it seems my intuition was correct, even if I didn't know why I needed to be here, other than to be close to them. I understand the calling now."

The breakfast arrived and both ate in silence. There was so much to consider, and no clear way forward. Selene would have to be told, but would it be too much for her to bear after all that had just happened?

Merope sighed, not sure which thought to think next.

"This immortal thing is becoming quite difficult in this modern age of photographs, internets, web cams, global security issues. This year Mathios will grow beyond me chronologically. And soon I will no longer be able to pass as a mother to them, maybe a sister. It will become more and more difficult. Meanwhile poor Nikolas continues to age beside me."

Ios chuckled kindly. He knew *exactly* what she meant, and how much more difficult it was to take on a new life as an immortal these modern days. It was one of the main reasons many of the immortals built vast secret empires and amassed such wealth, for it did allow them some anonymity, and an easier transition into a new life when needed.

"Well, your daughter has had quite a terrible start to the new year I am afraid. Some of her friends from Halifax let it slip that Jon had married Elysia earlier in the day, and that just about broke her, but that wasn't the worst of it. I am afraid that Lilith made her debut appearance last night in the club of all places. She slit Selene's hand and managed to taste her before I could stop her. We know now for sure that Selene is immortal, but she is also eternal. She carries the blood of an eternal, and there can only be one way for that to happen, Merope. Your secret is out. We can now be certain, beyond Elysia's tale, that it has been Lilith all along behind the many strange occurrences over the years, starting with your timeslide, when you fell from the sky, up to Elysia and her interference in Jon and Selene's relationship. And of course, the Labyrinth."

Merope held her hand over her mouth in shock and despair. She knew as well as Ios did, that this was the worst news possible where Selene was concerned. But she still couldn't figure out how Lilith would have known about Selene's existence, nor to suspect that she could be anything other than human or perhaps at best immortal. What was she after? Lilith was the goddess of many things, but the infertility in mothers and the murders of their infants was a rather enormous one. She may be powerful, sexual, independent, and strong, but she was just as deadly and vicious as any of her more virtuous and feminine attributes.

"I don't know what to say Ios. I am heartbroken for her over Jon. I really thought they would marry and settle together. But it is not what has been written in the stars then, not when someone with her power can interfere like that."

"Merope, your fall from the sky and flight through time wasn't written either. We have no idea how this will play out."

"Perhaps we should try to reach my sorceress Manto.

You can timewalk. Perhaps she might be able to provide some insight?"

"Insight into a situation happening three thousand years after her time? Is she that good?"

"Yes," Merope said with utter certainty. "Let her feel your energy Ios, and she will be able to connect, or I can come back with you."

"No, that is far too dangerous at the moment. Too much disruption in the threads will surely bring unwanted attention, and I can slide unseen. I will go, but not right now. I will go when the time is right and I will find her."

"Merope, Mathios knows pretty much everything doesn't he?" Ios asked as he placed his fork down for the last time.

"Yes, he was young, but too smart to not know better after Selene was born. He knew that she was not from Nikolas. So we told him what we knew, and swore him to protect her and keep our secrets. He has been such a light in all of our lives, he is really such a good boy."

Ios laughed again. 'Yes, a good man, that he is, and you are correct, he is extremely bright and doesn't miss much. He and his girlfriend Evangeline are at the house as we speak. Evangeline has come to know bits and pieces, but not everything in any great detail. I don't think she has worked out that Selene is not his real sister. She does know that we are not human, with the exception of Mathios and Nikolas of course."

"Ev? When did that happen?" Merope asked her eyes wide with surprise. "How did she take that?"

"In stride to give her credit." Ios leaned back and

sipped his coffee. "I imagine they will be waking soon, and it will be time to converse and plan. I am not sure what we will gain by telling Selene everything at this point. I think we should decide what is most important for her safety and leave it at that."

"Agreed, for now. If a labyrinth is indeed in play, then she needs to know, Ios. There is so much to tell her I do not know where to start, and perhaps, I should have started long ago."

"Despite Lilith's appearance, there is time yet," Ios said. "It will be hard to convince Selene that Lilith was just some mad demon after the blood tasting incident though. I have to be honest, I am not quite sure how to answer to that. Mathios did tell her that she was a demon in the taxi last night, and that didn't seem to faze her. She had a rather interesting introduction to the netherworld in Dublin over Christmas."

"Perhaps we can keep the focus on Jon and Elysia, and my arrival?"

"You do know your daughter won't be deterred for long, she will want answers, and soon."

Merope stood and waved at the hostess for their coats. "Yes, that's true. Gods but this is a mess. Please let's just see how things play out. Let Mathios know we are not saying anything more than necessary at this point. We need more information Ios, Lilith appears to be holding all the cards."

"Agreed. Let's get you back to mine and see what the light of day brings."

Ios helped her with her coat and they walked out together to the main foyer towards the taxi stand.

forty-three

Selene woke with a start. Taking a moment, she realised she was in Ios' bed.

Alone. And fully dressed.

Ok. Good. Nothing serious happened. But why am I here, and where is he?

She lay back down again as her head spun, and tried to recall the events of the night before. Bar, good. Dinner, good. Blood thirsty red haired demon woman, bad. What the fuck was with that?

She looked down at her newly healing flesh wound on

her right palm. New Years Eve kiss, awesome. Phone call from Sacha and Derry, good. News that Jon married Elysia, devastating. *Fucking fucking fucking asshole!* She raged silently, and tears began to fill her eyes again, but she wiped them away and stared up at the ceiling.

It's a new year and a new day.

She looked around the room and took in the space. It was a truly gorgeous house, and his room, though minimalist, was him through and through. Simple colours, of earthy greys and sea blues mixed with stark whites. There was a large painting of somewhere in Greece on the wall facing her, and it looked to be a scene from an ancient time. She rose and stood closer. The artist was so good, she felt she could have stepped out of the room and into the scene. It was a brilliant summer's day, she could almost touch the light and feel the heat rising from the sands. The colours of the Aegean sea mingled playfully with sunshine, and little wooden fishing boats floated close to the shore, where a small market was busy trading by the foot of a large castle.

She stood entranced, as if she could almost hear the ancient Greek as the figures began to move in her minds eye through the painting. She suddenly stepped back, catching herself before she lost herself in another time. Her skin felt hot to the touch now, warmed by the sun. She shook her head and smiled. *Timewalk huh. Just be sure you can make it home again Selene.* She looked at the title by the edge, which read 'Chios', and wondered where that was. She turned and grabbed her bag, and made her way to the ensuite. A good hot shower would wash the dust

342

away, and would surely make her feel a little better. After all the puke and tears she must look like hell, and probably didn't smell too pretty either. No wonder Ios hadn't stayed with her, she groaned inwardly.

Half an hour later, she made her way down the stairs to find the kitchen. Double espresso was way overdue. Seere was seated at the long breakfast bar table, reading the paper and munching his way through the box of donuts and croissants, a large cafetiere of fresh coffee beside him.

"Good morning, Seere." Selene said as she took the last step down. "Can I nic some of that coffee? It smells divine!"

"Hey Selene, how'd ya sleep girl?" he drawled like a true southerner with a broad smile as he looked up from the paper. "Help yourself."

Selene grabbed a mug from the shelf and sat down on a stool next to him. She poured herself a steaming cupful and bit into a chocolate croissant before answering. "Ok I guess, I kind of passed out up there. Where's Ios?"

"Gone to collect your mamma."

"Oh crap! I totally forgot she was arriving this morning! Where are Mathios and Ev?"

"Sleeping."

"Ah." Selene smiled. *Ya right. Sleeping. I just bet they are.* She was delighted for both of them, it was a superb match, both of her best friends together. At least something good had come out of last night's escapades.

They sat in companionable silence for a little while, reading and drinking. Selene rose and made a second cafetiere and offered more to Seere.

"How did you meet Ios?" she asked.

"Can't remember now, it was at least a couple thousand years ago. Us demon types travel around a fair bit. He's always been thick in the middle of things, he was quite a remarkable instrument of chaos in his early days. Actually he is still known as Lord of Chaos in our world, a real force to be reckoned with. Feared, y'know?. Powerful dude. I guessed it was better to be on his side," Seere chuckled.

Although Seere's response was casual and conversational, Selene almost dropped her mug. Demons. Back to that again, and the memory of Lilith, and the glaring slash in her palm echoed through her mind's eye. She looked down at her hand again. So, Seere was a demon too then.

"Why did Lilith taste my blood? And why did she taunt Ios with it?"

Seere looked distinctly uncomfortable, suddenly realising that he had already said too much. "I think that you had better have that discussion with Ios, Selene."

"Tell me what you know Seere, please. Why was she so vicious?"

"I don't know. I have no idea what she was after Selene, that's the truth. Demons kinda have a taste for blood. It gives us information, it tells us something about the person or thing we are dealing with, or shagging for that matter." Seere flushed a bit as he realised he had said too much again. "But there is something about your blood that is special. I don't know anymore than that, and

344

I am pretty sure Ios was as shocked as you were that she appeared last night." Seere said honestly. "As for vicious, that weren't vicious girl. Lilith can be evil with a capital E. Last night was like licking a lolly to her, whetting the appetite. Baby stuff. She had a specific intent in her actions, and we know she got what she came for. The fact that you are still here, alive and unharmed, it means something. Trust me when I tell you, she isn't someone to cross, nor turn your back on. She is considered the first demon, even before Sammael or Lucifer."

Selene's eyes widened with shock. That, she had definitely not expected to hear. But she held on to her thoughts of Ios.

"Is she like an ex-girlfriend demon or something?"

Seere began to visibly twitch in his seat. This wasn't good. This wasn't going to lead anywhere good. Ios was so gonna kill him. He remained silent for a while and sipped his coffee and ate another croissant.

"Seere? Come one, give me a heads up here. I know you two are tight, surely you can share just a little bit to help me out here?"

"Aw man, come on. He'll kill me. And I mean properly outright kill me." Seere looked desperately at her, but Selene didn't back down. "They spent time together yes, many *many many* centuries ago. They tore up the town so to speak, wreaking chaos here there and everywhere. They know each other well, really well, evil well. Ios is a very clever and long-sighted visionary creature. He has a good grasp of how the past can alter the future, even with a simple sleight of hand. Creatures like us don't do relationships like humans. We are timewalkers. It's hard for us to be stable. We are unstable elements so to speak."

"So they were intimate?"

Seere went green and sank into his seat. "Please Selene, no more no more!"

Selene laughed, the sight of this demon shrinking before her as she interrogated him over sex and love was pretty funny.

"Ok ok! I'll torture Ios later with all my questions."

forty-four

The main door upstairs rattled and opened, as Ios and Merope entered. The house was fairly quiet still, so Ios set her bag down and took her coat.

"Welcome to my home, Merope," he said and nodded at her to follow. He knew that someone was in the kitchen, he could smell the coffee and smell the fresh croissants. He led her to the stairs and they descended.

"Mamma!" Selene jumped off the stool and launched herself at Merope.

"Hello darling!" Merope replied lovingly as she

embraced Selene. "You look tired, but lovely my dearest. Oh how I have missed you! It's so wonderful to be here! Ios has told me you had a bit of a long night."

Selene looked at Ios and he smiled softly and gazed downwards. "Yes. Yes it was an interesting night. We were just chatting about that Seere weren't we?"

Ios looked sharply at Seere, who in turn smiled weakly and shrank a bit. "Uh, yeah, kinda."

"Mamma, this is Seere, a friend of Ios. Apparently he is a demon too. Did you know that?"

Selene paused for breath, and took in the closeness between Ios and Merope.

"Why do you two seem so friendly?"

Ios stood stock still, glaring at Seere, who shrugged his shoulders. How much does she know? He mouthed at Seere. Not much, was his response. Ios exhaled, relaxed, and reached for two more mugs.

"Coffee Merope?" he asked, ignoring Selene's questions.

"Good morning to you too, Ios." Selene said.

Ios poured the coffee, ignoring her snideness. Merope cocked her head and smiled at him.

"I'm going upstairs to see if Ev is up yet," Selene said with a pointed glare at Ios.

Merope waited until she was out of earshot. "So my daughter has a sweet spot for you then does she?"

Ios flinched a little but tried to control his emotions.

"As do I, I'm afraid. It isn't a feeling I am overly familiar with Merope. I think I may be the one that you would warn her against, being a little too old, a little too dangerous, and a little too not human."

Merope laughed. "Maybe. Yes, maybe. But you have always been so good to me. Let's see how time plays this out shall we? It's taken more than several thousand years for you to open your heart Ios, who am I to say no? And quite frankly, who am I to judge?"

Ios looked at Merope with eyes wide and full of gratitude, another emotion he was simply not used to feeling.

"Thank you."

He leaned on the kitchen counter across from her and sipped his coffee. His head was spinning a bit with all of these new sensations. It felt overwhelming. His honest intention had been to protect Selene, so how had that come to desire, or love even? It was still too much to contemplate right now. So was Merope's simple acceptance.

Seere looked up suddenly hearing footsteps. Mathios and Ev made their way down finally.

"Mamma!" Mathios exclaimed as he entered, grabbing Merope up into a huge hug. "How was your trip? Did you mind terribly having Ios collect you?"

"Not at all my lovely. We've had a lovely morning together while you sleepyheads have taken your time!" Merope laughed. "Good morning Ev, so lovely to finally meet you! Selene is always speaking of your adventures and hard work together."

"Thanks Mrs Kostantakos. It's great to meet you too." Ev said shyly, and reached for the coffee that Mathios held out to her.

"Merope, please."

"Merope." Ev repeated with a smile.

"So, everyone had a rather interesting night then," said Merope. "What with Lilith making a grand appearance and then the whole Jon thing. Dearest Selene, her poor heart."

Mathios stood beside Ios, and together they looked to be long lost brothers.

"We haven't debriefed with Selene Mamma, just amongst ourselves. She will be asking questions and we need to decide on what needs to be revealed properly for her safety. It doesn't seem fair to keep secrets from her."

"No, it doesn't. It makes me feel really uncomfortable being her best mate as well." Ev added.

"True my children true. However, we still do not have a grasp on the bigger picture here. And to be honest, I have my own reasons too. I will let Raphael know what has passed here, and that it is Lilith who is after her. The blood lust worries me beyond belief. We must know before choosing what to do, we are just working blind here at the moment, the best we can do is go on as normal, and keep our eyes open. Kristian and Osian are around and will keep a close eye, as will all of us the best we can. It really is all we can do for the moment."

"Kristian and Osian were there at the club when Lilith appeared Mamma, I am sure they will have informed Raphael." Mathios said.

Merope nodded and Ev looked a bit confused with all the new people they was speaking about, but decided she could get caught up with Mathios later.

"Where is Selene? Didn't she come back down?" Ev asked.

"She went to find you, and no she has not returned." Ios said. "She wanted to know why your mother and I seemed so friendly. Perhaps Merope, that part of the story is yours to tell, and that time may have come. She doesn't have to know the rest just yet, but your past can no longer remain hidden when we know she can timewalk, and can relive the past through your eyes. This is how she saw Elysia in your dreams."

Merope nodded. "Yes, that much will do, no more. Mathios, the rest is mine to tell too, please say no more until the time is right?"

"Of course, Mamma. You have my word."

Ev looked confused again but remained silent as she reached for a croissant and refilled her mug. Mathios smiled at her and moved closer, wrapping his arm around her waist and kissing her on the head. Ios and Merope smiled too, knowing that this was new for them.

Ios thought of Selene, still upstairs on her own, and decided he had better go and see what she was up to. He didn't bother climbing the stairs, he vanished and reappeared minutes later by her side, nearly scaring the daylights out of her.

"Shit! Do you really have to do that?!"

She was lying on her side, across the middle of the huge bed, lazily leafing through one of his arty books.

Ios reached over and tossed the book aside. He rolled himself on top of her and gently pinned her down with his hands. "Wake up on the wrong side of the bed this morning did we?"

"Ugh, get off you beast!" Selene said forcefully, trying to hold on to her annoyance with him. But she couldn't budge him, and finally she gave up in a combination of frustration and a fit of giggles as he kissed her beneath her ear.

"Demon! You are so annoying! This is so unfair!"

Ios threw his head back and laughed deeply. "Perhaps, lovely Selene. Perhaps."

He looked down at her and slowly leaned in to kiss her. He could feel the desire rising in his body as she responded in kind, and he fought to control it. He could feel her moving underneath him and he moaned slightly with pleasure. He knew given another moment he would lose control completely and take her, all of her. He could still sense the smell of her blood from the night before, it was overpowering and stirring his demonic nature. He forced himself to back off, and he ended the kiss with a smile.

"Come, everyone is waiting for us downstairs, and you mother wants to see you."

Selene groaned and forced herself to stand up with him, feeling a little lightheaded and giddy from the intensity of his kiss. "Ios?" she said, picking up a thread of a troubling thought unravelling in her head. "Did you love her?"

This caught him off-guard. "Love who?"

"Lilith," she said, staring into his eyes. "It's just that Seere said--"

"No, Selene," he said. *Love. There was the word again.*

"No. I do not know what Seere has told you. But no. Demons, immortals, creatures, do not love like humans do, we do not share the same sense of time or attachment. How can we? It is hard to describe."

Selene stood still, not really knowing what to make of his answer, so she decided to not press him further.

"Fine," she said, getting up and straightening her clothes. "Good to know I suppose," she turned and headed for the door.

"Selene...."

Ios chuckled at her snarky response. *I'm so too old for this. Several thousand years of chaos, mischief and primal sexuality, and here I am, falling for a newly born immortal, and an eternal at that. What is wrong with me?*

He shook his head and followed her down towards the kitchen, but everyone had moved up to the lounge by this time, where it was much more comfortable. The rain had stopped and the skies had cleared to reveal a sharp deep blue sky. Seere had opened the patio doors and the cool fresh air felt good.

Ios stepped outside and took a deep breath. He needed to find out more, he needed some freedom to move and timewalk through the threads in search of the truth of Lilith's game. *What was she after? Why Selene? Clever bitch, tasting Selene's blood like that. She had already known that there would be something special there.*

He would have to leave before nightfall. There was no way he could spend the night with Selene right now. It was too much, and it would distract him from where his head needed to be right now. *Done. Decision made.* He knew that she would be upset with him, but the timing between them wasn't right. There was too much at stake.

Merope watched Ios in silence, noting the changes in expression as his thoughts churned inside his skull. He hadn't changed much in so many years. He was as stunning as ever, and kind. Strange for a demon really, although she hadn't ever given it much thought over the years that they had known each other. There were so many different types of creatures of her time, he was simply another. And there had been good demons as there had been bad angels. The lines between them were blurry, too blurry. And the powers and magiks each had also made it hard to know at times whom to trust. Her King husband had taught her that hardest lesson himself. If it hadn't been for Gabriel and Ios, she may never have opened her heart or trusted anyone again.

With everyone so lost in their own thoughts, Mathios reached up and flicked on the telly. He surfed the channels hoping to find a match of some sort, just to ease the tension and give everyone something else to focus on. Selene joined them on the large sofa and leaned in to Ev with a smile.

"So, good night then?" Selene said with a grin.

"*Verra verra* good," Ev said blushing slightly. "Fancy a little walk around the village?"

"Can't think of a better idea! Let's go!" Selene leapt up off the sofa and turned to her mother. "Ev and I are going to get some air. Do you need to rest up a bit? We can catch up a little later this afternoon?"

"Sounds perfect dear, you go on. Ios will settle me

into a room and I will find some restful sleep. Don't you worry."

Selene smiled and bent down to kiss her. "Ok then, see you a little later. Love you. Bye all, we'll be back in an hour or so."

Ios nodded from the patio doors and smiled. Selene met his eyes and just held his gaze, expressionless, before turning away.

"Come, Merope, let me show you to your room," Ios said and stepped back inside. "You must be exhausted now."

"I am tired, and a good rest would be lovely thank you. See you later Mathios, Seere. Dinner perhaps?"

"Ok Mamma," Mathios stood and kissed her on both cheeks.

Seere smiled and nodded from the corner and continued to read the paper.

Merope followed Ios up the two long flights of stairs, then up a shorter one to the room that would be hers. It was beautiful and light, with soft lavenders and turquoise blues. The window overlooked the park behind the house, which was beginning to fill up with families as the sun continued to shine. "Thank you Ios, your generosity is much appreciated."

"It is my pleasure Merope. We have been friends for a long time. It feels good to reconnect, and to also spend time with someone in *this* time from whom I do not need to hide."

Merope smiled. She understood completely, on every level. Even with Nikolas, at times it was hard to express

355

how different these times were, and how at times it was very stressful to navigate being a lone immortal in a sea of mortals.

"I will be leaving you tonight Merope. I need to seek some answers, and I will take Seere with me. I can't just walk into Zemargad and state my desire. I will need allies and a certain amount of surveillance to get to the root of what she is after. We are missing something ancient, a prophecy or a legend, something like this. That's the key. I do not know how long I will be gone, you know well that time works differently above and below. You are welcome to use my home as your own for as long as you need it, and whenever you may need it."

"She will not understand Ios," Merope said. "But she will forgive you in time."

Ios looked at her in wonder.

"I can see how she feels about you, but she isn't ready, her heart has only just been broken freshly again. And she doesn't really even know who she is, being an immortal and eternal. She has no idea what that will come to mean, and neither do we. The time you take now will serve you both for whatever is to come, no matter how she sees it. She is young, and we are immortal. We have loved and lived so many times over, and we can see what yet she cannot. It is wise you go tonight. The gods be with you."

"Merope, you are wise beyond even your immortal years. Thank you for understanding, and for putting into words what I cannot even begin to coalesce."

forty-five

Selene stretched her arms up over her head and swung them around a few times, filling her lungs up with much needed fresh air. The energy in the house had been overpowering, and she was delighted to be free of it. The middle of her back was aching, throbbing away again, which it hadn't done in ages. Arm in arm, she and Ev made their way to the high street in the crisp cool air. They revelled in the silence all around them, as most of

London still slept.

"*So*, tell me something good then!" Selene said.

"I am in love. Capital L. Nothing new of course. I've been in love with Mathios since we met the very first time. You know that!"

"I do know, and I'm over the moon for you hun! I can't think of anyone else I would rather to be with my lovely brother! Are you sure you can handle him?"

Ev stood back and gave Selene her best 'Oh, I've already *handled* him' look and laughed.

"Ok, Ok! Too much information!" Selene laughed. "Seriously, I am happy for you."

"Me too!" Ev chortled, skipping forward a few paces.

"So what do you make of the whole demon thing? A bit weird right?" Selene suddenly turned the whole conversation.

Ev wasn't sure how to answer. "I guess. I mean, Mathios isn't a demon right? But that chick in the red dress was a bit freaky."

"No, Mathios is human. Unlike me, apparently. Lilith said I was immortal and eternal, and she held her bloody hand up into Ios' face, taunting him, like he would want to have my blood too. I don't know what she said to him Ev, but he went purple with rage."

Selene paused for breath. "I don't know what it all means. Why did she want to taste my blood? What does it mean that I'm not human?" Selene turned to face her friend. "I'm not human." Selene repeated softly.

"How messed up does that sound. Will you still be my friend?" she asked in mock seriousness.

358

"Aw y'know, I've always wanted my very own demon friend, or whatever you are!" Ev laughed and grabbed Selene up into a huge bear hug.

They continued further along the road. Pretty much everything was closed, but they could see a small café open across the road, so they looked at each other and headed straight there. A group of rowdy guys dressed in various remnants of tuxedos were just leaving, all in fine spirits and jostling and joking with each other, shouting and hollering their goodbyes as Selene and Ev reached the door. They waited as the guys made their exit.

"Selene!"

Selene turned and came face to face with a tall ginger-haired, slightly battered but very handsome looking rugby player still dressed up in what was left of a tux.

"Ryan!"He scooped her up in his arms and swung her around. "Happy New Year!" he shouted happily. He was still a little drunk, and she laughed as he placed her back down on the ground. "What're ye doing here? Where's Jon?"

Selene paled a bit at the mention of his name but managed to hold it together.

"Jon and I split up. He married someone else yesterday Ryan."

"What?" Ryan sobered with the shock. "He never! How is that possible? That was a bit quick like wasn't it? You were pretty tight when I met you in August. What a jerk!"

Selene and Ev both laughed and nodded in tacit agreement. "Ya. It's been a bit of a shock really, it's all happened so fast. Ev this is one of Jon's friends from Uni, Ryan, Ev."

Ryan smiled and held his hand out. Ev grasped it and gave it a firm shake. "Oh these strong women. Chiropractors heh. God, I so need you lot!" He ran his hands up and around his neck and stretched.

The other guys started shouting for Ryan to hurry up, so he turned and said a few choice words back. "Sorry!" he laughed, "it's been a long night and I haven't been home yet!"

"Well, looks like it was a good one. It's great to see you Ryan, Happy New Year." Selene said smiling. Ryan turned to her and smiled. He stepped forward and very gently held the back of her neck with one hand and her face with the other. He looked deeply into her eyes, bent forward and kissed her. Soft and light, but very lovingly. His lips were soft and gentle, drawing her in as they swept over her own. She was a little breathless as he pulled away, surprised that she had responded so well in kind.

"It's lovely to see you Selene. I hope we meet again soon." he said slightly flushed as he stepped back and released her, nodding to Ev and turning to go.

"Goodbye Ryan," Selene said somewhat stunned. He turned and winked at her, then vanished around the bend with his mates.

"Whoah girl. I think I may need to place you under house arrest."

"As far as weird things go, that was good weird. A bit wow. Actually." Selene said. "Maybe dating another human would be a good idea for a while."

"You giving up on Mr. I-am-a-demon so must be dark-and-mysterious then?"

"I don't know that there is anything to give up on!" Selene huffed as she settled herself into the booth. "He is so hot and cold. I just can't work him out at all."

"Yeah. I see that. I can also see he has some pretty strong feelings for you though, maybe he's just got commitment issues?"

"Whatever. He seems to have other-worldy hideous red haired demon issues as well," Selene said, pausing to read the menu. "Seere said that they had been friends for like ever, like thousands of years."

Ev looked up but said nothing. *Eggs flo. Large black coffee. Perfect.* They ordered and sat in silence for a moment. Selene watched Ev, and the emotions as they crossed her face, revealing her thoughts. She was happy, really happy. Mathios was a lovely guy, and it was amazing that this had finally happened for them. It made Selene feel more secure as well, with so much uncertainty around her.

They ate slowly, totally relaxed in the middle of a very busy café. It felt good just to hang out in their own bubble, no pressure, no demons, no dramas. Pure girl chat. Selene could almost pretend that the last twenty-four hours hadn't happened. *Almost.* She wondered if being a demon meant she would start to feel different. Was she a demon? She didn't actually know. Timewalking had spun her out a bit when she had been with Ios, and the feeling of slipping into other times and other peoples lives without so much as a blink of an eye,

361

was nothing short of unbelievable to her.

The last year had brought so many new things, and with it, its share of loss. Breathing thoughts of Jon away again, she tried to focus on what her life was now going to be like. Without him. And with not knowing who she really was, at least at the moment, she didn't know if she was angel of demon, or any other creature. The whole foundation of her life shaken, she looked up at the sky and sighed. Ev reached over and squeezed her hand tightly, nudging her forward. Leaving the café, they walked on a little further, then made their way slowly back to Ios' home as it was already starting to get dark.

"I wonder if Mamma is awake yet. Did you notice she and Ios were quite friendly?"

"I did actually. They don't know each other do they?"

"I don't see how they could. Although, Ios does have a Greek phone number on his card...maybe they have met before. If I am immortal, then shouldn't she be too? Seems a bit too coincidental doesn't it?"

"I am not so sure I will be surprised by anything ever again Selene," Ev said seriously. "I mean, last night was pretty wild, never mind things with Jon. That Lilith demon, and then Ios and Seere disappearing into thin air and whatnot. I don't know what to make of any of it."

"Ditto. Especially as that now also includes me. I haven't even begun to let that sink in."

They had arrived back already, and she wasn't sure she wanted to go back inside.

"I don't understand much at the moment. My life feels so out of my control, and I feel a bit lost. I feel like I am

362

stuck in a maze, and keep hitting a dead end laced with something evil at the end of it. But I can't see the way through at all. And I can't seem to get out either. And, on top of all of that, I can't fucking take it in that Jon is married to someone that isn't me."

Ev turned and looked at her, hearing the sob catch in her throat. She knew tears would come, but the shock was still too deep. She hugged her friend close and tight, but didn't say anything else. They released each other in time, and Ev looked Selene in the eye.

"Hun, you have a lot to wade through about your own life, never mind Jon. Ready?"

"Yeah, guess we had better make an appearance or they might send a search party."

Ev remembered the expression on Ios' face as Lilith departed the night before. It had been pretty full on, and pretty scary.

"Hello, we're back!" Ev called out as they walked into the house again.

Mathios appeared from the lounge and kissed her lightly on the lips. "Glad to hear it. We were beginning to wonder where you'd gone. Mamma is just up and having a bath. She'll be down shortly."

"Ok. I might go up and rest a while before dinner. I'm pretty shattered. Where's Ios?"

"In his study I think, it's on the top floor."

"Ok. I won't bother him, I just didn't want to disturb him if he was in his room."

Mathios gave her a funny look, and looked to Ev, who just shrugged. "Uh, ok then. Have a good sleep."

Mathios and Ev went back to the lounge, and Selene quietly walked upstairs. She dropped her bag, shed her clothes, and fell onto the bed exhausted. Within minutes she slept.

forty-six

Ios sensed her return. He leaned back in the large office chair and pushed it away from the desk. He still hadn't been able to make sense of Lilith's appearance at the club, how she knew about Selene, and why she had tasted her blood. The pieces just wouldn't fit together. He needed answers and fast. He knew Selene would be upset with him leaving, but he knew if he stayed he might never leave. The inertia towards her was just too strong. He knew she felt it too, but perhaps didn't understand why it was he kept pulling away. He could feel that her life was about to unravel, standing on a high precipice with too many secrets and so much yet unknown.

He wanted to be the one to be there for her, but his demon mind held him a step away. He rested his head against the wall, then gave it a sharp bang in frustration. In past times he would have taken her without a second thought. *What the hell is happening to me? Whatever it is, get a grip. If Lilith sensed any weakness or humanity or attachment, it would be very dangerous.* He knew he needed some time to wreak a little chaos, it had been far too long, and he had a reputation to protect. It was time to go looking for trouble.

He could hear the house making noise, the sounds of people laughing and the quieter sounds of sleep. It felt good to have a house full, and this too was a new sensation. He stood and stretched. He was still in loose fitting casual trousers, which hung low over his hips. He had left his shirt in his room, thinking that Selene would not be back until much later. It was already dark outside however, and he knew that thoughts would turn towards dinner at some point. And then he would go. He made his way down to his room, he froze by the door when he realised she was in his bed.

He stared for what felt like ages, just taking in her face, her closed peaceful eyes, the length of her hair; and the shape her body, wrapped only in a light sheet, revealed its full form. He could see she had dropped most of her clothing on the floor beside the bed. He walked into the room, his head telling him to turn away, his body crying out to touch her. He closed the door softly behind him, and walked to the bed. He stood there for a while, battling with himself. *Just for a moment. Only a moment.* He slid under the sheets next to her, and she stirred.

He rolled her over to face him, and she opened her eyes. They stared into the depths of each other for ages in the dim light. Breathing softly but rapidly, he pulled her closer and held her body against his own. Selene let her head drop back and lifted her face towards his. She could barely breathe. He was so close and his body felt so strong next to hers. He let his hand slide down her back, gently massaging the space between her shoulder blades - where the constant ache lived.

She sighed and relaxed into the ease. The tension of all her life lived there, and in moments she felt it come free, everything relaxed as he stroked and squeezed the skin and muscles there. She breathed in deeply.

"How do you know me so well?" Selene murmured, almost purring in his arms as he continued to stroke her.

Ios smiled and leaned closer to kiss her forehead, then her cheek. He nuzzled into her neck and breathed deeply, inhaling her scent. *Forever is how I want to know you,* is what he wanted to say, but he did not. He could not. *How am I going to tear myself away from her?* But the longer they stayed like this the more his resolve was slipping away. His demon nature was urging him on, *take her, get inside of her, have her.* She wanted him just as much, he knew it. *So what the hell is your problem?* The broken record of his battling mind continued to play on.

Then she was kissing him. And he fell. Hard and fast into her arms, rolling on top of her, pulling her more deeply into his body. Their kiss grew in demand, deepening as the passion between them began to lift into a full roar. They rolled over and over each other lips entwined, neither wanting to let go. They tasted each other deeply, thoroughly, and completely. Selene felt like she would never again come up for air he felt so good.

Then abruptly, he let go and sat up in full alert.

Ios hissed. "What is it?"

"Sorry man, you know I wouldn't interrupt unless—" Seere shifted from foot to foot in immense discomfort.

"Where?"

"Chios eighth century," Seere hesitated, then added, "BC."

"I will meet you there." Ios replied coldly.

He hadn't turned to face Seere, his eyes never leaving Selene, as she lay breathless beneath him. He rose suddenly, not returning to her arms. He knew things had already gone too far, and another moment and he would again be lost. *Damn. What's happened to your control? Damn it.* He just couldn't think straight with her, with them, being like this. As much as he cursed Seere for his appearance, it couldn't have come at a better time. He was pretty sure he wouldn't have been able to stop this time. *And what would be so bad about that?* The voice in his head chided him.

"There are things happening I need to attend to Selene, and I need to go." Ios said as he turned, flicked

the bedside light on and opened his wardrobe. Grabbing
odd styled loose fitting clothing, he dropped them on the
edge of the bed. He let the other trousers fall to the floor
not bothering to cover himself as she watched, threading
his legs through the new pair.

"Chios," Selene repeated her eyes glued to his
exposed body. He was beautiful, but there were many
deep scars layered across his torso and on his arms. "I
could step through time into that painting."

Ios looked up sharply. "*No*, Selene. Promise me, no
timewalking with Lilith on the loose. If you disappeared
and we couldn't find you, she would, and believe me, you
do not want that to happen." Ios returned to the edge of
the bed and pulled her firmly up into his arms in one
swift movement.

"*Promise me.*"

"Who the hell are you to tell me what to do Ios?"
Selene shouted at him and pushed him away. She stood
angrily in front of him, her body barely covered in her
lace bra and knickers. He caught his breath and looked
away. Still seething with anger, she smiled at his reaction
and stepped closer to him. She could see his desire for
her beneath his trousers.

"I am not a toy. You come and you go. You kiss me,
you hold me, and I can feel you want me. But then you
pull away and you're gone."

"I know. I'm sorry. There is too much at stake here
Selene. I want you more than you will ever know. But I
do not think, you want all that comes with me." He
reached out and gently stroked her cheek. "You know

nothing about me, about who I am—what I am. If you were a toy, I would have bedded you and been gone long ago. If you can trust me, then trust I need to protect you. Trust that there is much yet we do not know. I need to go, Seere is waiting, and this is important. Please, can you give the others my apologies?"

He paused and looked deeply into her eyes. "I do not know when I will see you again Selene. Time— time works differently there," he bent to kiss her without touching her anywhere else, and was gone.

Selene stared at the painting of Chios in the empty space he left behind and felt a knot of anger in her stomach, which was still fluttering from the sight of his naked body—*that* had just about undone her. She could of course try to follow him. She hadn't actually promised anything. But she knew she had better not. The idea of running into Lilith alone didn't appeal in the slightest. Truth be told, it frightened the life out of her. She put her arms around herself and fought off a shiver.

She let her mind wander back to his naked form, and felt her body sigh.

A shower. Yes.

Might as well finish what he started.

To be continued…..

Book Two: Ritual

"Many a night I saw the Pleiads, rising through the mellow shade,
glitter like a swarm of fire-flies, tangled in a silver braid."
Lord Tennyson

Book Two: Ritual

(excerpt)

"Who are you talking to?"

Ryan dropped his kit bag on the side and reached over for a kiss.

"Umm, no one, just muttering to myself, really."
Selene returned the kiss and gave a small smile. Turning she breathed a sigh of relief. She had actually been talking to Ios, but only in her mind's eye, rather than his actual presence. She had arrived home to an enormous bouquet of white roses, and had been setting them out on the table, talking as she did so, when Ryan had walked through the door.

"Nice flowers."

"They are, aren't they?" Selene turned to face him. "They're a gift from some close family friends. We hope to see them over the summer in Greece."

"Greece?"

"Yes, mamma mentioned she would like us to do a family trip when I graduate. Return to her proper home up in the mountains. I've never been there, despite having mostly grown up not far from it."

"Cool. I've never been to Greece," he paused wondering if he would be asked to join them. "It will be good for you to spend some time together. Any news on job stuff yet?"

Selene watched as Ryan circled the flowers with a keen eye, as if searching for a card. Hell. At least Ios never left cards, small mercies. He launched himself onto the settee and stretched out. She moved slowly towards him, knowing that right now, he would want comfort and reassurance. But she couldn't give it.

They had been spending more and more time together, with him spending many more nights with her at her home since talking about possibly living together. And it was proving difficult. Selene was feeling the pressure of time, and the presence of him being in her space everyday. The pressure of needing to be social with him whilst needing to study and take part in study groups. She felt at times she couldn't breathe properly, and her back ached for the memory of freedom.

She wanted to go to see Adam, but it would be hard to explain why she felt the need to go see a tutor, not only outside college hours, but at his home. She knew that Ryan would be away again over the coming weekend at a match, and she had already decided that until her exams were completed, she would remain in town. No more travel. And Ryan was not best pleased. Everything felt strained at the moment, and though it was easy to blame timing and the weight of the exams, Selene knew it ran far deeper than that.

She would be lying if she said it wasn't about Ios. But there was no way to come clean and tell the truth without getting into everything and causing hurt and pain.

374

But it was getting harder to hide her need to be true and free to be herself, whatever that meant. She wasn't sure, but this, this was hard. And she cared for Ryan. That made it even harder.

Ryan reached for her, "Penny for your thoughts?"

Selene smiled, reaching down and kissing his cheek. "Brainless at present. Nothing sensical."

At least that was the truth.

He grinned and pulled her down onto the settee. "Well, if that be true, then perhaps you will allow me to bring you fully into your body and out of study mode?'

Selene laughed. "One track Ryan is going to be your new nickname soon."

He was already pulling her trousers down inch by inch, having flipped her onto her back.

Lightning Source UK Ltd.
Milton Keynes UK
UKHW010258140720
366472UK00001B/65